Evac

(The Commo...

Al K. Line

Copyright © 2014 Al K. Line

Alkline.co.uk

Sign up for The Newsletter for news of the latest releases as well as flash sales at Alkline.co.uk

All rights reserved. This book or any portion thereof may not be reproduced or used in any manner whatsoever without the express written permission of the author except for the use of brief quotations in a book review.

This is a work of fiction. Names, characters, businesses, places, events and incidents are either the products of the author's imagination or used in a fictitious manner. Any resemblance to actual persons, living or dead, or actual events is purely coincidental.

Commorancy: *a dwelling place or ordinary residence of a person. This residence is usually temporary and it is vacated after a given time.*

Surprise

"I never knew, honestly I didn't. I've never been over this side... well, not for hundreds of years anyway. How could this happen? How could they still be here, living like this?" Marcus felt sick to his stomach.

It was a mess, a sprawling slum that couldn't even be described as a shanty town — that would give it unwarranted glamor. The horror confronting them made no sense whatsoever. With nearly every building in the UK unoccupied there was no end to the choice those still living had in terms of accommodation. Huge swathes of the last years of construction were little but rubble, whole city centers burned to the ground, and many a fine place was gutted, but the high quality building that had continued right up until The Lethargy meant that there were millions of homes still standing and in relatively good condition.

Yet here they were, untold thousands of human beings, all cramped into a decaying maze of hovels on the side of the hill that was slowly sliding down onto the sand then relentlessly onward out into the ocean.

All properties pointed to The Commorancy.

The makeshift homes housed people in various states of Lethargy — some had been there for years.

The group walked through the degradation and deprivation. These were people once Whole, many were once Awoken — now most were either cared for by their family or still cognizant enough to stay alive, clinging to life when they sporadically came back from their all-consuming stupor so they could manically consume whatever food they could find and scrabble in the filth to source fuel to warm their cold, aching bones.

It was like walking through a third world concentration camp where the inmates had no hope of rescue.

Hundreds of sunken, dead eyes followed the group as they took switchback after random switchback that slowly allowed them to make progress down the side of the hill. The narrow streets, little more than filth covered gaps between makeshift homes, were treacherous; each foot had to be placed carefully for fear of slipping in the mud, stepping in excrement, or stumbling into a body unapologetically lying in their path blocking their way.

Some buildings were nothing more than tin sheets tied together with rope, others were tiny brick-sided buildings, the work so poor they were already collapsing before a makeshift roof could be tethered into place.

Other abodes were shacks made from all kinds of salvaged materials: wood panels, fencing, car windows or anything else that might help to keep the weather out. A few young children scattered as they passed, skeletal things with pot bellies, matted hair and minimal clothing. You could tell that some were already in the clutches of the worst way to die imaginable — Creeping Lethargy. It could take years for them to die, each day just a little bit more of them taken away into The Void, a tiny piece of humanity washed away forever, leaving them that little bit emptier inside.

Nobody could look, it became more unbearable with every carefully placed step. This was a degradation beyond the likes of which any of them had known, ever imagined could exist.

Narrow passage after narrow passage filled with the dead and the dying, with no hope of salvation.

Many once inhabited shelters were mere piles of rubble, there to be scavenged by the next poor soul.

They walked, and they walked — there was no choice in the matter. They needed to get away, to leave the nightmare behind them before the misery pulled them down into its sticky embrace and swallowed them whole into a world where you could spend lifetimes trying to make things right but never succeed.

Every time they looked up they were reminded of where they came from. All views from on the hill pointed directly out to sea, to Vectis, to The Commorancy that was so tantalizingly close yet impossible to reach. Everything clung precariously to one side, the other was nothing more than a landslide of detritus, a tipping ground for those that could be bothered to take their rubbish away from their homes. They could see it all around them, the hovels became sporadic then there was only garbage curving around the hill, and down below, as the hill met ground level. The foulness piled up, backed up in waves up the hill, before it was eventually claimed by the encroaching sea. The roads that ran along the once popular promenade were already half eaten away, even though Marcus had re-fortified the defenses long ago. Other parts of the coastline had been cut back deeply by Marcus, to strengthen them and to ensure they were not taken by the sea, but this outcrop was left mostly alone as it had been the place he stood centuries ago and dreamed of The Commorancy, a sanctuary for humanity. Now he stood halfway down the steep hill staring out toward his accomplishment only to be mocked by the depravity threatening to suck out his sanity.

It was a cruel joke, a slap in the face for what he had envisioned and what he thought he had been achieving all these years.

Why were these people here? What were they doing? Why weren't they living in the countless towns and villages all along the coastline that would offer better comfort and security while they still had life left in them?

Marcus thought he had the answer, much as he didn't want to think about it until he and his companions got away from the horror.

The welcome to the mainland had started so well too.

~~~

Letje found herself sat against a weathered railing at the top of a flight of stairs, worried faces peering down at her. She had Constantine resting in her lap, clutched tightly.

"Ugh, I had the funniest dream. I had this whole thing where I was talking to my dad but he was Constantine really. It was so real, like he was really inside him." Letje shook her head, her hair tickling her eyebrows as she dispelled the dream — or tried to at least. Something wasn't quite right here. It felt almost too real.

"What? Why are you looking at me like that?" Letje peered from person to person, concern and discomfort vying for dominance on every face apart from Marcus'. He was just grinning broadly, weirdly raising one eyebrow and nodding his head at Constantine.

She looked down at her little friend. *Hello Letje. Again. It wasn't a dream, it really is me.*

Letje passed out, again.

When she awoke she found herself overcome by a foul stench that was impossible to ignore. It made the air heavy, it sucked the joy out of the world, and it made a mockery of the whole notion of olfactory senses: they weren't designed to be greeted with such an onslaught, surely?

"Ugh, I just had the strangest dream — again. I think... um, hang on a minute." Letje battled with the foul air and peered at Constantine, she was getting a serious case of Deja Vu.

"Daddy? Daddy is that you?" She peered into the eyes of Constantine, the heavy lids making him constantly look like he was either about to go to sleep or had just this second woken up.

Yes Letje, it's me. Please try not to faint this time my dear, otherwise this could go on for days.

"Okay Daddy. Um, do I need to talk out loud? And what is that smell?"

"We are about to go and find out Letje," said Marcus, "and your father is right, please don't faint again, it's really rather dangerous you know."

No Letje, you don't need to talk out loud. But we do need to have a serious conversation young lady, certainly about your age — and boys.

Letje was now sure beyond doubt that this really was her father, only he could manage to say 'boys' like it was a swear word.

Letje smiled at Constantine. Or was it Daddy now? She couldn't very well call her tortoise Daddy though, could she?

"Do you need some help?" asked a fretful Sy, standing close, ready to come to her assistance if she should pass out again.

"Hmm? Sorry, this is a little overwhelming, too many voices all at once. I think I must be going a little mad."

"Don't worry, you'll get used to it," said Marcus, smiling weakly. "Sort of." Marcus sniffed the air, trying not to let the stench make him retch. "Okay, I know this is not the right time Letje, but we need to be on the move. We need to find out what is going on here, and let's not forget the assault on The Commorancy. The Eventuals know we are on the mainland so let's get moving, we need to get out of here and get away from the coast. In a few miles we can rest up and we can go over this." Marcus pointed at Constantine that was now Yabis, indicating the rather odd situation the creature, and Letje, both found themselves in.

Letje stood as if in a dream, making sure she held on tightly to Constantine, her father? The group crested the side of a steep hill, ancient stone steps cut into the stubby grass still remarkably functional after so many years. As they rounded the corner, looking out to sea, and to Vectis, a wall of foulness descended. They thought it had been bad before, but with the gentle breeze coming in from the sea they were hit full force with the obscene odors from the terrible shanty town sliding inexorably into the water.

The vision of such misery was worse than the smell emanating from it.

Letje could do nothing but try to block out the madness. If she was to get through the next few minutes then she had to focus.

Stay calm Letje. Just try to forget about me until we have some quiet time and can talk properly, said Yabis.

So, you can read my thoughts too. Well, that's just great. What if I don't want you to? It's lovely to hear from you Daddy, and you obviously know how much I missed you, but, well, Letje flushed just thinking about it, *you know, what about boys and things? Ugh, we definitely need to talk.*

We will, and I promise, I won't interfere.

Letje could feel him smiling in The Noise.

Yeah right Daddy, I'm sure you won't.

A Descent into Madness

Marcus' thoughts were reeling. He kept having visions of the shanty town, unable to get it out of his mind.

They had made their way down through the growing stench, all the way to the crumbling promenade where mountains of detritus were either piling over the broken asphalt down onto the sand or were backing up the hill. They clambered over the filth, circumspectly making progress eastward, the mess slowly giving way to greenery. Once they had made their way along the coastline, then headed deeper back to where Marcus had cut away the unstable coastline so many years ago, the smell, sight and sound of the isolated town of The Lethargic slowly melted away.

They rounded a corner and it was as if it had never been. As if it was nothing but a nightmare vision of what a post-apocalyptic England could be. Now, in total contrast, they were confronted with the beginnings of a thick forest with short grass welcoming them brightly. Fields full of bright yellow flowering Canola plants climbed up gentle hills in the distance. It was easy to believe farmers were still tending their land and would be out on their tractors soon enough to harvest the seed for oil.

Marcus knew they wouldn't of course, old hedge boundaries had simply kept a few fields true to the crops last sown by man three centuries ago.

They sat in a lush field on the edge of the forest, sucking down deep lungfuls of salt and pollen tinted clean air. Old farm equipment covered in moss and ivy made an ideal home for families of sparrows and gave the perfect place to sit and take stock of the madness.

"What on earth was that? I feel like I've stepped into some kind of armageddon," said Sy, shaking his head to try to clear away the assault on his senses. He daren't look at his shoes, it would bring back too many memories of what they either trod in or over.

"Those poor people," said Umeko, tears streaming down her face, just as they were on Stanley's and Kirstie's. The others weren't in much better condition. The air, though welcome, hung heavy, as if it too had succumbed to The Lethargy and the sheer misery of those that clung to the coast of England, drawn by a power they could never reach.

Baby Dale whimpered in his blankets so Kirstie adjusted them enough to settle the babe before a whimper turned into a shriek.

Marcus and Letje were silent, each lost in their own private worlds of confusion, despair and incomprehension.

"What have I done? It wasn't supposed to be like this. Those people have no hope, no life, no chance of ever getting to The Commorancy. I couldn't help them even if they made it. I can't do anything for them, apart from end it all for them." Marcus' head threatened to crack open like a dropped coconut. Events had twisted out of his control too quickly. With The Commorancy safe now the other him had done what he knew he would, what the him sitting on the mainland would have done in his place, he was considering leaving too. It was understandable, so long together, so long being him, the tenuous link between them threatened to snap, and he felt it like a kick to the guts just as the other Marcus did. Even though it was him that was holding off from sharing his experience through their unstable connection, to spare such confusion, it still made him feel like he had lost a part of his own personality.

Their tie may break soon enough, but it went without saying that their combined knowledge of future events meant that the him without the responsibility of drawing Varik away would pursue what both of them had long dreamed of, but never able to seriously contemplate actually doing.

And the poor people on that foul slope of misery? It was his doing, wasn't it? Marcus put his head in his hands and found it impossible to stop the swelling tide

11

of human despair emanating in The Noise from washing over him — leaving him cold and dreaming of finally embracing The Void.

"Letje? Letje, are you alright? I'm sorry that you had to witness that, especially after finding out about your father. Why don't you go and take ten minutes and have a little talk with him? I'm sorry, it can't be longer as we need to move, and soon. Otherwise..."

Letje just stared at Marcus, her eyes glazed, the blank look on her face an indication that shock wasn't far from taking her down into a beautiful blank peace.

"Let me try," said Astolat, putting a hand on Letje's shoulder. "Letje? *hedgehog, sticky pink stuff.* Letje, can you hear me? *grr, no more doggies. whoops.* Come on, let's go sit over there." Astolat guided Letje over to a small hummock and sat her down on the sloping grass. She made sure she was settled then left her with the tortoise and went back to the others.

It was obvious she needed to be alone with her father to even begin to try to understand her new reality.

Dead Dad

Letje was distraught when her father passed away. It wasn't only the end of her childhood of innocence of a sorts, it was the end of the family line that stretched back to the beginnings of The Lethargy itself. Each male sought a wife, and that wife bore a male child, but it fell apart over time, less and less of the males staying Whole their entire life, children being born to younger and younger parents to try to keep the line going.

Letje was the anomaly, the end of the line. Her mother had given birth to a daughter, something that had not happened to her family since the first relative entered The Commorancy back at its beginnings, and Awoke with a blueprint to pass down the ability to stay Whole to each male child.

It all gradually unraveled as knowledge was lost through the generations. Eventually the power of the males waned, along with the knowledge of how to manipulate your body to keep it functioning optimally and the ability to ensure Whole children came into the world.

When Letje's father died it meant that the long custom was finally at an end.

She felt a heavy weight of responsibility now — she may not have been a male but she was certainly as good as one, and she intended to make her own line that would stay much healthier. Hers would flourish over the centuries, rather than wane as ancient lore and knowledge became warped, lost, then sadly forgotten.

Her father had instilled in Letje a deep sense of tradition, yet he also wanted to be certain she understood that nothing was forever. Although the family had tried to keep Whole, to build a lineage that ever expanded, it hadn't worked out like that. He told Letje of the ways things were, of the struggles through the centuries, and of the way the male line had carried on. He never made her feel bad for not being a boy, he taught her that she was special. Unique. Although he had done what he could to pass on the genetics from his side of the family to a boy, she had decided that she would be better than any male, and that was what had happened.

He told her that great things were waiting for her. Inside of her was amazing potential, all she had to do was unlock it. He told her of The Commorancy and the beginning of their family, and he told her of the importance of hanging on to being Whole, to always strive to Awaken.

As she entered her eleventh year her mother passed and her father was all that was left of their family. Then he too began to lose interest in things, to stare vacantly at Letje, often not answering when she asked him questions. Letje found herself performing more and more of the duties needed to run the house, until she did everything. She cared for her father, washed and dressed him, fed him and forced him to sip water. He just stood or sat there, unblinking, unmoving, shallow breaths all that remained of the once inspiring man that made her laugh, taught her so much, and cared so very deeply for her.

Then he died.

Yet he refused to die.

Yabis Sandoe had made plans to ensure that his daughter was never left truly alone.

~~~

It was dark, dark and strange.

Yabis Sandoe had died, and he had broken the rules that govern the Universe. He retained his sense of self even though his body lay in a heap on the patchy grass outside his kitchen door that was in serious need of repainting. He heard his daughter weeping, heard her talking to his inanimate corpse, heard her saying how much she loved him and she didn't know what she would do now he was gone.

He felt her lift him up and watched through heavy lidded bright black eyes as she planted a tiny kiss on the top of his strange, scaly head.

Yabis was a tortoise and his daughter's best, and only friend in the whole world.

He blacked out moments later, his new existence too alien and strange feeling for his mind to currently cope with. It would take time, there were many adjustments to be made if he was to retain a sense of self in the small body he felt he had no choice but to make his home.

~~~

After the passing of his wife, Yabis and his daughter were alone in the world. It was a melancholy period and he could sense that it was only a matter of time before he too succumbed to The Lethargy. So he made his plans.

He couldn't bear the thought of Letje being all alone, and knew the dangers that were at work in the wider world. He felt that if she were to survive, more — to thrive, which he knew she must, then she would need some help along the way. The problem was, there was no doubt that his body would fail him soon, and once that happened Letje would still be but a young girl.

He decided that for him to be there when she needed him, which may not be for years, then he would inhabit, or hopefully cohabit, the mind of her best friend. Constantine was a great find, when he stumbled across the sleepy tortoise whilst out on his travels he had thought him a good gift for his daughter. He would teach her responsibility as well as being a lifelong companion if cared for properly.

Now the hard-shelled little creature was destined for another purpose. Yabis had inhabited the bodies of creatures before, and always respected the minds he encountered. The trick was to enter in such a way that you retained your own sense of self, no easy thing when you had to deal with a completely alien mind and the overriding urges that went with such bodies. All creatures were hard-wired for self preservation so instincts were nigh on impossible to overcome. You could fight them for a while, but they always won out eventually.

So he practiced.

Whenever he could do so safely he would tread lightly in The Noise and seek out the presence of the tortoise. It was a compact, light pin-prick of light sat there all deep purple and scallop edged, a tiny beacon in an infinite sea of creatures jumbled around the past, present and many futures. The Noise could overwhelm you in a heartbeat, so deep focus was imperative. Once he joined with Constantine he would slowly make his presence known — never a sudden appearance. He would gently fade into existence so the creature accepted him. It was hard at first, such intrusions were rarely welcomed. But over time he became a familiar presence for the creature, and with the rather sedate and laid back attitude the tortoise had, Yabis relatively quickly became a welcome friend.

The main issue was one of personality. Occupying another creature meant that your mind slowly melded into theirs, staying Whole and aware was no easy thing to achieve. But it could be done, had been done in the past, and some had even made permanent transfers over. He heard about them from his own father, and not only hoped, but prayed they were not myths but actual fact.

He practiced, and he practiced again, often getting up in the middle of the night and sneaking into his daughter's room to pick up Constantine and take him outside to become a part of a new whole. He found that the more readily he was accepted the easier it was to retain his own identity, until one day it felt just as natural as waking in the morning, all sense of self still intact.

Then the time came for a permanent occupation.

To say he was nervous would be an understatement, but he thanked The Void that he could at least still feel such emotions. Soon there would be no such luxury. Already The Lethargy was knocking at the door of his awareness; he had begun to slide and there was no way to stop it. Days would pass in a stupor until he finally returned to consciousness in random places, his daughter looking into his eyes with concern.

It was time.

With every cell of his body he urged his mind to stay aware. He was at the end of the line now and he knew it. The Lethargy had almost totally claimed him, and although he hated his daughter caring for him he didn't want to leave, so clung to his rapidly diminishing existence like a limpet to a crumbling rock.

Finally it was now or never.

He had found himself out in the garden by the kitchen. The sweet smell of the growing herbs wafted on the breeze, the wind tickled his stubbly beard. Letje and Constantine were a little further down the lawn — she picking flowers to brighten up the house. He was a wreck of a man and it wouldn't be long before he lost all consciousness and it never returned.

He focused, straining to keep aware. If he blacked out now then he would be lost forever, a ghost, not alive, not dead, not even able to enter The Void. So he concentrated. He found Constantine, the tiny purple scallop in The Noise, and entered the creature's body as he always did: carefully and with respect.

Yabis looked at his daughter from his low vantage point, sat on the path while she chose the best blooms. He munched slowly on a crisp lettuce leaf while he re-entered The Noise and overlaid it on the scene in the garden. He searched for the ethereal umbilical cord that joined his body to his tiny new home, and saw the link, noted the tenuous nature of his life-force, the darkness weaving like smoke through it — the contamination that was The Lethargy.

Yabis mentally cut the connection. He heard the dull thud of his body falling from the chair and landing on the ground. He felt himself picked up, heard Letje crying out his name, and knew that he would be able to watch over her, to reach out and contact her when the need arose.

It was far from perfect, but being a tortoise was better than being dead.

Yabis had family commitments, and he intended to be there for his daughter no matter the price he had to pay.

~~~

"It's really you then?" said Letje, her surroundings coming back into focus. She peered into the black eyes of Constantine, her father? "You aren't dead? You're a tortoise? You're Constantine?"

I am. I'm sorry, but I wanted to be here for you, to make sure you stayed safe, that you were alright. And that you had me here if you needed me. Did I do the wrong thing?

"What? Um, I don't know. No, of course not, it's great to talk to you, it's just a lot to take in."

Letje me dear, just talk via The Noise, no need to speak out loud. We can talk privately whenever you want, just us. You and Daddy.

"Okay Daddy." Letje let herself connect with the vast Noise, felt the tiny presence of Constantine, her father, and spoke without speaking.

How long have you been him? Constantine? No, don't answer. Since you died right, when you died you became him, entered him? Right?

Letje felt the ponderous blinking of Constantine's thick eyelids, it was as if she was in there, inside her friend, with her father.

Yes, since I died. I couldn't leave you alone, my beautiful girl, my poor little girl. I knew you would need me one day, and I was right.

I always needed you Daddy, I loved you and mum very much — I still do. Letje looked at her little friend again, the thick legs wriggling in the air as she held him up to her face. *It's really you? Really? I'm not going mad?*

No Letje, you aren't going mad, it's really me, really truly me.

So what should I call you? Daddy? Or is it Constantine Alexander III still? A terrible thought came to Letje. Daddy, did you...?

No, don't worry, Constantine is still in here safe and sound. He's actually a very friendly tortoise, although to be honest he isn't the best conversationalist I've ever met.

Oh Daddy, he is only a tortoise. So, what do I call you now?

Just call me Constantine my dear, I've got used to it now. I have been here for a while, and that's what you have been calling me up until now anyway. Does that sound alright with you?

Yes Dadd— Constantine, that sounds just fine.

Good, now look Letje, I know you're afraid, and disappointed too, but I do want you to know that I'm here if you need me, and that everything is sure to work out just fine in the end. I promise. I'm not saying it's going to be easy, or that it isn't going to test you to the limits, but you will be alright, just be prepared for anything. And I mean anything.

Okay, but can't you tell me mo— Letje was interrupted by George nudging her leg, startling her. She felt her heart miss a beat as she jumped and almost dropped Constantine.

"Oh, hello George. How are you?" George just stared at her whilst pointedly ignoring Constantine entirely, then turned and walked back to the others. Marcus was beckoning her over, mouthing that it was time to leave.

Well Constantine, I guess it's time for us to go. And Daddy?

Yes my dear.

It's lovely to speak to you again. I missed you so much. Mummy too.

I missed you too Letje, and there isn't a day that goes by that I don't miss your mother.

Marcus Groan

Marcus felt alone, more alone than he had ever thought possible. He had felt isolated and desolate in the past — had screamed in The Disco Room until he was hoarse, cried in The Room For a Thousand Tears until he felt little more than a dessicated husk, and had howled like a banshee in The Room For Deciding If You Are Mad until he felt like his guts would explode from his belly and evacuate his sanity once and for all — this was different.

He genuinely was alone.

The other Marcus had left him and gone to the mainland.

He had remained — to clean up the monstrous mess caused by Varik and The Eventuals.

"I don't know where to start." Marcus poked a finger into his cheek as he thought for a minute. "Wow! What's wrong with me? I must really be out of sorts." He stared down at his assassin clothes, got out of The Assassin's Chair, and shook his arms vigorously. The

Assassin's Room was so small he almost hit the sides. "Of course I know where to start."

With a flicker of a smile forming, Marcus went to get changed into a more suitable outfit for the job at hand. As he crossed the rope bridge he wondered how well he was doing on the mainland; hopefully Varik would be getting his comeuppance some time soon. The link to himself was so tenuous now that he could no longer simply experience himself as if he were split in two, for better or worse his reality was firmly his own. There was no duality, and it made Marcus feel like half a person.

He didn't like it one little bit.

What he disliked the most was that he knew that he was blocking himself on purpose in The Noise, as normally he could get the connection and update the experiences in a kind of fast forward recap of the time since the last contact. In a second he could gather himself in and know everything he had done — there were never gaps. Now the disparity had extended since he got on the train and it left him disorientated, disjointed, and very annoyed with himself.

Just what exactly was he up to?

He suspected what it was, and although he was loathe to admit it, it was exactly what he would do. But he still held a grudge, so he decided as he walked the bridge that there was no way he was going to miss out on the fun.

The break.

Time away from The Commorancy.

Freedom.

He was going too.

No, he couldn't. He had responsibilities. Didn't he?

~~~

You can't tell them that though, can you?

No, I guess not.

Look, I understand. I really do.

Well, of course you do, you're me, aren't you?

Let's not get into that again please. We'll be saying how this conversation is impossible next, as how can we argue with me.

Well, now you come to mention it...

Marcus rolled his eyes, he hated these conversations in The Noise. He preferred to talk to himself in person, it made it less weird. Less like he was going mad, or mad already.

Can you come here? You know I don't like to talk this way.

Me either, I'll be there soon. You do understand, right? I can't do this, not when we know what has to happen. Tell me honestly, no don't bother, we both know anyway, don't we?

Marcus rolled his eyes, what was wrong with him? Why did he keep talking to himself like he was a different person?

Marcus made his way to Marcus, it was what they both wanted. *What's wrong with me? I feel like I am not quite me any more. There are secrets, things I'm not telling me. If I have them then he, me, Marcus, has them too. Am I me any more if I don't share everything? Are we still the same?*

Marcus tried not to think about it. Now here was another little bit of himself he had to block from sharing in The Noise, just in case Marcus didn't actually have any secrets and it was just him.

He did though, and Marcus knew he would. It was him, after all.

~~~

Marcus came to with a shudder and looked around blearily.

Damn, just another dream, wasn't it? It had to be. Marcus, the other one, wouldn't agree to him leaving The Commorancy, not with so much to do, so much work left unfinished. Not to mention all the guests, all the cleaning up after The Contamination. Surely he would say no.

But hang on, if he, him sat here in a chair in The Orientation Room, wanted to leave and thought that maybe he would, then it stood to reason that the other him would agree to it — he would have to, they were the same. Weren't they?

Or had they diverged too much already? Had too much happened away from their home for them to ever be the same person again? But still, if the other him were here, if they had swapped places, then he would be thinking exactly the same thing, so it stood to reason that whatever he decided, whatever he did, was what they would both agree on if the tables were turned.

That was right, wasn't it?

Sometimes being two people got rather confusing, but still, it had been better than being alone.

All alone.

So alone.

Marcus put his head back on the desk, hoping sleep would take him once more. Anything was better than the crushing loneliness that threatened to take away the only thing he had left: his own mind.

A change of clothes had completely failed to lift his spirits, so Marcus knew that things really were very wrong indeed.

Smelly Hair

Fasolt sniffed the air yet again, there was a pungent smell that had been tickling his cilia for days now — it was following him wherever he went. He turned in a circle, his naked body immune to the frigid morning. The first few days after his baptism and return to being a compassionate human being had seen him shivering like a wet dog and hunting in vain for something suitable to wear.

Then realization hit him like a bag of rocks to the face — he was Awoken, powerful, extremely powerful. What was a little bit of a chill to the likes of him? Taking no longer than a beat of his heart, he set his internal temperature so he always felt nice and cozy, like back when he had to have the fire roaring and layer upon layer wrapped around his scrawny body. He now felt perfectly at ease with his nakedness. He wondered what he had been thinking all those centuries, wrapped up so tight, seemingly unable to consider using his knowledge of The Noise to warm himself without the need for clothes. Just another part of the wickedness, he guessed, a way to even be cruel to himself as well as others.

Well, that was over with now, he was a new man. He felt like he had finally awoken to the world he lived in, astonished to find it such a joyous place. How could he have gone along with his son's plans to eradicate humanity? How could he have looked forward to his own death for centuries when there was so much beauty in the world? It seemed crazy. Sheer madness.

Now he reveled in the feel of the grass beneath his feet, savored the sensation of sticky mud squishing between his toes, and laughed like a child with a new toy at the sun shining in the sky, even as the clouds mostly did a good job of hiding it away out of sight.

Some things never change, he noted. Same old dull British weather as it always was. But still, it felt good to be alive. More. It felt absolutely glorious.

Fasolt had been walking ever since he was spat out of the water onto the shore, naked and half dead, yet more alive then he had been since his first birth such a long time ago. It may have been a different person, a different world, it was certainly a very different time. Now the world was as if made for an evil fairytale. Where people had powers, where lives could apparently be lived indefinitely, and people like his son and Marcus were past being mere eccentrics — becoming tyrants of the most extreme kind history had ever seen.

And him? Fasolt? He was a tyrant too, he had no doubt about it. He had, only days ago, controlled the minds, such as they were, and bodies of ten thousand Lethargic. If that didn't make him some kind of uber-tyrant extraordinaire then he didn't know what did.

None of it seemed real.

He marveled at the world as it now was. It was funny, but he hadn't really thought about all the crazy things going on, just accepted them for what they were. He had been so caught up in his own weird existence that he had failed to see just how bizarre a place it really was now.

He carried on walking as he thought, even though his body was tired. It would take some time to get used to such activity, he had been idle for centuries, spending all his time in The Noise. His legs were weak, his back hurt, and his feet and hands were as soft as a baby's. But not to worry, they would toughen up soon enough. He knew that he was to be out in the world at large for some time to come so was in no doubt his body would adjust even without him tweaking it himself. He also knew his son would be rather elusive, and that it would take maybe months before they met again. Oh what a surprise that would be.

Fasolt was a powerful man, so kept his presence hidden from The Noise — he didn't want his son finding out he still lived until the time was right. Otherwise it could be his life forfeit before he hopefully encourage Varik to see the error of his ways.

Fasolt stopped and sniffed yet again. What was that smell?

He continued but was pulled up short, his head yanking back, almost snapping his neck.

His hair! That was it. It had caught on a branch laying on the ground, and it was then he realized that it was him, his hair, his body that was the source of the olfactory annoyance.

He stank!

How could this be possible? How could he be smelly when he only came out of the sea days ago? He had gone decades, longer, between washing over the last few hundred years, how could a few days make you so stinky?

Sitting down on the ground and crossing his legs Fasolt pondered his new self. It was then that he understood what it was to be a real person, one that wasn't caught up in esoteric mumbo-jumbo and purposely shutting down such insignificant things as taste and smell. This was what it was to be human. This was the whole point to it.

To smell.

To taste.

To hurt.

To feel hungry and be in love and have your heart broken and care when others died. It was a part of the package, all of it was important, all of it was worth fighting for. And you should never deny yourself the experience of it all.

So you needed to wash if you didn't want to annoy other people, or even your own nose.

Fasolt dipped into the periphery of The Noise, just enough to search out a source of cleansing water. It wasn't far so he sorted out his hair by hauling it in like a one-sided tug of war, and carried it to the stream bundled in his arms like the prized possession that it was. He really did need to sort out some kind of system for it though. He would have to learn some knots, or how to wrap it around his head, if he was to make any sort of progress as he roamed the British landscape looking for a completion to his salvation.

~~~

The moss was a delight.

The coolness tickled his skin even while steam rose as his body tried to maintain its ramped up temperature. But the feeling, oh the feeling of such a simple pleasure.

Fasolt had once again been walking for days so was grateful for the rest. This time he had a few belongings with him, ones he made sure to make use of daily.

Coming across a small farmhouse, or what was left of one, he dug around in an ancient oak barn and found a battered leather satchel, obviously built to last a lifetime and more. He sat in the rotten straw and buffed it with a rag — it cleaned up rather nicely.

He entered the main house, ignoring piles of bones and rotten clothes in a well worn chair — the person must have finally succumbed to The Lethargy at least a decade ago, if not longer. The bathroom gave him items he had not used for centuries: a strangely gritty but very effective soap, a toothbrush, some kind of toothpaste, and something weird smelling he assumed was a shampoo substitute. No longer mass-produced, all manner of ingenious ways were used by Whole to keep their bodies clean, and this particular home seemed to have done quite well with homemade solutions.

With his satchel full of ablution items, he hunted around in wardrobes and dressers for a while until finally deciding that he liked being naked — why wear clothes when he was nice and warm anyway? It seemed kind of silly. The kitchen offered up nothing of use apart from some small knives, but thinking better of it he went to a well stocked tool shed and came up with a folding switchblade that would be useful for hunting along with a couple of other pragmatic items.

Then he was on his way once more.

He rose from the delightful moss and jumped into the stream, washed away the dirt of the day and then brushed his teeth vigorously. What a strange sensation, and how joyous, to run his tongue around his mouth and for it to feel smooth rather than rough and full of the detritus of decades. He soaked his hair for ten minutes as the water took time to penetrate such thick coils, and then shampooed for all he was worth. Rinsed and rung out his hair felt alive, like it wanted to rise up into the sky and grow longer and longer until it reached the sun.

Returning to the moss, clean and no longer desecrating the pure ground, Fasolt sat and attempted to control his crazed locks. He finally came up with a way to spiral them around his head, tucking loose strands into the top. Those that were too thick to cope with he wrapped around his neck a few times to shorten their length.

He felt reborn once more, clean as only soap and shampoo can make you. He sniffed the air — nothing. That was a good sign, and grabbing his satchel he promised himself that he would stay clean and pure from now on. No more Mr. Stinky for him.

~~~

A mission plan, that was what he had needed. And now he had one he was surprised to see how much distance Marcus and his group had made in a matter of days. He needed to pick up his pace but his body simply wasn't up to it yet.

He knew that if he found Marcus then sooner or later Varik would turn up too. Where there was one, eventually there would be the other.

He had to stop Varik making a bad mistake, so he pushed his body onward and ignored the bleeding feet and the aches in his body — it would all get used to the new environment soon enough, and what a marvel it was to be so free. So alive.

Reluctant Flight

Bird was not happy.

Bird was away from home.

Bird missed his family.

Lately he was getting rather annoyed with Master. Being kept away from his mate and newborns was really beginning to make him resentful.

Once Varik and what remained of his church had made it back to the mainland, Bird was called upon to relay the route Marcus and the group had taken, and he was getting fed up with being summoned so often. Each day Varik would request he soar high and allow him to take up residence in Bird's head to see for himself what was happening. It was slow work and it was always an intrusion having such company.

There was a time when Bird didn't mind the company, but as it increased in occurrence so it became less and less welcome.

Now here he was again, after Master had just vacated his head, having to make the long trip back to his nest to feed his young and soar with his mate, who he missed terribly. This was the curse of being Awoken, he knew. He understood what it was to love, he was self-aware, so an innocence had been lost, but it had been centuries since he was but a little chick, and he had almost forgotten what it was to be a free creature, unfettered by thoughts or emotions. His mate had brought the freedom of what he should have been, what she was, back into stark relief. He wondered what his life would have been like if he hadn't been caught up in the sweeping cleansing of the planet all those years ago, when he was Awoken, rather than washed away by The Lethargy.

It didn't matter. He was proud to be so old, so full of knowledge, but it came at a price — the loss of innocence. Yet at the same time he knew that over the years some of his small chicks would be like him. He knew a long and glorious dynasty awaited his descendants, and that he too would be part of it — living countless normal lives, staying strong and agile, enjoying The Blue for centuries to come.

Things needed to change first.

Bird couldn't keep returning to Master, keep going off for days at a time at his beck and call. He was his own Bird, he wanted freedom.

It was more than that though. Master had changed, he could feel it every time he perched on Varik's calloused shoulder.

Master had grown evil, crazed and bitter. He was currently far removed from the pure creature he once was. Long ago Bird had understood what Master wanted: to eradicate the remains of humanity, who seemed like they were no longer wanted by the planet. It made sense to him as it was all that he knew, having met Master the day he was Awoken.

But now?

Now he wasn't so sure. He gained knowledge as he grew older, understood that things were maybe not as simple as Master liked to think they were. Life was complicated, and humans, some of them, maybe deserved to live. He sensed it with the female, the one that he had watched pluck the acorn from The Oak.

She was different, destined for great things. Her death far from a foregone conclusion as Master liked to think.

Bird soared high, not even needing to flap his huge wings as the thermals were strong at such altitude. He headed back to his family, his real family. He was coming to the conclusion that it no longer included Master, abuser of favors, thoughtless in regards to Bird's ever increasing reluctance to share his mind with him.

Still, they had been together a long time, hundreds of years, so it was no easy friendship to break.

For now he would continue with his assistance, although thankfully for today his work was done. He had shown Master a glimpse of Marcus and his companions, making great speed through a generous green carpet with a smattering of trees.

They rode horses, beautiful pure white creatures that somehow seemed more than happy to allow the humans to sit on their backs.

More creatures enslaved by humans, thought Bird. Maybe Varik wasn't so wrong about wanting to see them terminated once and for all.

Tasty Smell

Marcus' virtual Jacobson's organ, or veromonasal organ as he liked to call it since it sounded more made up, went into overdrive. The taste of odor molecules hit the structure and told him of the danger. Once only the province of the now extinct rattlesnake and a few other creatures — long ago victim of The Lethargy, Marcus had honed his smell/taste combo so that it was heightened tenfold. His tongue darted in and out comically, not tasting, but smelling the air as his retracted tongue sent the molecules up to the bridge of his nose where the imaginary organ resided, or didn't reside — he got confused about such details. It didn't smell good. No, that wasn't right, Bird smelled fine, it was what it forecast that wasn't so welcome — discovery.

Marcus signaled for the others to take cover, but it was too late and nobody was paying attention anyway. He sent a whisper through The Noise and this time they all directed the horses into the cover of a thick forest meandering away into the distance as far as they could see. They had been trotting along in the relative open as even though it was dusk and they were tired Marcus wanted to get a little more distance between them and Varik, but it would be time to stop soon enough.

Now they had been spotted it was futile trying to hide, but even a few miles into the forest would at least give them an advantage. It would take at least a day, if not more, for Varik to catch up with them, so they could rest for a few hours, tend the horses, then get a few hours sleep.

Once in the woods dusk turned instantly to the blackest of night.

Marcus ramped up his vision, pupils as big as saucers, and slowed to a gentle walk while he waited for the others to become accustomed to the darkness. The horses seemed to know where they were going anyway, so he led the way and the others followed close behind.

The deeper they got the quieter it became, even the birds were getting ready to settle down for the night. They came to a clearing by a small stream and the horses decided this was to be camp for the night.

Who was Marcus to argue? After all, it was the horses that had been so generous in giving them a head-start on The Eventuals two weeks previously. Since then every day had been a battle for shelter, food and trying to stay hidden at the same time. Hunting had gone poorly at first until the memory of the shanty town had been forgotten. Such depravity had sunk them all into a mire of depression — especially Marcus.

But he suddenly snapped out of it, knowing that dwelling on such things was going to do nothing for their chance of survival, let alone make it a partially enjoyable journey through the ever improving British countryside.

"Thank you Ahebban, you have been most kind in giving us a ride these last few weeks. Without you I think we would have had a much harder time getting some distance between Varik and his Eventuals." Marcus weaved his hands through the white mane of the huge colt, untangling it as best he could. He had been hanging on too tightly again he knew, and didn't want to spoil the beauty of such a fine creature.

You are welcome Marcus, said Ahebban through The Noise. *But now it is time for us to part ways I am afraid. We have things to attend to, and I know that you will be fine without us now.*

Marcus responded silently in The Noise. *Thank you my friend, I won't forget this, or you. It's good to see you doing so well, if, er, a little differently to how I remember.*

Well, you always did have a knack for understatement Marcus, said Ahebban, laughing in The Noise while a loud neigh broke the silence of the settling forest.

The other horses came alongside from the rear, the group dismounting, encouraged in no small part by the horses shaking of their heads under the lightest of suggestions from their leader.

With a flick of the ear and a shake of the tail Ahebban galloped off at speed, the herd following close on his hooves.

"They didn't even say goodbye," said Letje sorrowfully.

"They did to me," said Marcus. "But they aren't really like that Letje, horses are not big on small talk or what we would think of as being polite. They did their part, bringing us this far, and for them that is enough. They don't need good-bye's or thank-you's, they aren't wired like that. Apart from Ahebban, and he said his farewell.

"Such a shame, they were beautiful," said Umeko, staring after the ghostly shapes of the horses before they were lost forever, swallowed up by the wild countryside that was their unspoiled home.

George looked at the departing animals with sheer malice; he'd had a bad few days. Nobody seemed to care that he was a lot smaller than them and it took an awful lot of energy to keep up with their erratic speed. He hoped they didn't return, and that the pace from now on would be somewhat more sedate. He really needed a lie down.

So that's exactly what he did. He turned in a circle three times, found it not to his liking so moved, repeated his actions, dug at the ground to make it 'just so' then lay down and was snoring a few seconds later.

"Right, I think it's time for a bite to eat and a nap, then we will be on our way again. Tomorrow is a very exciting day, it's going to be one of those days you will never forget."

"Why, what's happening?" asked Sy, keen to hear of something happy.

Marcus just smiled, a glint in his eyes that could unnerve you if you thought too deeply on the powers the man had.

~~~

Letje was as sore as a bride the morning after her wedding, and just as euphoric. The warm glow enveloped her like an intense love, heat radiated from her body, her cheeks flushed a deep satisfied pink.

Riding horses was fun! But boy did it hurt by the end of the day. It certainly activated muscles that you didn't even know you had. Each evening she, along with the others, would dismount and try to stretch out their sore limbs. The stamina needed just to ride all day was unexpected, and the soreness of her thighs and bum, not to mention her back and her arms from gripping tightly onto her rather erratic ride, meant that she was either sore, recovering from being sore, or in the throws of anticipating being sore once more.

Still, it was incredibly enjoyable and everybody's spirits had lifted once they began to make such good progress. The height helped immensely as it opened up the beauty of the mostly unspoilt countryside; it was shown to them in ways impossible if they had been traveling by foot. It was a shame it was over, but she certainly wouldn't miss the chafing of the thighs and the, dare she say it? The smell. Horses were really rather windy animals, and if you didn't happen to be at the front of the herd then it got to be somewhat unpleasant after a while.

~~~

"It's horses," said Letje. "Real life horses. Cool. I've only ever seen them in books before, never an actual real one."

"And they are here to help us pick up the pace," explained Marcus, as they were surrounded by the largest and most beautiful animals Britain had ever seen. Centuries of unfettered wild living, with access to the increasingly abundant natural food supply of the countryside, had seen the creatures grow stronger and larger than ever before.

Hello my friend, how are you?

Marcus replied via The Noise. *Honestly? I have been better, but that isn't to say it's not invigorating to be out having an adventure. And you? You look well.*

For a horse you mean?

Well, yes, there is that. I didn't like to ask really, didn't want to be rude.

It's rather a long story if truth be told, and I'm not sure you want to hear it, you may be a little disappointed in what I've done. I felt like a bit of a fool at first, but now I'm

45

amazed I never did it sooner. I think I'm the first actually. To die and stay alive in a different form. Ahebban was proud of his achievement and had been quite excited when he picked up Marcus in the vicinity, arranging to meet and help him via a conversation in The Noise.

Ah, the things I could tell you. If you ever meet a crayfish just be sure to be polite. Oh, and, of course, there is our little friend over there. Marcus pointed at the battered leather duffel bag.

You mean the girl? Special that one, no doubt.

She is, but that's not what I meant. "Letje, can you come here please?"

"Me," said Letje, rather unnerved, pointing at herself like there were any other Letjes in the vicinity.

"Um, yes. You."

Letje sidled over and Marcus asked inquiringly, "If I may?" gesturing at the holdall.

"Sure, okay."

Marcus pulled out Constantine/Yabis.

Hello Mr. Horse, said Yabis.

Damn, so I'm not the only one. Hello Mr. Tortoise. Bet I did it before you though, right?

Marcus interrupted what he knew could carry on for some time; what he knew was a rather strange looking sight to the rest of the group. *Can we do this later? Let's get safe and we can all get to know each other a little better.*

"Hey, I heard that. You were talking in The Noise, right? You were a person?" asked Letje, pointing at the horse accusingly.

Neigh.

"You were," said an indignant Letje.

That was just a horse noise, Letje is it? But yes, I was a person.

Seems like it's catching Daddy.

Bet I did it first though.

Marcus was getting exasperated. "Can we please do this later. People are trying to kill us you know."

Fine, said Ahebban. *No need to get huffy. I am here to help.*

~~~

Later that evening, in the relative safety of a surprisingly ample country home, a wreck, but still standing tall and proud, a strange group of companions sat, stood, lay and paced in a large ex-ballroom. To say it was a mixed grouping would be an understatement, mused Marcus, sitting himself on a blanket, trying his best to keep centuries old dust out of his nose but much more importantly — off his clothes.

Ahebban stood in the middle of the assembly of horses, humans, tortoise, and goat, finding the grouping just as bizarre as Marcus, not to mention the rest who had less experience of such outlandish situations.

Everyone could hear Ahebban's story as he related it via The Noise — there was no need to speak out loud.

The story went that he had left The Commorancy Awoken and eager to get out into the world after a relatively short, by Commorancy standards, stay of a mere 37 and one half years. That was a total of 49 years ago now since he left. Since then he had decided to get back to basics and had ridden around the country on a bicycle, something Stanley approved of and asked for details about. Routes were discussed briefly until everyone got bored, so Ahebban got back to his story.

He had been enjoying his time so much that one day while out riding he grew distracted by the sight of a group of horses in a field just off the animal track he was using as his cycle-route to weave through the trees. He took to the rougher ground and dropped the gears down low so he could make it through to get a closer look. He was so intent on looking at the proud animals that he didn't notice a huge badger hole just down the bank he was trying to do his best to navigate. The front wheel went smack into the hole, luckily no badgers lived there any more, and with a jarring of the bicycle he went flying over the handlebars and straight into the unwelcome embrace of a rather unfortunately placed stump of a tree that had been hit by lighting at some point, and was now all just sharp splinters and not a lot else.

As he lay there, impaled through the thigh, femoral artery sliced and irreparable even with his

Awoken knowledge, he felt like a fool having to meet his end so soon and in such a banal manner after all he had gone through. The fact he had the power to live a life of countless centuries really rubbed salt into the wound

As he stared at his leg pumping blood and smiling at the irony of it all, he noticed the horses were gathered around, staring with interest at him. There was no fear, they had so little to do with humans that there was no longer any knowledge of what to them was a very nonthreatening creature. He noted that one of the horses stayed back, lying on the ground, making a pitiful noise. Through The Noise, and while he still could, he asked politely of the nearest horse to take him to her, to see if he could help. The horse bent its front legs down and with blood leaking his life out into the leafy ground he hopped until he could grab the mane, desecrating it with his dark blood. He got onto its back with a comical lack of grace and was escorted to the crying mare.

She was giving birth, but he was too late. The newborn foal had been too long in the birth canal and starved of oxygen it was a stillbirth. He saw a chance to do one last good deed and entered the body of the creature, hoping it wasn't too late. Once inside he quickly sourced the way to pump a massive supply of adrenaline to the heart, restarting it. Oxygen poured back into the lungs, and more importantly the brain. The young foal's chest heaved, the body shook, and was animated once more. But it was no use, the young foal's spirit had already gone, and for good — it was impossible to bring a life back from The Void. Ahebban sadly went to return to his last moments on earth as his body slipped away.

And irony of ironies, he too was dead. His body at least. His essence of a person however, much to his surprise, was still firmly rooted to The Now, and he was stuck inside the body of the newborn foal, not even sure how to go about standing on four legs.

Let's just say it took some time to get to grips with being a horse. Walking on four legs is not as easy as it looks.

You should try having a shell and a retractable neck, said Yabis. *Now that is something that takes considerable practice.*

Family Time

"Are you absolutely sure you don't mind? I feel as if I'm letting you all down terribly." Umeko tugged nervously at her bottom lip, hating that she was being so selfish, yet knowing how important it was she stay.

"Of course we don't mind. I think I speak for us all when I say that the most important thing of all is children. And now you have that chance." Marcus put his arm around Umeko, reassuring her.

"My father always said that finding a husband and starting a family was the most important thing for all of us Umeko. We need to have more people if we are to have any hope of humanity surviving. And now you have your chance." Letje peered into Constantine's holdall, still finding it hard to talk about her father now that he was actually here, albeit in a strange form.

They were stood out the front of the ranch style house, the large balcony a rare luxury for homes in England. Ryce was inside, staying out of the way so that they could say their goodbyes in peace.

The moment Umeko had set eyes on the man, she knew. Knew that he was the one for her, the other half of her she had been waiting for her whole life. More than that, he was to be the father of her children — their children. Fully Awoken inside the Commorancy, Umeko had focused on one main goal: to become fertile and have the chance of a family.

Middle age in the old conventional sense meant she would be close to never being able to bear children, but it meant little when you were Awoken. She was now hundreds of years old and before she was accepted as a guest by Marcus she had dreamed of being able to get pregnant. Now it could happen. She had dedicated herself to altering her body chemistry to allow for children, in the process she became even more beautiful. She shone with inner vitality that overflowed and affected all those around her.

As soon as they encountered Ryce it was as if she truly blossomed as her name signified: plum blossom child. Her skin virtually radiated happiness. Her deep plum complexion took on a shine that was almost blinding, as if she were a piece of fruit too tempting to ignore. She felt her body stir at the sight of the rather scruffy bearded man, Umeko actually felt her hormones go into overdrive.

Ryce didn't stand a chance. He was captivated from the second he laid eyes on her. Pheromones captured him and Umeko's radiance shone directly at his heart. The encounter was, as far as Marcus could recall, one of the most bizarre and uplifting meetings he had ever heard of, let alone witnessed

They had been traveling for a number of weeks, hiding out, moving surreptitiously, making their way slowly yet surely to a place Marcus was keeping very tight-lipped about. Varik was always just a few steps behind them, his bird a real problem when it came to hiding. Yet for some reason it hadn't been seen for a few days and Marcus knew through The Noise that it was safe for them to travel in daylight for a change. So they walked down the center of a once large road, now green and verdant with grasses and wild plants of all description. Butterflies startled from their nectar feeding as they brushed past the high plants, glinting in the sunlight as they fluttered off to continue their dreams of life somewhere else. The seed heads of hundreds of dandelions floated gently on the breeze, making the air a haze of white. It was a sticky day and all around was the background buzz of insects busy making the most of the remaining warmth of summer.

Ancient rusted cars now covered in plant-life and home to hedgehogs, birds, insects and even the occasional fox made lumps in the road like natural hillocks, strange outcroppings on the otherwise perfectly flat surface.

The group were spread out in single file, taking up the width of the road, enjoying their own individual peace. Lost in personal daydreams they walked steadily yet without rushing, enjoying the heat, the intoxicating smells of countless blooms, the ripe summer gathering them up and wrapping them in its natural beauty.

Umeko felt as though she was living a dream — a lightness filled her head as the heat shimmered in the distance, the haze of bright flowers making a mirage so beautiful it was as if the old paintings by Monet she had seen in books had come to life just for her. She plucked a beautiful shocking blue flower from a tall stem and twirled it absently in her hand, then tucked it behind a perfectly formed ear.

The road cut deep into the undulating hills that flanked it. High banks, the excavations from the road's construction, stood tall on either side, now covered in thick forests of oak and numerous other native trees. Hundreds of birds chirped their contentment at the return of the forests to the once overly farmed and almost sterile landscape; they bred and proliferated like they hadn't done in thousands of years.

As she walked without conscious thought, Umeko saw rabbits lopping around on the banks close to the road where the grass grew short enough for them to tunnel their burrows. Young bunnies gambled energetically, rolling and playing with their brothers and sisters.

Then Umeko had a funny feeling in the pit of her stomach and stopped dead in her tracks. The world went silent and there was but one thing in her vision. A man.

He stood but a handful of paces away from her, and she knew there and then that this was to be the father of her children. She knew with an ache in her heart and a longing in her belly that she had found her source of happiness at last. She had found the other half of herself, the missing piece of what it was to be human, and why humanity simply had to make it through the terrible place it currently resided in. Umeko found love.

The others in the group stood and kept silent as the man approached. Through The Noise it was obvious there was no danger from the stranger, and each one of them knew that they were witnessing something special.

The man approached. He was six feet tall and rather scruffy looking. His face had a thick beard but was obviously trimmed quite recently. A mess of short black hair sat on his head like a bird's nest needing a spring clean and he was beginning to gray at the temples. A thin face showed a Roman nose with thick full lips, and although his build was slight he was wiry and strong looking like only those that travel a lot by foot and survive off the land can be.

He wore faded denim trousers and functional walking boots with a black shirt open at the neck. He hefted a substantial rucksack on his back, with a sleeping bag and pots and pans that swayed slightly as he walked with what Umeko thought of as a gentle confidence.

The overriding feature was his eyes — so pale as to be almost colorless. They sparkled with joy, like diamonds in a crystal clear pool, as he stared at Umeko with wonder. He stopped for a second to shed his rucksack, then continued to move toward Umeko at a leisurely pace. It was as if he wanted to etch into his memory forever the first time he laid his eyes upon her. He took in the radiant plum skin, the high cheekbones and pouting red lips, the glorious hair on her head, the slender fingers and slight but full figure. It was obvious he wanted to commit every detail of her to memory before he said a word, just in case it broke the spell.

He noted the flower behind her ear and smiled, and once again was drawn to her radiant face. He obviously had a realization just before he reached her, and as he took the last few steps he withdrew something from a pocket in his shirt.

They stood face to face, hearts hammering in their chests, eyes taking in the soul of the other, and the man held out a tiny but perfect wild plum in his open palm. It was the exact same color as Umeko and she put out her hand to take the gift.

"For you, Wife," said the man, smiling so broadly he was at risk of losing it off the side of his face.

"Thank you, Husband." Umeko took the plum and bit into the sweet soft flesh, then offered it back to the man. He took a bite and licked his lips as juice trickled down his chin.

Umeko reached for him and held him tight, kissing him on his plum flavored lips.

They held hands after their kiss, and the introductions to the rest of the group were made.

Tears dropped gently to the reclaimed road from the eyes of all as happiness sang on the breeze and whispered in the trees — there was hope after all, you just had to find it.

~ ~ ~

Marcus married them the next day. He knew that they would live an exceptionally long and happy life full of children, grandchildren and generations of a healthy line that would not only be Whole but would Awaken — just as Umeko would teach her husband how to Awaken over the next few years. He said little about this, simply reveling in the moment, letting them enjoy the promise of a happy future together.

Kirstie caught his attention that evening as everybody enjoyed the happy day.

"I'm staying too," said Kirstie. "I talked with Umeko and Ryce and they say it's fine. I hope you don't feel like I'm deserting you, but with the baby it just feels like too much of a risk. I'm sorry." Kirstie began to cry, her decision one of concern for her child more than for her own safety, yet she still felt bad about leaving, especially now that Umeko was not going to continue either.

"It's fine Kirstie," said Marcus. "I knew it was coming. You can hardly be expected to traipse around the country when you have the little man to look after. I wouldn't expect it of you. And anyway, this is how it's meant to be. Soon Umeko will be with child and Dale will have a little playmate, maybe even more once her girl grows up. So, don't feel bad, some things just work out how they should."

Kirstie stared hard at Marcus, trying to read what went on behind eyes that knew so much yet gave nothing away. "You knew, didn't you?"

Marcus held out his hands. "Knew what?"

"That this would happen — all of it."

"Haha, you think too highly of me. But there were hints, suggestions of what your future would hold. That you were destined for friendship, company, and to help rebuild things. You belong here Kirstie. It's going to be a great future, just be sure to look out for one another. And strangers."

"We will Marcus, we will." Kirstie hugged Marcus tight, then stepped back and looked at him. "Look after yourself Marcus, and look after the others, especially Letje. She's so young still, so very young."

"Don't worry, I will. Now, come on, let's go enjoy the rest of the day. We will be leaving in the morning so let's make the most of it. I quite fancy a drink actually, I wonder if Ryce is a bit of a homebrew expert, he seems to be good at most things."

Mike Takes a Trip

Mike had slept late. Again. It was getting to be a regular thing, and Kirstie could really do with some assistance. Early pregnancy was making her feel less than her usual energetic self, and Mike would have been a lot of help if he could rouse himself earlier, rather than later. He had always been a heavy sleeper, but this was getting ridiculous.

Kirstie went into their simple but comfortable bedroom, more a living, breathing Room than a conventional space. The wooden walls were alive, the lifeblood of a ficus that sat squat above the compact space. Kirstie stomped over to the bed, trying to wake him before she arrived. Nothing.

She pulled the sheet back from Mike's face and put out a hand to shake him by the shoulder. Then she stopped. A clammy sweat sprung like a million geysers in miniature all over her body and she felt as if she was going to either faint or throw up — maybe both.

Kirstie slumped onto the bed, Mike still not waking from his deep slumber.

How could she not have seen it? Her, with all her newfound insights into things natural after so many years being Awoken, and she couldn't see what was staring her right in the face.

Mike had The Lethargy.

The father of her unborn child was never going to see him grow up and become a man. Kirstie had spent so much time obsessing about her boy that she had failed to look at Mike in the proper way; she failed to see what was now obvious. Mike would never grow old with his family, this was why he slept.

The Lethargy had him in its slippery clutches and his life was already being sucked out from him to be sent back to The Void a wisp at a time. Kirstie tried to stop the hammering of her heart — it couldn't be good for the baby, surely? She did her deep breathing until gradually the sickness and the sweats began to fade, in their wake a hollowness came to fill their place. A vision of things to come, the emptiness that would be there when Mike finally passed into irreversible Lethargy.

Kirstie didn't know how long she had been sat there, but finally Mike roused himself. He sat up in bed and smiled at her, eyes groggy from sleep, hair wild as it always was in the morning.

"Hello my wife, and hello little apple. He is that big now right? The size of an apple?"

"Hello sleepy — my husband. And no, not yet. He's still about the size of your thumb. Tiny."

Mike held up his thumb and stared at it suspiciously. "Are you sure? That's awful small. I hope he's going to come out on time. Hey, what time is it? Feels late."

"It is late, so c'mon mister, time to get up and at 'em. Things to do, places to go and all that."

Mike pulled back the covers and smiled at Kirstie. "What, right now? What's the rush?"

Kirstie smiled at her husband.

~~~

Mike never got to see his son, he died before he was born.

It broke Kirstie's heart.

The birth was straightforward and although she didn't know it Marcus was on hand with every piece of equipment possible, just in case it was needed. As it was, Kirstie was alone when Dale came into the world, both coping just fine without any form of outside help. A concerned Marcus watched via monitors, getting hardly any sleep for weeks before the birth. He was probably more nervous about the whole thing than Kirstie herself.

She was confident that what her body was telling her was correct: that she was fine, the birth would go well, and her baby would be born Whole. She desperately wished Mike could have been there to see his son come into the world.

Since the day she first realized that Mike had The Lethargy, that after hundreds of years of a Whole life he had finally succumbed to the dreaded curse, she had vowed to make the most of their time together. Later that day, summoning up more courage than she thought she had, Kirstie sat him down and told him.

"I know, I didn't want to worry you, that's all."

"Worry me, what about you? How long have you known?"

"A week or so I guess, maybe two. I just wanted to be sure you and the little one were fine, no point worrying you unduly is there?"

"Mike, we're a team. We promised to be honest with each other, to tell each other everything. How could you keep this from me?"

"I know we promised, but, well, I guess I just didn't want to admit it really. I thought I could ignore it, maybe try to find a way back. After all these years, so many normal lifetimes, I thought maybe I could fight it and try to deal with it. Well, that didn't work. Ha, I should have known. Why would I be able to beat The Lethargy when it has killed billions? Still, gotta try, right?"

"Oh Mike, you silly thing, you should have said something. What are we going to do? You can't have it, you just can't. It's not fair." Kirstie was trying to be strong, but it all fell apart in an instant. It just got worse.

Then worse still.

Mike never asked Kirstie to kill him, as her father had done. He wouldn't put that type of pressure on her, he loved her too much, knew what it would do to her. As the days passed into weeks, then the weeks bled into months, and his mind and body let him down more and more often, Mike came to understand the true nature of The Lethargy.

He was in a rather unique situation. Having all Marcus had learned at his disposal, the specialist nature of the Room, and the daily practices he had done for centuries, meant that he was alone in becoming Lethargic after such a life. Nobody else had survived so long, learned so much, and succumbed. Sad as it was that even those inside The Commorancy could become afflicted, Mike understood that his situation was special, and delved as deep as he could into the root of the stealing of his identity and his very being, and did what he could to understand it, to pass on vital knowledge.

It didn't matter, he still died.

He never did get to see his son.

That Was Quick

Astolat lay in the grass, her final resting place. As her body turned cold and wild dogs circled ever closer to their free lunch Astolat was already far away.

She was with her new family now, not that she knew it. The timeless Void had claimed her once more, taken her back into its cold empty embrace, eliminating the pain, the suffering, the blip of a life she had thought so important. Now it was as if it had never been — she was once again reborn.

Not for the first or the last time, just another temporary stay in a body of one kind or another, of which there had been countless.

There would be countless more.

In The Void she was readied for physical life once more. If there had been such a thing as time then she would have been queued for almost fifty thousand years, but as there was no such thing it was a stay neither long or short. She had no body to experience it with, all there was was nothing.

Reborn, she was sucked away from the emptiness and entered a body new to a world that was galaxies away from the life her essence had once inhabited. From the point of view of Astolat's stay on planet earth it was a million years in the past — irrelevant and meaningless to the newborn. There was nothing to remember, nothing to forget, no past, present or future, just states of being that played back and forth across the Universe in a never ending dance that spread out in all directions — infinite in all things, merely there.

The creature she was born into was hurtling through space in a vast construction that itself was once many other creatures, and would be countless more. A sentient being in its own right, it was older than many races, had seen more than most other creatures in the Universe, and was vastly intelligent. Inside it the lives of its passengers played out as they traveled on their never ending journey around the ever expanding Universe, mapping, discovering, wondering at the beauty that they encountered, at the ends of civilizations and births of new ones.

The woman known as Astolat was no more, but something else was there in its stead. Astolat had not even been born for countless millennia, yet inside this new birth was a spark of memory of what it would be, what it had been, and what it was most of all: part of The Void. Each life was as nothing, lived then returned to where it came, traveling as if as dust, vibrating around the Universe and time as the games unfolded, as they had countless times before and would until the end of everything, then doing it all over again as new universes came into being with a snap of cosmic fingers.

The mother cradled the newborn, staring with almond shaped eyes, watching its pasts and futures through The Noise, marveling at the variety of life in the place it called home: the vast, empty Universe its race played in for generation after countless generation.

It smiled at the things her child had been, what it would be, and made a slight adjustment to her own body chemistry, releasing the milk it would now give to the ravenous new life, allowing it to become instantly self-aware, knowing all she did, seeing what it had done, what it would do, allowing it the privilege of making its first decision, the one that all newborns of such a high caste were allowed to make.

Where to next.

~~~

"How can she be dead? I can't believe it, she was just talking to me a few minutes ago, then she went off to... you know, have a pee." Letje found it hard to come to terms with the fact she had just been talking to Astolat, trying not to giggle when she burst out with silly words about donkey bums and floppy rabbit ears.

"I think that answers your question Letje." Marcus pointed at a young man in his early twenties, tattooed red from head to toe, a short bolt through his forehead. Astolat was a good aim and had hit her mark, but not before her own life was ebbing away. The slice right through her leg the death blow she had never seen coming. "This is why we need to stick together. No going off on your own."

"Not even for a pee?" asked Letje.

Marcus raised an eyebrow, nodding his head at Astolat.

"Okay, yeah, point made."

Marcus bent and gently closed Astolat's eyes, then stood and turned to the ever shrinking group. "I'm sorry but we really do need to stay alert. I can't see everything that could happen. Although our deceased red friend over there is, well, was a fool, he was still adept enough to keep himself hidden from me, from all of us. Nobody picked him up through The Noise, so we need to stay close to each other, always have at least one other person with you at all times. Now we need to go, we may not have been able to sense the killer of our friend, but you can bet The Eventuals know he is gone. They will be here to find out why soon enough."

On it went, day after day. No peace, hardly a chance to rest. Locations were chosen more carefully, nowhere too overgrown or with too many opportunities for The Eventuals to ambush them. But it grew harder and harder to stay motivated, to stay alert, and, finally, to even care what happened any more. The days were spent holed up wherever Marcus felt was safe, the darker hours spent trudging across the countryside, skirting towns and villages, and following roads not used by vehicles in centuries. Often they followed animal tracks used daily and now clearer of nature's ceaseless forward march than the once pristine roads man had been so proud of.

Fishing

"Well," beamed Marcus, "I think we all know what this means, don't we?"

"You don't mind?" asked Stanley, concern on his face, battling with the smile that he knew would surface at any moment.

"Of course not, it's like it was all made just for you Stanley, it's your idea of heaven, right?"

"Absolutely. Look at it, it *is* heaven on earth."

"Just like your first perfect day all those years ago, isn't it? When you skipped work and went fishing, were alone and happy. Eating fish and swigging booze straight from the bottle."

"Hey! How do you know about that? I never told you did I?"

"Well, not exactly, but you thought it lots, and sometimes I can't help but pick up on such things. You know that by now Stanley, you have the same thing going on inside of you too, right?"

"Well, yes, but I don't ever peek, it's rude," said Stanley, the closest to affronted he could get in such a beautiful place. Already he was itching to pull out the rod he had found on their travels and used to feed them countless times already.

"It is rude, very rude. And I apologize, I am just a busybody at heart, I know."

Stanley could feel the pull of the place, it was sucking him in and he knew there was little he could do to resist its draw. This was why he was here, what it had all been for. This was his destiny. It had been a few months now since they had left The Commorancy, and their numbers had dwindled down to just the four of them. Stanley didn't mind, he enjoyed the closeness that only a small group of people with a common goal — in this case survival — can have. At the same time he understood that something wasn't quite right, that there was something missing. This was it. This small patch of England, this feeling, this vibration.

"What's that, um... thing? I don't know what to call it. A feeling? No, just something about this place." Letje couldn't express what it was, Stanley and Marcus just smiled at her. Sy furrowed his brow, trying to figure it out too.

"It's Stanley's home, that's it, isn't it?"

"Yep."

"It is," confirmed Marcus. "This is what Stanley was born for, to be right here, at this time, with us. All those years, the things he has learned, the life he has led, The Contamination, us leaving, being chased, the sorrows, the good bits, all of it, it's the line of history that had to happen to bring us here, to now."

"Somebody care to explain to the youngster what's going on then. I feel like the odd one out here." Letje was out of her depth — again. She wished for the million and first time that she had got a Room.

Stanley tried his best. "This is my place, where I am supposed to be. I don't know how else to explain it really. It just feels right. More than right. It feels like I am only a part of it all here. I can feel it calling me, vibrating, waiting for me to arrive and complete the circle, fill in the gap, bring what was missing. Something like that anyway, it's hard to put it into words. It's too complicated but too simple at the same time." Stanley didn't know quite how to articulate such a simple thing as belonging to a place, all he knew was that this was where he was meant to be. Where he *had* to be.

"So it's like you are just a piece of the actual whole? Like the place will be Awoken now that you are here?" Letje thought she was beginning to understand.

He's met his fate Letje, he belongs to this landscape, to this environment. Everyone has a similar destiny inside of them, it just takes a long time to find it. Most never do. I think it is why The Lethargy actually came into existence. Nobody was where they were supposed to be, everyone lived in the wrong place, some even at the wrong time.

Thanks Daddy, I think I'm getting it now. I wonder if you're right — about The Lethargy?

When have I ever been wrong? said Yabis, somehow managing to smile during their conversation via The Noise. Letje still couldn't really figure out how he managed it and doubted she ever would.

~~~

They wandered over to the house, a sprawling baroque frontage to a respectably sized country house. They crunched over an ocean of gravel in need of serious weeding, which led down to what would have once been an immaculate lawn, and would be again in a few years time with careful tending from Stanley.

Stanley was lost in a dream-haze of euphoria. He had finally found his home, his true home. But it wasn't the house that was at the heart of the place, it was the natural surroundings that were what drew him, what called him and wanted him as a part of them. It was nature at its finest. Once tamed, it had grown wild, gradually returning to settle between outright overgrown wildness and the remains of a once daily tended garden. Now the balance was in tune. Dominant plants and trees, beautiful shrubs and wild flowers, had fallen into harmonious collusion to make for a truly stunning environment that Marcus had come so close to achieving within The Garden Room — almost. This was different, the whole area vibrated with perfection waiting to be completed, and Stanley was what was missing.

"This is what it is all about," mused Marcus as they wandered around the outside of the building, huge geraniums shouting out loud greetings with their bright red flowers, now gone rogue and growing vigorously all around the building perimeter. "This is the truth. This is man and nature in harmony, one complementing the other. A house for people to live in, a nice house that respects its surroundings, and the plants and the birds and the animals and insects all having a home too. This is what it should have been like, how people should have built, but there were too many, not enough space for them all, and look what happened. But this?" Marcus spun and held his arms out high. "This is true perfection. A place that is calling you Stanley. You will make this even more beautiful, and it is your home. Where you are supposed to be. Stunning."

"We all know what the best part is though, right?" said Stanley, looking down the gentle slope to the half hidden lake, a truly natural lake with impossibly perfect rocks erupting from the grassy banks, some huge, moss covered and standing like silent sentries, others small, impossibly delicate.

"The lake?" ventured Letje, knowing just how much Stanley loved his fishing, or just sitting by the water's edge, doing nothing but enjoying the peace when he could. It made her long for her own house; she hadn't realized quite how much she had missed the home of her family for generations, and her very own lake too.

"The lake." Stanley nodded his head and was already walking down toward the clear water.

"Don't you want to look inside the house Stanley?" asked Sy.

"Not at the moment. I know it will probably be a nightmare, there is so much work to do in there I would rather not let it depress me just yet. Not that I mind, it will be great to restore it to something magnificent, and I have plenty of time to do it. So I think I will have a look at the lake first. You all coming?"

They made their way down to the water's edge, an impossibly flat rock that curved gently into the water making for a perfect fishing spot. Stanley stared into the water, seeing through The Noise the teeming life under the surface. There were fish in abundance. Trout and other species had thrived for centuries here, undisturbed by anything more threatening than a heavy downpour.

Stanley was convinced that he could see the world vibrate. It was as if a perfect balance was now to be found in this small part of the United Kingdom, as if it was finally made pure. The air rippled as if in a heat haze, impossible as the fast-encroaching autumn was chilling the air. He could feel the rock vibrate beneath his feet, humming its gratitude for finally being complete. He could swear that even the fish were pleased to see him, understanding the natural order of things and knowing that he would be a gentle caretaker for their needs, only taking out of the water what he needed, nothing more. Never greedy.

Stanley smiled, he had found his home at last.

~~~

The house was a mess, a true decorator's worst nightmare.

Stanley just smiled. He wasn't in any hurry, and besides, he knew he would have company soon enough. Not today, not tomorrow, but over the coming years he simply understood that the house, or rather, the whole estate, called... what should he call it? Such a place surely needed a name.

"Good Vibrations. What do you think of that for a name for the estate? I think it fits. And it's a blast from the past too, for those of us that remember. Right Marcus?"

"Very fitting. There certainly are good vibrations here, now that it has you Stanley."

"I like it too, but what's it got to do with the past?" asked Letje, determined this time not to miss out on something everyone else seemed to know.

"Don't look at me, I haven't got a clue," said Sy, wilting under Letje's scrutiny.

"It's a song from back before The Lethargy, by a group called the Beach Boys." Marcus started to sing, everyone laughing at just how bad a voice he had.

"Wow Marcus, I assumed you would be good at everything," said a shocked Stanley.

"Haha. Nobody's perfect, I always did want to be able to sing though."

The house was in a very sorry state. After hundreds of years of neglect it was amazing it was still standing, but quality shone through and although many windows were broken, paint was peeling from the walls and furniture was covered in mold and the countless deceased bodies of generations of insects, the actual structure was surprisingly sound. Deep coving still joined wall to ceiling, elaborate cornices were everywhere, and thick skirting board still highlighted the thick oak boards of the floors.

As they roamed the house Stanley felt more and more at home. It was as if the building had been waiting for him, waiting to be restored to its former glory. To one day be a home for a man that had spent centuries alone, happy in his Room with only himself and his newly Awoken insight into the world as company.

Stanley left the others in one of the huge downstairs rooms and roamed around the extensive building. It was very large, some would say too large for a comfortable home, but Stanley was now used to The Commorancy, where space seemed to be infinite.

He walked the corridors of his new house, staring at pictures of past owners, long dead, paint peeling under cracked varnish. He walked on red carpets, frayed and threadbare even as the last owners succumbed to The Lethargy. Now they were little more than dust.

But the place had promise, he knew he would restore it. More, he knew there would be others. Others would find this place now that he had. Now the owner was back people would be drawn to it like moths to a rare electric light bulb. He would make the place burn with those bulbs again. He would set up wind generators, maybe even a hydro-electric system — there must be plans somewhere — and he would let the newly decorated rooms burn brightly with electricity and roaring fires warming the house, welcoming guests.

Stanley went down the stairs to join the others, running his hand down the glass-smooth banister as he did so, smiling as he reached the bottom step where he placed his hand on top of the newel post. It was topped with a huge acorn, rubbed back to pale bare wood on the top from thousands of hands over the years that couldn't help but give it a rub for luck.

An acorn, now that's fate I believe. It's what set all this in motion after all, a simple acorn plucked from a tree.

Stanley's Room

Stanley had thought he knew himself quite well when he entered The Commorancy. After all, there had been plenty of time to familiarize himself with his own sense of self — now it was obvious he was sorely lacking in his knowledge.

He had believed that the time he had spent with only his thoughts for company, after The Lethargy eliminated everything that had made up his life thus far, had given him the freedom to really understand what it was he actually wanted out of life — the truth was that he didn't have a clue. He thought he knew, but the Room given to him by Marcus made it abundantly clear that Marcus, from questionnaires, strange and complex seemingly random things he had been made to do, and countless details amassed via extensive research, knew Stanley an awful lot better than he knew himself.

How else could he explain the contents of the Room he had been given, and the level of knowledge he had gained whilst idling away the centuries? It was as if Marcus had somehow peered into the very essence of what made him a man and constructed his Room to draw out his true nature slowly but as surely as the eroding of the British coastline. It was scary if you thought about it, so Stanley decided that he would not think about it at all.

When Stanley first entered his Room he assumed it must be some kind of joke, or at the least that he had been mixed up with somebody of a very different personality to his own, or more likely it was for an alien species or something, it jarred that much with what he was expecting. To say it was a Room wasn't even correct, as Stanley found out over the years. His 'Room' actually consisted of multiple spaces over more levels than he cared to think about. He never did get to see it from the outside, or if he did then he didn't recognize it, but it must have been an at least moderately large skyscraper with numerous Rooms on each level, and what he could only assume was some kind of complex rotational system where he found himself going through the same door but it leading to a space he had never encountered before. It was dizzying, confusing, annoying, exciting and downright mind-boggling, in no particular order.

Yet he loved it all looking back on it. It had made him the man that he was today, and he intended to take every advantage of what he had learned, to enjoy the rest of what appeared to be the chance of a very long life indeed.

The first thing that Stanley had encountered, when the door was closed behind him and Marcus wished him good luck, was a series of moving platforms beneath his feet. The minute he stepped into the Room, as the door slammed shut, the floor had begun to move. One minute he was at the door, the next he was on the other side of the Room, pieces of the floor moving in random directions, as well as up and down, on thick hydraulic legs. Peering down between the gaps he saw nothing but darkness, cold air blowing upward hinting at dangers unseen.

What the hell? I'm too old for this. Stanley thought he may as well have been told to...

"Stanley. Stanley!"

"Eh? What? Sorry, I was miles away. Thinking about some things."

"Oh, didn't mean to interrupt. You go back to your thinking, it wasn't anything important."

Stanley looked at Marcus. "You sure?"

"Absolutely, I can see that you have a bit of catching up to do still. It was a pretty mad time for you in there wasn't it?"

"Yes," said Stanley cautiously. "Not prying into my thoughts are you Marcus?"

"Wouldn't dream of it Stanley. Carry on, as you were. Are you alright there though, on the stairs?"

"Eh?" Stanley noted with interest that he was sat on the bottom step of the stairs. Well, if he had to think then he had to think. He had learned over the years that keeping his head straight meant giving in to such things when they came to the surface.

Now, where was I?

He thought he may as well have been asked to play and win at one of the video games the kids had all raved about, or be told to dance — he had absolutely no rhythm. How was he supposed to be jumping about on platforms at his age? Craziness.

So he sat down and waited it out.

And waited.

And waited, and waited some more.

Until in exasperation Stanley got to his feet and tried to figure out the predicament he found himself in. He began to focus, to watch for patterns — there were none. To try to time the movements — they were random, or to see if he could manage to jump between the gaps that never seemed to shrink enough to make leaping over the void a good idea.

So he sat, and allowed himself to empty. He let himself go, thought back to the first day he was truly happy, alone at the lake fishing after he realized the world as he knew it was over. Slowly he came to understand what was so special about that day; he had been close to not only The Noise but also The Void. The same stillness settled over him until slowly he came to find himself in tune with the strange movements of the floor. He found that although there was no pattern there was a future that allowed him to simply step from one platform to another without any risk, and that being able to see such a future meant that he was beginning to Awaken.

Stanley got to his feet and with his glimpse of the perfectly aligned future that allowed him to walk as normal through the Room he turned to his left, sidled forward until his feet were lined up along the edge of his platform, and just walked, without thinking, without fear, without even looking down, trusting in the future he had chosen to follow. Less than ten seconds later he watched a door opening into another Room, one that looked a lot less crazy, or, at least, a lot less shifting, which was a start he supposed.

It went on like that for years, crazy Room after crazy Room. Each time he thought the next space seemed normal it got weirder and weirder as the spaces showed their true natures to him. Some he spent years in, others he passed through in the blink of an eye, or had zero memory of at all — he just found himself opening a door and entering the next one. At first he felt scared turning the handles as Marcus had warned he was, under no circumstances, to try to leave his Room until the time was right. Then he figured out Marcus was referring to his final Room, not any of the intervening ones. Still, it got the old heart-rate up quite a few times.

Time passed, somehow always at a speed that seemed right for Stanley's mood, although if he thought about that it made no sense whatsoever. Still, it was how it seemed, as he never got bored, never felt that he had been in The Commorancy too long, and he always imagined that what was happening was supposed to happen, everything going at a pace that fit perfectly with his slow Awakening.

On and on it went. Endless Rooms, each teaching him a lesson somehow, even if he didn't understand it until many Rooms later. He found himself slowly but inexorably moving higher and higher. He could sense it somehow, even if there was nothing as straightforward as an elevator or a floor number to indicate his ascent. He just somehow knew.

Then one day he found himself transformed: fully Awoken. There was no sudden enlightenment, no miraculous insight into the nature of things for him, it just gradually all came together over the years until he became as much as he could be. He became fully Stanley. A man that had been alive for a lot of years, although he had no idea how many. A man that was Whole, Awoken, and wouldn't be dying any time soon.

Stanley realized he was in his final Room. He knew it, felt it as a physical truth. There was no more he could learn, not in a Room at any rate. He had achieved what he was meant to achieve, and soon he would leave for good.

It was a shame though, Stanley really liked his new life. His solitary existence was bliss, and he wondered if he could actually be called the same Stanley that entered the strange place so long ago. Did it matter? Probably not. He was who he was, he had changed as he had experienced so much and come to understand so much. Now he was different, but deep down he was still the same person he was sure, just one with a lot more understanding. A man that was truly alive in every sense of the word, truly deserving of the life that had been granted him — a thing so rare it was a gross crime to waste such a beautiful gift.

Stanley got to his feet, feeling light and overflowing with the life-forces all around him.

"Right then, I wonder what Marcus wanted?"

He went to find out.

Lies and More Lies

Stanley found them in the kitchen, sat around a table that was made in the 15th century and had been polished daily for centuries by servants of the same family line. Letje had wiped it over with a cloth and the countless layers of wax sprang back to vivid life, bouncing back the light coming in from the generous windows that made the kitchen the definite heart of the home. It was huge.

"It's huge."

"We know, nice isn't it?" said Marcus, admiring the opulently fitted out kitchen.

Stanley inspected the space, noting first of all the stunning condition of the table. Now there was a table you would be proud to eat your supper from. Using a table-mat of course, you wouldn't want to spoil it or anything. He began to look around the room, noting the mix of old with what used to be thought of as thoroughly modern. There was a beat up Aga, but additionally two electric ovens in a mass of cupboards that also housed a microwave, a coffee machine and a few other gadgets he had no idea about as to purpose.

There was a massive center aisle, with a sink and breakfast bar, black marble worktop now white with dust apart from the footprints of some small animal or other. His dreams of what he would do to the place were interrupted as he caught the conversation around the table.

"What? Sorry, I was dreaming of cooking the fish from the lake on the Aga, and wondering how to set up the electricity."

"No problem Stanley, and I can help with that. I have a lot of experience of that type of thing you know. I was saying, I need to tell you all something, to get it off my chest so-to-speak. An admission of guilt if you will. The truth."

"Okaaaaay," said a wary Stanley. "About what exactly?"

"About why we are here. Why we left The Commorancy, why we are now just the four of us. Well, plus Constantine and George, but you know what I mean."

"And soon to be three," said Letje. "Stanley is staying, aren't you Stanley?"

"I am, it feels right."

"Of course, of course, and that is a part of what I want to talk to you about. The real reason for everything that has happened of late. The truth."

Evacuation

"I get the feeling I'm not going to like this. Is it bad Marcus? Something really bad?"

Marcus squirmed in his chair, finally getting up and walking around the kitchen, running a finger through the dusty countertop, drawing lines of black in the dust of time.

"Please, sit down. This is going to take a while."

Once everybody was seated Marcus made a request.

"If you would all just listen to what I have to say without interruption then this will all go a lot more smoothly. I need to tell you, it's important, but if I get stopped I don't know that I will ever be able to get it all out, tell you everything. Deal?"

The deal was made, Marcus told his story.

~~~

"I, me, um, that is to say, me and the other Marcus have been—"

"What?"

"What are you on about?"

"Two Marcus's, that explains a lot," said Stanley.

How did you do it?

Marcus sighed deeply. "What happened to our deal? I haven't even finished a sentence yet. Please, let me tell this."

"Sorry."

"Me too."

"And me."

I'm sorry too.

"Right, okay fine. Now, please let me just tell this..." Marcus waited to see if there would be more interruptions. Letje, Sy and Stanley just sat there looking innocent and keen to hear the story. Yabis/Constantine sat on the table top, eyes blinking lazily.

"Maybe I need to start this differently. Now, I know that both Stanley and Sy are very old in one sense, but most of your lives have been spent in your Rooms, so it's different than it is for me. My time has been lived from each Now to the next Now, a linear time if you will. Although much of it has become somewhat jumbled, and I am the first to admit that often things get a little out of whack for me in terms of what I have done and even where I am, I have lived all of these years. In the Rooms, deep in Lessons, or in The Noise time can be different: fast or slow, it depends. But either way it's not the same as simply living each and every day of three hundred or so years like I have.

And there are two of me..." Marcus waited, nothing but curiosity, maybe even dubious stares.

"I can't, won't, go into just how this happens to be the case at the moment, it would take too long. But I do need to tell you the truth about why we all left The Commorancy. The truth of the matter is that I wanted an adventure. I was going mad, still am I suppose, and on top of that you all needed to come to the mainland

and be in certain places at certain times. Umeko needed to be in The Commorancy, but she then needed to be back out walking down that beautiful overgrown motorway when she met Ryce. Stanley, you needed to be here today, this is your home and you had to be here at this point in time for you to understand that. Astolat, well it's obvious that timing was crucial for that too. And Sy? Letje? You will find out in due course why you needed to be a part of this ever-dwindling group, but there is a reason for all of it. For why we came here the way we did, why we left when we did, even why we have traveled the routes we have and the way we have.

Oh, and did I say that I wanted an adventure too? That was a question by the way, you can talk now." Marcus smiled weakly, hoping that the rest wasn't going to be too much worse.

"Okay, apart from the whole 'double Marcus' thing, which really does explain a lot, are you saying that you can see the future?"

"Good question Sy. And the answer is yes and no. I can see futures, countless possibilities. Some are stronger than others, and the closer they get the less chance of divergence there is. So the nearer we get to what I think is the most likely outcome, the better I can help it happen."

"That doesn't make sense," said Letje, frowning. "If you are interfering and the possible future only happens as you saw that it might and then made it happen then if that wasn't what was going to happen then you wouldn't have seen it, so it must have been the only possible outcome, right? Or, um... no, wait, that's not right." Letje went over what she had just said in her head, her concern evident. "Okay, if you saw these futures, and knew certain things had to happen for the right one to happen, then it means you would have to control everything for that to come to pass. Plus it would mean everything that has already happened would have had to have been under your control too." Letje trailed off, it was too confusing.

"Well, this is the problem with such things, it gets too complicated and you could go mad trying to figure it all out. But I saw what could happen, what should happen, and made sure I did my best to make it happen."

"Marcus, are you saying that this adventure so far could have gone another way? That the outcome could have been totally different? That people didn't have to die? Calvin didn't have to fall? And Astolat? The Contamination could have been stopped?"

"Yes, that's exactly what I am saying. Haven't you thought about it yet? Letje, I picked you up in a helicopter, we could have left the same way right?"

"I never thought about it. I assumed you wanted Varik and The Eventuals to follow us a certain way."

"I did, and the way we left certainly meant they were distracted then followed us. But look, I could have just blasted them out of the water. The Commorancy has the capacity for hitting such large targets — they were within range."

"So...?"

"So that isn't how it happened. I mean that isn't what was supposed to have happened back before it did. What has happened is what was supposed to have happened, and all so that what will happen for the foreseeable future is what was, is, supposed to be the timeline that is our future for the reality we live in."

"Because there are countless other timelines, right?" Letje remembered her teachings so far with Marcus, and the infinite timeline lessons were some of the most vivid, if the most confusing at the same time.

"Exactly."

"But Calvin and Astolat died," said Stanley pointedly.

"I know, but what a life eh? And I can't see all that happens, I mean is going to happen. I don't even always know what it is, I just know what should happen so that the right future is the one everyone is heading towards. What I can tell you, and it puts it into perspective, is that right now Calvin, well, not him, what was him for a while, and has been countless other things and will be until the end of time, is right now staring out of his home high up in the air on a floating island. And you know he would have loved that. Astolat? Well, I haven't seen that, which leads me to think it is something even better, but way in the past. Um, yes, that's about right."

"How do you know that about Calvin?" Letje asked suspiciously.

"I followed his path into The Void while I could, and thousands and thousands of years from now that is what happens."

"Huh? It hasn't happened yet?"

"No, but it will. Time means nothing in The Void, it may as well have happened yesterday. But look, I just wanted to explain about all this, about leaving The Commorancy, and the way we did it. Plus, let's face it, it is kind of exciting isn't it? All this adventure, being chased, strange encounters with dead men being horses, a talking pet tortoise. I don't even know if you have met the crayfish yet have you?"

"Why, what about them?" asked Letje, hoping it wasn't going to be something gross.

"Let's just say they used to be a guest, when *they* were a *he*."

Letje gulped, remembering the time she had feasted on them when she went walking for a few weeks. Boy were they tasty, but she thought there was something odd about them at the time. "Oh."

"I haven't quite finished, there's more. I may have not been absolutely, one hundred percent truthful about The Rooms either. I know I said that you were all next door, sort of, to each other nearest the perimeter, and that was why you had to be the ones disturbed, but that wasn't quite true. Fact is that although you were in Rooms one through seven there are countless other people in Rooms all called that to them. I told you there are many more guests, it just keeps it straighter for me, for us, to keep records if each seven Rooms are classified with a system, so you could have been in an original Room three or one of the countless incarnations that came after."

"So why us? Um, sorry, are we allowed to speak again," said Sy, getting more confused by the minute.

"Why you? Because you were the people that were supposed to be disturbed, had to be disturbed, to make The Contamination stop. I'm sorry, it's hard to explain, but if you hadn't been taken from your Rooms then The Contamination would have succeeded, one way or another. I know all this sounds like a mass of contradictions and like none of it really had to happen as I could have blasted them out the water, but that future led to nasty things, things that shouldn't happen, and weren't what was supposed to. What was supposed to happen has, did, will, as long as we do what we are here to do, and that kind of just means that everything is right and proper. Even though The Commorancy was disturbed, and I broke The Rules and disturbed my precious guests. Or in your case Letje, it meant you never even got your Room in the first place. But hey, I never had a Room, and I turned out alright... I think." Marcus looked at the faces of those around the table, hoping, knowing, that they were now his friends.

Stanley, laconic and matter-of-fact as always, summed up the feelings of the others perfectly. "Right, well that's that then. Thanks for telling us Marcus. Anyone fancy a nice cuppa? Oh, damn, no teabags." Stanley was disappointed, he really did fancy a nice cup of tea.

"Aha, never fear, Marcus is here." Marcus rummaged in his pack and pulled out a tin full of tea from centuries past.

"Where did you get that from?" said an astounded Stanley.

"I got it the other day. I have a lot of caches of things all over the country stored in airtight containers. You can't be having an adventure without a nice cup of tea now and then, can you? Make mine extra strong, so the spoon finds it tough to move please."

"You got it," beamed Stanley, feeling that, all things considered, it had been/was going to be/is a pretty good day after all.

"Any sugar?" asked a less than hopeful Sy.

"Wait one second," said Marcus, as he rummaged around in his bag, finally pulling out a tiny tin. "One lump or two?"

"Wow, really? Actual sugar, like the real thing?"
"Yep?"
"Then two please. Wow, cool."
"Letje?"
"Is it like honey?"
"Sort of, it's sweet like honey, but different."
"Just one then I think. I don't want to be greedy if I don't like it."

"Oh, you will," beamed Stanley, licking his lips, already off to find wood to see if he could get the Aga working.

"Tea, real tea," he sang to himself as he literally skipped out the door.

Well, that went better than I could have expected, all things considered, thought Marcus.

"Um, Marcus, about this whole there are two of you thing...?"

Oh well, I thought it had gone a little too well.

Moving On

Marcus had mixed feelings about saying goodbye to Stanley. He had really come to like him, and was glad of the quiet man's company. But he knew that Stanley was where he was supposed to be — that was what came first. As they said their farewells and turned a corner, waving before they were out of sight, Stanley gone from their lives forever, Marcus really wished that things could be different. They weren't — couldn't be.

Marcus sighed, not because of the farewell, but because of what he knew was coming next. It wasn't what Letje would say, or what they would then do, and do after that, and after that as well, it was the fact that he felt he had already lived it so saw little point in having to go through it all over again. Things were unraveling, becoming jumbled, lost in pasts and futures, mixed in with visions of strange occurrences back at The Commorancy where he tenuously tried to hold on to an ever more elusive sanity, even as he explored Rooms never before encountered. The only problem being it was no longer him, if it ever had been, and he didn't know if what he saw had already happened, was happening now, or was just one of countless possible futures in the infinite number of universes that were right now playing out in every possible way through the all-encompassing Void that made up the whole.

Here it comes, thought Marcus, trying to act like he hadn't already had the conversation he was about to have. Was he actually getting bored?

"I want to go home for a while, just to check on things, to see something familiar. Plus I would quite like Sy, and you too Marcus, to see it. It really is beautiful. Nothing like The Commorancy of course, but still..."

"That would be wonderful Letje," said Marcus, smiling and nodding agreeably.

"Sounds good to me," said Sy, beaming at Letje, his admiration for her growing the more time they spent in each other's company. Although Sy had found himself having to make a real conscious effort to stop staring at her bum, it really was getting rather embarrassing, especially for a man of his age.

"Really? Phew, I thought you were going to say that we had to be somewhere else Marcus, that we couldn't go."

"No, it would be fun Letje. We will have places that we have to be, so we can't stay for too long as it will take a while to get there, but it should be safe enough if we are careful, and we must stick together closely. You two must not leave each other alone. We are down to just us now, I don't want anything at all to put you in danger, so promise me."

Letje and Sy stared at each other, the relationship obviously building fast; Marcus could see it in their eyes. They promised, and so they set off to make a short stop at Letje's family home.

The trip was mostly uneventful. Keeping away from the crumbling urban sprawls and sticking to traveling mostly through the night meant that they were safe from many dangers, although wild animals, especially dogs, were an ever-present concern.

Marcus was able to subtly steer anything that picked up their scent well away from them, but it meant he had to be constantly vigilant, and it was draining when he had so many other problems. He was constantly dipping in and out of The Noise, checking on the progress of Varik and his church members, hiding their own presence from him, dealing with animals, finding shelter and food, and trying as best he could to manage the fragmented sense of time that was playing havoc with his abilities on all levels.

But progress was made, the pace they set was good. Luckily both Sy and Letje were fit, with great stamina. He was especially impressed with Letje who, unlike the men, didn't adjust her internal body chemistry to allow for such sustained activity — she was just naturally fit.

Guess that's what seventeen year olds are like, mused Marcus, looking around at the small village they had skirted, recognizing it and smiling to himself.

"Hey. Sy, Letje, want to go have a bit of fun?" whispered Marcus conspiratorially. "I remember this place, I set up a really cool Room just a half mile from here. Want to go see if it's still there?"

Marcus could see their inquisitive natures would find it impossible to say no, they were very alike in that regard, so he simply said, "Follow me, it could be fun. You'll like it too George, and you have been very good so you deserve a treat." George stared at Marcus blankly, he had been in a bit of a funk since leaving Stanley. He liked it there and thought that maybe they were finally going to stay put for a while. No such luck.

~~~

Marcus pushed open the graffiti covered steel door, centuries old detritus of countless teenagers who had come to drink, eat or just spray the walls were pushed aside slowly as the door eased inward, revealing nothing but blackness and stale air.

"Come on, what're you waiting for?" said Marcus eagerly, stepping over the piles of rubbish and marching confidently into the darkness.

Sy shrugged his shoulders at Letje and they walked into the murky interior. Letje grabbed Sy's hand as the darkness enveloped them. Sy smiled contentedly, as happy as he had ever been.

"Shield your eyes," warned Marcus, as he fidgeted with the hidden security pad — the best lock he could come up with at the time without drawing undue attention to his activities.

They stood on a narrow gantry high above a stark imposing space, empty apart from the object down below in the center of the Room.

"What is it?" asked Letje. "And what is this place?"

"Years ago, and I mean many years ago, it used to be an old pump house to serve the village. It got shut down. They built a better one closer, then it just got used as a place for kids to hang out and drink cheap booze. Of course all that stopped rather suddenly, and then I came across it and added it to the collection of Rooms I managed to get built away from The Commorancy. It's not as spectacular as some of those back home, but it's still pretty cool... I think."

Sy turned to Marcus. "What do you mean you think? You're getting me worried now. I thought it was going to be a fun thing. What else could it be?"

"Um, just give me a moment will you? I'm trying to get the order of Rooms right." Marcus did some mental arithmetic in his head, trying to place the time and resources used to alter the space below them. The silence seemed to pulse while Marcus thought, then remembered. "Ah, yes, now I remember. Please, listen carefully, and do exactly as I say. I think it's probably best that we run now. Fast."

"What? Why?" said Letje, as Marcus turned back the way they had come. It was too late, the door shut behind them, their exit cut off.

"That's why," said Marcus, pointing at the contraption below that was unfolding like an impossibly complex paper fortune teller, which is exactly what it was — with a difference.

"Doesn't look that dangerous to me," said Sy. "What is it, some kind of game?"

"Yes, we used to call it a fortune teller, sometimes a whirlybird. You used to make them out of paper, fold it up in a special way, then you would sing a rhyme and whatever you landed on then unfolded you had to do it. This one is a little different though, bigger for a start."

"Well, can't we just leave? It's down there and we're up here?" Letje tugged at the door, it wouldn't budge. "What about the keypad?"

"It won't work, I don't know the code to get out. It's on one of the folded up pieces in the fortune teller, we just have to find out which one it is."

"Which means we have to play, right?" asked Sy, his uneasiness growing by the second. It sounded simple enough, which meant it most definitely wasn't going to be.

"Exactly. We have to play." Marcus began to descend the steps, warily.

"Marcus?" asked Letje, as she and Sy followed him down toward the somehow menacing fortune teller.

"Hmm?"

"If this is dangerous then why did you build it?"

"Oh, you know, just to keep things interesting. And actually I didn't build it, Hoffen Hubenstager did. He was what you would call a rather eccentric physicist, and after he died of The Lethargy I... well, I tracked down quite a lot of his inventions in his private lab, and most of what he had been working on for his current employers. It was quite an eye-opener, I can tell you. He was a very hands-on type of man, more an inventor than anything else, but he was mostly well known for his works of art, what you would call speculative art."

"So how does it work? This, what did you call it, speculative art?"

"Oh, this isn't anything like that, this is a theoretical future fortune teller and one of the most dangerous things I have ever come across. I don't want to play at all."

"Come on Marcus, what could it do?" asked Sy, trying to keep his voice light, and failing.

"It could alter the whole future I have been trying so hard to ensure happens. It could make events occur that have no right to happen and it could mean the end of everything that we know and love. Or it could just be fun and we will be out of here in a few minutes."

"Really," said Letje, her hope restored.

"No," said Marcus. "Sorry, that was in bad taste. Well, come on, let's hope we get out of this alive."

~~~

Hubenstager had foretold of The Lethargy years before it decimated not only human populations but also animal, plant, insect and microbial life. The Lethargy was an outlier, an anomaly in the entire history of the Universe that was simply never meant to have been — then Hubenstager wrote of its coming, so it had to come to pass.

It was one of those paradoxes, one of the faults with living in one of the universes that was perfect enough to lead to your birth. With endless numbers of them it was inevitable that everything would happen, and this Hubenstager foretold of The Lethargy and lived in the one universe where his prediction came true.

Nobody knew of this telling of a future event apart from Marcus. Hubenstager had written it in a journal, one of countless Marcus had read once he discovered them. His theoretical work had led him to be convinced of the need for multiple, if not infinite universes. Many were empty, but countless had conditions perfect for stars, planets and life to form. And each life in each universe would have their lives played out in an infinite number of ways — it was, according to him, the only possible stance if you wished to explain the existence of anything at all. The odds were so stacked against there ever being any 'stuff' at all that the only possible explanation was that there were so many different universes that it stood to reason it was impossible for him, and everyone else, to not be there. There was no other explanation, and he had done the math to prove it.

He was ridiculed and praised in equal order for this so never published about The Lethargy, but then oddly turned his attention to more esoteric arts, namely making strange machines based on the abstract physics he contributed so much to. Immersed in his complex work he had begun to get glimpses of a world where The Lethargy swept across the globe, becoming more convinced it would happen, and it did. He left no word as to what it actually was, where it came from, or why it happened, just that he was sure that such a thing could, and therefore must exist.

Marcus often wondered if it was the mere conceiving of it that brought it to life, but knew deep down this was not the case, although he too had no idea exactly what The Lethargy actually was.

"Let's play," said Marcus, after recounting the odd man's history. He walked toward the incredibly complex looking machine and then said to Letje, "Pick a color, any color, and speak into that grill there."

~~~

Two days later three sweaty people emerged form the dark to be greeted by a very annoyed looking George.

"Sorry about that," said Marcus, "shall we be on our way?"

"Sorry! You get us locked in a Room with a demented giant fortune teller built by a man that believed there are infinite universes and thought it was a good idea to build a machine that could turn your insides to jelly if you failed to complete one of its mad tasks. And all you can say is that... ah, forget it. Let's go." Sy stomped off into the woods.

"Gosh, bit grumpy isn't he?"

Letje stared at Marcus, unable to say anything at all. She simply wanted to forget about the last few days and never, ever, ever think about them again.

Neither did anybody else, she assumed. Letje caught the look on Marcus' face out of the corner of her eye. She pointed at him accusingly. "You enjoyed that, didn't you? You knew all along what was in there. You knew it and you still took us inside." Marcus said nothing, just smiled, looking as innocent as a dog locked in a room with the cushion stuffing covering the floor.

"What! As if!"

"And all that about whatshisname, Hoppenwhatever, you made that up, didn't you? You built that, and I bet that it couldn't really turn your insides to mush at all."

"Come on, let's catch up with Sy," said Marcus, bending down and apologizing to George. He stood and walked off, then turned and said, "Kind of fun though wasn't it? Got the old heart beating, made you feel alive."

He winked at Letje and waited for her to catch up.

My Children

Bird was sad.

Bird had never felt such an emotion before, never wanted to again.

It washed over him and threatened to drown him in its all encompassing cold embrace.

Varik would pay for what he had done.

Bird had wanted to return home to his mate and his growing offspring. His visits home had become more and more sporadic over the previous few months as Varik grew increasingly desperate to eliminate Marcus and his companions. So Bird had been called upon time and time again to watch from above, to follow them and report back to Varik against his will. Varik could see through Bird's eyes but the further away he was the harder it was for him to get a clear picture of where the group were. It meant he regularly called Bird back to him to better read the flights he had taken and get a clear picture of exactly where they were.

It meant Bird was able to go to his family less and less.

But he had finally made it home after doing a duty he was beginning to find very wearisome. He liked it when Master was at The Sacellum and he could do as he wished. Being forced to travel so far, and stay away for so long, was not something he was enjoying at all.

Master had grown dark, and serious; no longer the creature he once was.

He was bitter. Bird began to understand what evil was.

The natural world had no place for evil. It was only the humans that could act in such ways.

Bird was stood at the edge of the nest, his mate directly opposite, the white stripe on her head shining in the weakening sunshine. She keened loudly, ripping through the air as if to tear it apart.

In the nest lay one of their chicks.

Dead.

It had fallen from the nest. A nest that needed repairing. Bird's mate had not had the time to maintain it properly as she was so busy finding food for the two always ravenous youngsters.

The other chick was well-fed now its father was back, and sleeping happily, unaware of such a loss. The mother had retrieved the chick from the ground far below, bringing it back to the nest, not understanding it would never grow to soar in The Blue and wonder at the ground below and the activities of the humans.

She nudged the mangled bundle, trying to get it to move, and looked at Bird imploringly, begging him to do something — to make it alright.

Bird did something then that he had never once done before — he gave her knowledge. He packaged up a bundle of information and he sent it to her, forced her to take it in and to understand what and why this had happened. He had been made to stay away because of Varik, a human that had become more and more deranged. This man was no longer Bird's companion, but a slaver that would not release him. It was this human that had done this to their family. Stopped Bird from returning home to care for his family properly, much as he had wanted to.

His mate understood what she was being told, and took flight rocketing upward. She turned and plummeted back down, arrow straight, heading for the ground below. She landed back at the nest minutes later with a meal for her one remaining chick. A huge hare that would keep the young one content for hours to come.

Together they spent the time repairing the nest, making it safe and secure for their little one, and then Bird brought yet more food for their still hungry chick.

Then together they took to the wing.

Family stuck together, and this family wanted blood as payment for the death caused by Varik's manipulation of the natural order of things.

Burning Ears

Marcus knew he was being talked about by Marcus, he could feel it through their now inexorably tenuous link. No, it wasn't the link at all, it was something else, it was The Noise, the disturbance of his secret being told. Marcus hoped for Marcus' sake that he was somewhere extremely private and was sure he could trust the people he was talking to.

Marcus was bored.

It was business as usual. There were no more Contaminations, no howling Lethargic roaming the corridors, desecrating his home.

No Orientations either.

They had decided that until the threat of Varik and The Eventuals was dealt with then there would be no more new guests. The risk was too high, and as each Whole was so valuable there seemed little point in risking something that could wait a while until events unfolded.

Marcus was hanging on to Marcus at large by the most delicate of threads, but the unfolding of a story told hundreds of miles away was making the connection somewhat stronger. He assumed that Marcus was letting his guard down somewhat, caught up in his story of himself, letting their connection get just a little bit more solid.

But he still had no idea what he was doing on the mainland, and really wished it had been him that had gone on the adventure. Still, if he returned it would have been him, the memories, the whole experience, would be his just as if it was him that had gone.

It didn't help one little bit.

What if something went wrong? If he didn't return? He would have missed out. But then if he didn't return would he want to know of his own death?

He thought about it for a while, sat in the middle of The Weightless Room, cross-legged, arms out to his sides, feeling the strangeness of his organs trying to get used to the severe lack of the gravity they had become very accustomed to.

Marcus had been playing a dangerous game: as his sanity slipped he decided to purge certain memories of recent conversations with the other him. Now he half-believed he truly was coming home, even as wisps of memories hinted at this being anything but the truth. Deep down he knew it — chose to forget. Almost.

Putting thoughts of his other self out of his mind, he simply enjoyed the Room. To occupy himself he had spent the last few weeks entrenched in myriad chores that had been neglected for way too long. He went through countless Defense Rooms, checking cables, oiling chains, greasing gears, wondering why he had used such and such a device to commence the various ways The Commorancy could be defended. He marveled at the contraptions, tempted in certain Rooms to press plungers, flick switches, turn knobs or, rather bizarrely in one Room: The Happy Clappy Room, clap three times, pause a second, then clap four times more. He very nearly came close to doing it, but after considering whether or not he really wanted to retract the roof and send 18,739 balloons with a Website address on them where people could begin the twisted route to The Commorancy, he thought better of it. Plus he didn't fancy waiting for the nozzles all around the Room, poised to be activated and blow up the balloons.

He left the Room shaking his head, wondering if it was him or Marcus that had designed this particular Room. Knowing, of course, that it was him and only him. It was all him, it always had been, always would be.

He was alone.

As he floated in the middle of the vertical weightlessness tunnel, reaching up seven stories, he thought of some of the other Rooms he had uncovered while he roamed his home these last few weeks, taking a mini holiday of his own after so much death and the unheralded interruption of his guests.

Some of them had been truly stunning, some downright bizarre even by his standards. There were quite a few he hadn't even known he'd built, the memory completely lost in a haze of time and split personality, where each individual experience was never always fully passed from one of him to the other.

Marcus didn't often get surprised, so what surprised him the most was the Rooms he himself had designed and built too many years ago now.

He had wandered down metal gangways, suspended over machinery that ran his home — huge things, steam roiling upward, automatic equipment that ran flawlessly for the most part. Yet at the end of the gangway he crouched low and entered a small Room via a glass door that contained what he calculated roughly in The Noise were close to 100,000 butterflies of all description.

How were they there? How had they survived so long with nobody to tend them? But it was beautiful, a crazy tropical paradise with plants crammed into every available space. Orchids grew in notches in trees, huge ferns dominated, and the ground was covered in a lush carpet of fragrant flowers that swarmed with butterflies. It must have been designed to take the steam from the machines and at the same time keep the Room a perfect hothouse for the insects; the automatic feeding and watering systems had taken care of the rest. He stood there, covered in butterflies, making a mental note to visit the Room again soon. Although the insects seemed perfectly happy with no intervention from him.

Other Rooms were simply mad, a nightmarish vision of a young man's state of mind when he built a home he planned, or at least hoped, to inhabit for centuries if not millennia to come. A home to be passed on to the next Keeper once his time came.

One such Room was one of the oddest he had ever seen, although he got the distinct feeling there were more extreme surprises to come if he carried on his opening of doors. It was just as well that via The Noise he could stare at the doors and see exactly where the hidden circuitry was, otherwise he would have no clue as to how to open them and gain entry to the weird imagination come real that was contained behind the doors he took so much pride in.

The Room For Making You Dizzy, that was the rather understated name for the Room he had been in before he lost consciousness and awoke to find himself deep in a pool of water, soaking to get rid of the bodily fluids that had covered him from head to toe five minutes after entering the very, very bad idea for a Room for anyone apart from your worst enemy.

Marcus had got down on his hands and knees as he walked down a corridor open on the left hand side to a view of a towering glass cube set in a walled compound. The glass Room was empty apart from a single wooden stool and a periscope — he liked that Room, it was an old favorite. As he walked along the corridor he noticed something shining down low — a miniature door handle. Crouching down he realized that if he got on his belly and scrunched up tight he could open the tiny door, the smallest he had ever seen. Before he had got his shoulders through he was already feeling extremely sick, but as he had pushed his arms through first there was no going back. A moving floor was pulling him in, the door itself aiding the floor with peristaltic pulses that he could not prevent depositing him inside.

Once dragged through, the tiny door slammed shut behind him.

Boom!

The noise echoed around the chamber, obviously not coming from the door itself. It didn't make it any less menacing however. The floor continued to move, pulling him in deeper. Or were the walls moving? He was no longer sure. Then the ceiling began to move, or was that the floor? He seemed to have been spun upside down, the ceiling had descended or the floor risen until he couldn't even begin to try to move. He was squashed flat.

How ironic if he were to die, squashed as flat as a pancake in a Room of his own devising. One thing was for sure: nobody would ever find him down here through the tiny door.

Lub-dub-lub-dub-lub-dub-lub-dub...

He felt his head spin as blood rushed to his ears — they were already pounding to the beat of invisible drums causing his heartbeat to fluctuate wildly.

Then he was gasping for air. He was sure he was inverted, trapped between the walls, or the ceiling and floor, he no longer knew, or cared. All he knew was that he had to escape. Then he dropped. Smacking into the floor with a loud thud. The wind knocked out of him, he quickly got to his feet, only to fall again, this time sideways maybe?

Then things got really bad.

He was spinning, faster and faster. Nothing like the whirling dervish he had been on occasion in The Disco Room though. No, this was really, really fast. He put his arms out to his sides to try to maintain some balance, but seconds later he was flung against a surprisingly soft wall.

While all of this had been going on there was a god-awful song playing over and over, a woman he remembered drove him crazy centuries ago, singing about love and longing like she meant it, when she was obviously just the result of some kind of reality TV show with a lot of money backing her.

On it went. Louder and louder, until it got deeper and deeper, and his bowels began to loosen.

Ordinarily he would control his body and all would be well, but it wasn't working, nothing was. Then the walls began pulsing, throbbing in and out, bulging toward him and squashing him. Out they went again, the colors constantly changing.

Red.

White.

Black.

Orange. Then blinking faster and faster — all the colors of the rainbow in a split second, driving him mad and making him vomit violently.

Then his ears began to bleed.

Then his eyes cried red.

Silence.

It all stopped.

The Room pulsed white. Blinding. Jets came from all sides, washing away his bodily waste, cleaning him. Then the tiny door opened and the ceiling lowered, the walls moved in, and he was pushed out through the tiny gap the same way he was pulled in.

As he lay out in the hallway trying to breathe again he heard a manically happy voice, recorded years ago — his voice, saying, "Thank you for taking the time to experience The Room For Making You Dizzy. Please come again." As the door slammed shut he heard the final words from his long ago recorded voice, "Surprise!"

Marcus staggered to his feet. "Damn right surprise. Thanks for nothing."

Shaking his head and dreaming of getting clean then visiting The Room For Clothes, Marcus had to at least congratulate himself for making something that was anything but boring.

Once again he really wished he had built a Room For Afternoon Drinking, which was exactly why he had done no such thing.

~~~

Whirr.

Bzzz.

Whirr, bzzz.

Whirr, bzzzzzzzzzzzzzzzzzzzzzzzzzzzzzzz.

Fft.

Zlopp.

"Ow, ow. OW! What the hell...?"

Marcus pulled himself upright off the pastel blue padded floor that matched the walls, and rubbed at his elbow. Lost in thought he had completely forgotten that time was limited in the Room. Built that way on purpose, obviously, so he didn't just spend hours floating about in free-fall and allow his organs to get all messed up and his finely tuned chemical balances to get completely out of kilter.

He could have had longer if he had changed the default on the timer, but thought that half a day would be long enough.

Wow. What have I been doing for half a day up there? Marcus had lost track of time, and looked up at the distant clear roof high above, as if the overcast sky could give him the answer.

He got to his feet, checked his internal clock as he had left his watch out in the anteroom, and was delighted to see that it was past 5 pm.

"Vino o'clock," smiled Marcus, keen to finally be able to go to The Room For Evening Drinking.

It had been a long day. It would be an even longer evening — all alone in his sprawling home, with thousands of guests locked away in their own private dreams, where they would finally become Awoken, their worlds containing countless possibilities.

Sometimes it actually got a little depressing.

Huxian

Sy was a man of action, not a thinker.

Sitting around idly waiting for things to happen just wasn't in his nature; he had tried that and all that happened was that he got bored, depressed, then bored again. He preferred to be out doing things, even if those things were rather solitary. But it was a damn sight better than moping around the house wishing things were different — at least when he was out walking, sometimes even running, although his thick frame wasn't built for extended runs, he felt alive and as if his existence had some meaning.

So he roamed quite a lot, sometimes only going out from dawn to dusk, other times he was gone for weeks, exploring, always carefully, towns and villages and trying to understand not only the world he now lived in but the world that had been taken by the unstoppable encroaching Lethargy. Some of what he found made him so physically ill and depressed he wished he had decided to stay at home and been bored. But he always dove back into his travels with renewed optimism — he was the kind of guy that always looked on the bright side, he liked to think.

There was no point being sad about the things he had missed out on, and anyway it wasn't all good back before The Lethargy — for a start he couldn't think of anything worse than walking and having to stop for cars, pushing buttons and seeing little green men that told him it was safe to cross a road. How crazy a world was that? It made him shudder just to think about it.

Time with people, company, shared experiences, that he would give almost anything to have, but it just wasn't to be. The people he did meet were either too wary to trust him, too untrustworthy for him to stay long in their company, or were dying slowly and there was nothing he could do to help. If he wasn't such a positive guy he could have got borderline suicidal. Through it all Sy continued with his trips away from home, and as he passed through his teenage years and matured he found that he became more and more capable away from home comforts.

He was slowly becoming a man. All he needed was a wife, somebody to love and to love him in return, but it never seemed like that was going to happen.

He had one kiss, one kiss only. The girl that kissed his younger self had now been dead for centuries. She never even got to grow old enough to become the beautiful young woman she would have surely been.

Of all the times that he wandered the shattered city streets and tatters of ancient villages there was one encounter with a group of people that had always stayed with him — an encounter that probably had more to do with him finally deciding to gain entry to The Commorancy than any other single factor. He met the fox-men.

Winter had been harsh the year he found himself miles away from home and in serious need of food. His muscles screamed at him about the lack of sustenance, the hollowness in his belly a constant reminder of the hunger that threatened to overwhelm him and leave him to die pitifully in the stark landscape.

Sy was wrapped up in countless layers of good quality clothing he had collected over the years. It was so frustrating to continually grow out of your clothes as your body matured, so a lot of his time as he exited his teenage years had been spent searching for suitable attire that would fit his ever expanding frame. Always seizing opportunities as they arose, when he found clothes he hoarded them, knowing they would fit soon enough. Now he had finally stopped growing and had plenty to wear without having to worry, so he was wrapped up nice and warm. It was just as well since the snow had began to fall in earnest, the ground already thickly covered after only a few hours of snowfall that began early that morning.

It was very peaceful, the silence of the snow falling turning the landscape into a blankness that drowned out everything but his own breath and footsteps. Criss-crossing the ground were tiny bird tracks and the occasional four-legged tracks of rabbits or other small creatures, but for the most the snow was pure and undisturbed, a freshly fallen blanket of perfection he felt guilty for disturbing with his clumsy feet. Sy was unsure if the snow was a blessing or a curse. It brought with it an inner peace but made the going tough. Already his calves were aching from the drifts he found himself struggling through, and the wind that whipped at his scarf covered face was biting at his cheeks, setting his teeth on edge even though his body felt nice and warm.

The one bonus was that he could easily follow the animal tracks, so he should find food soon enough. It turned out to be wishful thinking. As Sy followed the marks he did encounter, which were not as common as he had thought they would be, he soon discovered that the snow made it almost impossible to actually see anything. He would follow a trail only to find that tracks had been swept away by the strong winds, or that he was half blinded from staring at the ground so long that he wouldn't be able to fire his small crossbow and hit anything unless it was stood a few paces in front of him and promised to stand still while his snow-blindness dissipated.

Hungry as he was, Sy gave up hunting as a lost cause and decided to head back to the relative comfort of the small village he had been based in for a couple of weeks now. The house he had chosen had low ceilings and small rooms, so although he kept banging his head on the ancient oak beams it meant he stayed very warm as it was so easy to heat. He knew the countryside well, and even with the snow descending ever more rapidly, repeatedly wiping out many familiar landmarks, he could still use a number of large trees to orient himself. He decided to set off across a series of large open fields that descended down the side of the valley and led to the outskirts of the village — it would save a lot of time and he might get lucky and capture something to eat on his way. If not then he would make do with the dusty tins of ancient dog food he had found hidden in a small pantry in the cottage, even though his empty stomach flipped cartwheels at such degradation.

He set off in the direction of his temporary home, looking forward to burning the well matured wood he had gathered in copious amounts the first day he had arrived.

~~~

"What the hell?" Sy had walked down the gently sloping uppermost field and all of a sudden found himself flailing in mid-air before landing softly on his backside in a snowdrift that came up to his chin. He struggled madly, fear bringing sweat to his skin that instantly cooled and sent his body temperature dangerously low. He crawled out of the snow to find himself on a narrow cleared path, obviously freshly done no more than an hour ago. Shaking the snow off himself he stood only to find that he was confronted with a large wall of dirty glass, topped by the field he had just stepped off.

It was a home, a once modern piece of expensive architecture now almost totally invisible. Built to offer stunning views over the valley for the rich commuters that commissioned it, it was an eco-house built into the hillside that had been gradually hidden even more by subsequent generations. Looking closely, Sy noted that the glass was not quite as spectacular as on first impression. It was a mish-mash of different panes, parts patched with boards, along with a few original pieces that stretched from the floor to the low roof and were wider than he was tall.

Sy could see nobody outside, so walked up to the glass and peered inside, cupping his hands either side of his face to stop the blinding reflection of the gathering snow.

Oof.

Sy hit the ground before he had the chance to get more than a rudimentary glance inside, which would have been enough to send him running down the hill if he hadn't been smacked over the head by a wooden club and fallen unconscious to the floor.

~~~

Sy woke to a splitting headache, a tingling all over his body as his temperature rose, and a pair of wide eyes staring down at him with unmasked curiosity.

"You Whole?" said a gruff voice that came from somebody out of his line of sight. The young girl continued to peer at him, so close their noses almost touched. She needed a wash.

"What? Eh? What happened?" Sy shifted, pushing forward to sit up, sending her scampering away to stand beside a small man with a mass of black hair and a thick stubbly beard.

"Ah, yes, well, sorry about that. Young Xylia here is a bit of a naughty vixen and—"

"I hit him over the head with my club, didn't I Daddy?" said the excited young girl.

The man frowned at his daughter. "Yes, you did. And don't interrupt, it's very rude."

"Sorry." Xylia pulled her furs tighter around her body, then dragged her heavy hood up over her head and went off into the corner of the strange room.

"Why?" asked Sy, rubbing the back of his head, feeling the large lump that made him wince.

"She was just being cautious. We don't get many strange men peering in through our windows so she did what she thought was best. And why were you peering in through our windows young man? Eh?" The man got to his feet and Sy realized that he too was dressed head to toe in furs, red and white furs that were rather expertly stitched together in a pleasing patchwork.

"I fell off the... the roof I guess. I didn't know there was a house here, I was just walking." Sy was coming back to his senses, and was getting a bad feeling about the place. A quick glance around revealed quite a few makeshift beds, parts of the space curtained off, with countless skulls on the walls or piled up in corners; skins in various stages of being cured covered almost all available surfaces. There were piles of logs and kindling next to a large wood-burning stove with a chimney that disappeared at an angle through the steeply upward sloping ceiling that obviously followed the gradient of the hill.

The man walked toward Sy, then stood over him, looming menacingly. Sy got to his feet, grabbing for something to steady him as his head spun wildly. "Hey, what's going on here. I don't want any trouble." Sy's gear was in his pack on the floor, he could see the top of his crossbow, could get to his knives, maybe, if the man wasn't so damn close.

"Relax, we don't want any trouble either." He backed away, sat back down to show he wasn't a threat. "I'm sorry about my daughter, but you can't be too careful you know?"

"I'm sorry too. I guess it would come as a bit of a shock having someone peer into your home like that." Sy looked around again. He felt way too many pairs of empty eye sockets on him — it was creeping him out in a big way. "Who are you people?"

A freezing cold blast of wind came and went in an instant as a door he hadn't noticed opened and closed. A huge bear of a man shook the snow off his long oily hair. "We're the fox-men, and who might you be?"

Sy stayed for two months.

~~~

The fox-men, as the small family of male dominated adults called themselves, had been living in the same building all their lives, as had their ancestors, right back to before The Lethargy. They were a very close-knit family unit and had remained Whole, although children were seldom born. They modeled themselves on the fox, a creature that had done remarkably well since urban dwelling had no longer been possible and they made their way back into the countryside where many had always thought they belonged.

It was explained to Sy that foxes lived in small family groups and had strong hierarchies that kept their units manageable and stable. They used terminology unfamiliar to Sy, referring to their collective as a skulk, the younger ones were often called cubs or pups, with males often called dogs, and females vixens. Words that obviously were in no way meant to be degrading, which took Sy a while to understand.

He fit in well with the group, and his prowess at hunting cemented his place within the skulk. This was no easy invitation to receive, strangers were hardly ever allowed in. But mates were needed for the few growing children, so both Whole males and females were brought into the small community if deemed suitable, but only ever if they were Whole.

It was a life that was basic, not always comfortable, but it was steady. There was company and camaraderie, and food was always plentiful — if a little monotonous. There had grown around the extended family a fervent belief in the mystical qualities of the British red-haired fox, and every single one of them was totally devoted to the creature. They nursed sick animals, raised young if parents had left them for whatever reasons, and when they died they celebrated the fox's return to The Void by making sure that its body was put to good use. It was animal worship in a microcosm, elevated over the six generations since The Lethargy until it became as strong as any religion.

They refused to wear anything not made of fox, from skins to furs to amazingly comfortable and warm footwear that even had shoelaces fashioned from treated sinew that was flexible but incredibly strong. Bones were used for weapons, meat was eaten and blood was drunk, all to revere the fox that had fared so well once they left their scavenging ways behind them and resumed a hunter's way of life. The cessation of fox-hunting as a sport and the lack of road traffic led to an explosion in the population, and the cunning creature grew more and more important to the family as it found itself increasingly isolated from the tiny pockets of humanity dotting the countryside.

Fights were not uncommon amongst the men, as being the dominant male held a number of much sought after privileges; the battles were bloody and often lasted for hours. But once a winner was obvious there was never any animosity. The victor never gloated, the loser wouldn't sulk for long. It was the natural way of things and what was done was done, they were still a family. That was what counted.

It was a strange time for Sy. He knew that they wanted him to stay, to wait for the young Xylia to grow old enough to take a mate. Sy knew he couldn't live in such a manner though, much as he longed for a life that held a promise of daily human contact and a warm and eager body to lie with him through the long nights.

Sy stole away one night, battling with himself every step of the way. The fox-men may not have been interested in anything outside of their own little skulk, but there was warmth, love, family and a mate for Sy if he had stayed.

He thought about them often over the years, and knew exactly why they had suddenly dominated his thoughts: family. Maybe the chance of having one of his own was finally a possibility once more?

Duck

"What do you mean it's for cannibals?"

"I mean its design would indicate that they hung people on it, well, skewered would be a better word, I guess, and roasted them. Look, it's huge, you wouldn't need it for much else would you?" Sy was trying to be diplomatic in how he worded things, but it was rather futile really.

"It could be for deer, or boar or something," said Letje hopefully.

"How would you explain that then?" Sy pointed to the pile of bones off to one side. The human skulls were a rather obvious sign of exactly what had been consumed.

"Suppose. It's... a dead giveaway. Geddit?" Even Letje knew her words had been in bad taste. She was feeling nervous and, as usual, said something stupid. Sy just stared at her, mouth open, trying to decide whether to laugh or admonish her for such morbid humor.

"Anyway, there doesn't seem to be any sign of them any more does there? And I think it will be a perfect spot to hole up for a day or two — until Marcus gets back. You'll stand guard, won't you George? George? Where is he?"

"Not sure, I guess he isn't too keen on barbecue. Can't blame him really," said Letje, looking around for George.

Marcus had asked them to wait for him, to not go too far from the woods where he had suddenly said he needed to attend to something and would be back shortly. That was over a day ago now and Sy and Letje, left with George for company, had carried on through the thinning trees until they came across what could only be described as a rather macabre, yet long-vacated, compound. They didn't know they were at the sight of Varik's most recent previous excursion out from his Home, where he had dealt out suitable punishment to those that would consume the flesh of others.

Now the place was crumbling, the occupants long ago devoured by scavenging dogs. All that was left was the pile of bones, bleached white and shining with early morning frost, that had been piled up as a trophy by the cannibals that lived here many years ago.

The roasting spit, complete with turning wheel and hoist chains, was little more than rust now, and as Letje put a hand to the wheel the whole thing came crashing down into the pit. She jumped back, a gouge in her arm bleeding profusely.

"Careful!" shouted Sy, dashing to the rescue, holding her arm up high and squeezing to stem the flow. "Let's get inside, see what there is to use as a bandage."

"Okay. But I'm glad that horrible contraption is gone, it gave me the heebie jeebies."

Sy smiled at the use of words. "Don't worry, I'll clear it all away after we get your arm seen to. Look, there's a well, let's see if it still works. We can clean up the cut and see about something to eat. Mwaaaa."

Letje smacked Sy on the back with her good arm. "Sy, don't even joke about such things. That's terrible."

Sy smirked back. "What? After the 'joke' you just told?"

The well was functional, but bucket and rope were long gone. Sy pulled out a length of cord from his pack and tied a tin cup to the end, dunking it in and hauling it out, all mock effort and eye-rolling.

"My hero. Thanks," said Letje, as Sy passed over the cup, enough water in it to wet her mouth and nothing more. "I think we need to find a stream. What do you think about going in the house though? Safe?"

"Definitely. Look, the whole place is abandoned. My guess is somebody didn't take too kindly to people eating people, and... who knows, but I doubt it was pretty. Anyway, you forget what I can do now. There's nobody inside, nobody for miles around. Let me just get some more water and we can clean you up."

Sy hunted around the closest outbuilding and came back with a metal bucket, finally getting a decent haul to clean Letje's cut.

They searched the house but the place was little more than a refuge for rodents and spiders. Ancient mattresses strewn around every room were in shreds, litter for the mice and the rats.

There was nothing Sy was convinced was suitable as a bandage for Letje, and by the time they had finished their search the cut was already healing anyway.

Sy stared at it, amazed. "Where's it gone? How did you heal so fast? It looks like nothing more than a little nick now."

Letje just shrugged. "What do you mean, isn't that what happens to everyone? I always heal fast, and mum and dad were the same. I thought that was what happened to everyone."

Sy looked at her accusingly, very bemused. "No Letje, that is most definitely not what happens to other people. I think our kids are going to be some seriously powerful children you know, they are bound to..." Sy realized what he had said, but it was too late now. May as well get it all out in the open.

Letje stared at him with eyes as deep as oceans, so before she could say something that would only depress Sy he walked her quickly out of the house and into one of the spacious barns, away from the depressing habitation that was not exactly ideal for what he figured he may as well do sooner rather than later.

~~~

"Duck," said Sy.

"Where?" joked Letje, ducking to avoid the low oak beam, now black with age and as hard as iron. A broom swung gently by Sy narrowly missed her head — she batted it away easily.

"Haha, very funny. You're about as funny as a monkey on crack."

"What's crack? I don't get it?" asked Letje, confused.

"Damn, you kids, don't you know anything?"

"Hey, you were born hundreds of years before me, I think some of your reference points may be a little out of date by now."

The banter had been going on for some time now. Letje knew there was no denying that they made a good team. Both were feeling much more comfortable being in a small group of two rather than with everyone altogether, and they felt they were a lot more effective this way. At least Letje hoped this was the case and it wasn't just her.

They were alone.

"Sy?"

"Hmm?"

"Do you think that we will be killed? I mean by Varik or his acolytes, the ones with The Ink?" Letje didn't mind admitting that she was scared, there was no shame in that. Everyone else seemed so grown up, so accepting of the madness that was going on all around them, if in a somewhat sporadic way. It could be days, weeks between encounters, but The Eventuals always caught up with them in the end. She had the sneaking suspicion Marcus was actually enjoying it.

"I think there is a very good chance of it, yes." Sy rubbed his heavy forehead, trying to think of something reassuring to say to Letje. "But, on the other hand, I do want you to be my wife, and it won't be much of a marriage if one of us gets killed, now will it?"

Silence. Then more silence. It stretched on for lifetimes.

"Um, well," said Sy, shifting uncomfortably, "I guess I had that coming."

"Sy, what do you mean, be your wife? I'm just a little girl compared to you. I don't know anything like you do. You're a grown up man with hundreds of years of experience, I only found out recently I'm seventeen not fifteen. I would love to be your wife, you be my husband, but how would it work?"

"It would work because we would love each other Letje, that's how it would work. And look, I know I may be, what? Over two hundred and fifty years old or whatever it is, but let's face it, I've kissed exactly one girl, when I was a boy, and spent most of my life locked up in my Room in The Commorancy. Sure, I have all this knowledge and insight now, can do crazy things in The Noise, but at the heart of it I'm still just a young man. Does that make it sound a little more appealing?"

"Haha, yes, it kind of does. Well?"

"Well what?"

"Aren't you going to do it then?"

"It?"

Letje had to accept that he may be ancient but Sy was still not the most insightful of men, especially when it came to girls anyway. "Ask me?"

"Oh, right, damn!" Sy got down on one knee, ignoring the dust, the dirt, and the aching of his back. He took hold of Letje's hands in his. "Letje Sandoe, light of my life, beauty in a world of Lethargy, the brightest star in the sky, the—"

"Get on with it silly, you'll make me blush."

"And I think you are more beautiful than ever when you do. Okay, Letje Sandoe, will you do me the honor of marrying me and being my wife? I promise to protect you and care for you, and raise our children to be spectacular."

Letje smiled down at her husband-to-be, happier than she could ever remember. "I will."

"C'mon, let's go find somewhere better to spend the night."

"Good idea." Letje looked out of the barn door, hanging off its hinges, ready to crash to the floor at any second. A glint caught her eye. It was the sun reflecting off a cracked human skull sat atop a pile of once consumed people. She didn't think it was a good omen on the day she was proposed to, but she doubted there were many places where reminders of what humanity had become were not there to taunt and depress those of a morbid disposition. It was just as well she was strong-willed and didn't let such things bother her.

She wished her father could have been here to witness the proposal though, that would have made it just about perfect. He was still in the house in his duffel on the floor — she hated to admit it but she did forget about him sometimes.

Marcus in a Tree

Marcus felt happy even though he knew he shouldn't. Death should not be a precursor to a feeling of contentment, but he couldn't help himself — the tree was just so nice. It welcomed him with open branches, the sap vibrating up the trunk signaling it was more than happy to have a visitor for a while. It had been alone for centuries and although it didn't mind that in the least, it was still nice to feel the presence of a person, something that used to happen all the time.

Countless times a day it would feel the presence of people, now it had been centuries since it last felt the touch of a human hand. It wondered what had happened to them all, but saved the questions, content to just feel the warmth emanating from Marcus' body, the hands touching its rough bark.

Marcus was in what used to be a popular park, a place that was open fields for the walking of dogs and the sheer enjoyment of being outside. The ancient willow was always happy there, with kids swinging from its branches, strange men loitering there after dark, dogs marking their supposed territory. Even groups that would hang out late into the night sat around it on the wet grass, drinking from bottles and never picking up their litter. The tree enjoyed it all. It even liked the countless marks left by the people: names etched into nerveless wood, hearts with lovers' promises. Sometimes even a snowman was built close-by. The snow collected by shaking its branches and the heavy burden released, allowing its numerous limbs to spring back into position.

Then it all stopped, and over the years then the centuries it grew tall and strong, but everything went quiet. It forgot about the people, such things were not even distant dreams any longer. Gradually the marks on its lower trunk grew higher as the tree grew, and the litter stopped. As humanity was eradicated so was its open view of the fields. Other trees joined it, the grass grew high then was dominated by a forest that carried on for miles in every direction, obliterating the attempts made to tame the landscape by the humans.

Then it awoke to Marcus' touch.

It remembered the past and was happy for the company.

Where had all the people gone?

It didn't matter, maybe in a few more centuries they would be back, or not. Either way it was still a nice day and the sun was warming its leaves, allowing the tree to create sugars to grow even taller and maybe one day reach the orb in the sky that shone so invitingly at night, forever changing shape back and forth, then repeating at regular intervals. One day it would grow tall enough to give the silvery light source a proper greeting.

~~~

Marcus smiled at the thoughts and memories of the tree.

How glorious it must be to live such a life, to be so free and so detached from any form of worry.

The price we pay for being human I guess.

He continued listening to the tree for a while, before his own happy thoughts took precedence.

These were private thoughts, things that he would tell nobody, share not even with himself.

The lives of men are not always there merely for others to gain entertainment from.

Old Friends

"And where have you been?" asked a rather cross looking Arcene, arms folded across her chest.

It was hard to believe it really was her.

"What? Um, well, I've been away for a bit, not long." Letje was confused, this wasn't what she had been expecting at all. "You look... different. Clean! Come here you."

Arcene ran over to Letje and with uncharacteristic warmth flung her arms around her and hugged her tight. She began to cry. "I came to visit and you weren't here. I thought something had happened to you. I wanted to see you. It's been terrible Letje, things aren't so nice out there any more. People are horrible." Arcene sobbed into Letje's jacket. She could feel the warm tears on her skin as Arcene snuggled at her neck, they were coming out of the young girl so strong. A river of grief finally breaking free of its dam.

Letje looked at Sy and Marcus, raised eyebrows telling them she didn't know what had happened, why

Arcene was here. She had talked of the girl a little, about their meeting, hoping that she was alright, but she hadn't really ever expected to see her again. Arcene had just seemed too wild and independent — never at her house although she knew Letje was going to visit her. Eventually the sobbing stopped so Letje took hold of Arcene's shoulders and stepped back to get a look at her.

"Well, I must say, I didn't recognize you at first. You're spotless. Well, you were before the tears messed up your pretty little face. Here." Letje wiped the drying tears away with her sleeve. "That's better. Now, let me get a look at you. Are you alright? And is that my t-shirt you're wearing?"

Arcene looked guilty, yet defiant as always. A hint of the wild child Letje had met what felt like many lifetimes ago.

It wasn't that long ago though, was it? A few months? More? Maybe a year? Not long really.

"Sorry, my clothes were a little messy. I didn't think you'd mind. And look, I found the animals, they got out." Arcene pointed to the coop and the pens to the side of the garden. There were a few animals back that Letje had released before making her trip, she thought it best not to tell Arcene she had let them out as she didn't expect to return.

"Well, that's great, and I see you have been busy?"

"Um, yeah, hope that's okay?"

"That's fine." Letje tried to keep the horror out of her voice as she looked at the ravaged vegetable plot. It looked like a rabbit had decided a shotgun would be the best way to dig up some vegetables. Arcene obviously didn't have very green fingers.

"Now, let me introduce you, and then we can go inside and you can tell us all about what has happened."

"Okay," said Arcene, looking at the men with a newfound wariness. Then she perked up instantly.

"Hey, is that a goat? Is it dinner?" She ran over to George, patted his head then jabbed at his ribs. George trotted away and hid behind Marcus.

"Um, no, he isn't supper, he's my friend. This is George, and I'm Marcus."

"Sorry," said Arcene, head lowering, all joy gone in an instant. It was like a cloth had been rubbed across her face wiping away the happiness. "Your friend, your pet." Arcene burst into tears and ran into the house.

Letje looked after her with concern. What had happened to her?

Inside, after the introductions had been made, Arcene perked up again almost instantly, just like the girl Letje had met when she stole her rabbit. But she was also different somehow, there was a depth to her eyes that wasn't there before. Arcene had obviously encountered quite a lot since they last met and it was evident, no matter how much she skipped about and smiled, that a lot of what she had dealt with was not exactly uplifting for a ten year old. The arrival of Letje had certainly been very welcome, which was enough to tell Letje that Arcene was done with being alone.

~~~

"I don't want to talk about it, not yet," sulked Arcene, when Letje asked what had happened since they last met.

"Okay, that's fine. When you feel ready then you can tell me. It's great to see you though, and looking so clean as well."

Arcene smiled, then got up close to Letje and whispered in her ear. "What was it like? In The Commorancy? Did you get your Room?"

"No, not quite," whispered back Letje. "Something happened so we are on the run at the moment, and it might be dangerous." Letje thought for a moment, then said, "And why are we whispering?"

"I don't know those men, and Marcus might get angry if I ask too many questions." She looked around warily, double checking they weren't within earshot.

"Oh, don't be silly. There's nothing to worry about, they won't be angry, and Marcus won't mind if you ask such things. But we can't stay here for long, it's too risky at the moment."

Arcene seemed to have stopped listening, and was already dancing around the kitchen, voice getting louder and louder, firing off a barrage of questions all about The Commorancy. Where was it? What had Letje done? Who was after them? What were they like? Had she seen much on her trip?

"Whoa, all in good time. For somebody that I haven't seen for almost a year I think that if I am to answer your questions you will have to answer some of mine too."

Arcene went instantly still, the smile gone from her face, but only for a minute. "Okay, that's fair. It was horrible though, and I sure am glad to see you Letje. You're like my big sister now, is that okay? I've never had a sister, I think it'll be fun."

"Sisters," agreed Letje. "I've never had one either, I think it would be great."

They hugged then went to go and look around the garden. Letje had seen the mess as soon as she arrived, but Arcene seemed convinced that she had been doing a fine job of getting it productive again in the few months she had been at Letje's home. Letje didn't have the heart to tell her otherwise.

Being Marcus

It was only the next day, once everyone had settled into Letje's home and had a good nights rest, that Arcene's curious nature got the better of her. She was actually proud of herself for holding out so long. "What's it like? What do you see?"

They were sat out in the garden, the last of the summer eagerly devoured before such outdoor living would mean shivering in the cold damp air. Letje had made a large pot of tea, a honey laden concoction from plants cultivated in the garden for generations. Marcus grimaced but murmured polite thanks, Sy, Letje and Arcene seemed to be genuinely enjoying the beverage. The worn wooden furniture was comfortable and they all sat around the table, enjoying the smells and the sounds of the buzzing of insects — working furiously before their numbers were decimated as the cold weather settled until the following spring.

"What's it like Marcus?" asked Arcene, the second she finished her previous sentence, clearly in awe of the man. She knew little of him, but it was obvious just by his presence that here was no normal man.

"What's it like? What's what like?"

"Being you. How do you see things?"

"Arcene, it's rude to ask such questions you know. Maybe Marcus doesn't want to tell you personal things."

Arcene poked her tongue out at Letje. "What? I only asked. I wanted to know."

"It's fine Letje, I don't mind. Arcene, I can tell you if you wish, but it may be a little hard for you to understand some of it. You are still young after all."

"That's okay, I still want to know."

"Me too," said Sy.

"I guess I do too. Is it so very different Marcus? Different to how we see the world?"

"Very. Sy, to some extent you will understand a little better than the two ladies. As you have fully Awoken you see some things differently. And Letje, you have seen glimpses of it, know that there is so much more to the world than what you have experienced so far. But I have spent hundreds of years exploring The Noise, Awakening so many different things inside of me, that it's hard to remember what it was like before. Back when I was just a young man, a boy really, and none of this had happened." Marcus shifted in his seat, aware that he was going to change the way he was viewed by these people forever.

"How do I explain this? And where to start? For now let's forget about what I see inside myself, what I can do internally, and the way it happens. Let's focus on the external world, what I see and feel."

"Are there all kinds of ghosts and magic beings floating about? And demons?" interrupted Arcene.

"Haha, no nothing like that Arcene, it's a lot more interesting than that. Although I have seen ghosts, of course, and all manner of spirit related entities, but lets focus on the world as we know it. As you know it." Marcus took a deep breath, aware that what he was about to tell could have a deep impact, especially on Letje and Arcene. His focus was on Letje, not wanting to put her off Awakening and gradually reaching her full potential.

Here goes, thought Marcus, breathing deeply again. "I see everything. I see the flowers weeping, I see the grass joyous with the rain and the sunshine. I see the roots of the trees lit up like fires underneath the soil, the thousands of insects that shimmer in The Noise depending on the tree for sustenance. I see the life and death of countless creatures — I can see their lifespan counting down like the sands of time, and I see it in people too. I can look at you and I can see your thoughts, I can see the neurons firing as they pass through sections of your mind. I see where you think, where your emotions burn bright orange or the darkest black.

I see your past, present and future, and I see the well of tears that you will shed in a lifetime. I see the connections between all things. I can see the bees and their hivemind and I can see the death of a single one affecting the whole course of history, human and insect. I see the magnetic lines that pull on everything circling the earth and giving the birds their paths through the air. I can feel the tiny minds of the shrew and the infinite slow dreaming of the planet itself. I see the leaves rot and the food they deliver to the insects beneath, and I hear those plants losing their sparkle that are stuck in the endless loop of The Lethargy.

I hear the pain of humanity, see the history of a person spreading back into the mists of time, their lineage contained in their genes. I see their families and I see the past of all things. I see the passage of time through a simple thing such as this chair I sit on here. I feel it and I see the people years ago that made it, picked it up and carried it, and delivered it to a home many miles from here, where it was sold and brought to this place. I can feel that history, see it all.

I see The Noise in all things, the emptiness of it all, the stuff that makes us up. This planet and all things in the Universe is as nothing when compared to it. I see that, I see the way it all comes and goes, each tiny piece of matter connected to the next. Trillions upon trillions of strands reaching out from each thing, every event that has ever happened, is happening or will happen, all spreading out into untold histories playing out just a tiny shift from our own reality.

I see the beginnings of us all, the dust from stars older than this universe, reborn and traveling for countless millions of years, just to become a tiny part of your little fingernail. And when you die it will pass through incarnations countless in number, becoming something else, always enduring, yet totally insignificant.

I see the running of streams under the rocks, feel their currents, feel the gaps in the present, tiny disjointed pieces where things not meant to be can slip through the cracks, impossible things.

I can read pages of a book faster than I can turn them. I can make the minds of men turn into monsters and I can control The Lethargic as easily as I can tie up my own shoelaces. I can become the animals and the insects, and I could even join with the trees and watch the play of life unfold in ways so alien to our own that I would be lost forever.

There is more, but I choose not to see it all. I have seen, and do see, more than any other person in our entire history... more than I should."

There was silence. Marcus looked up, to see Sy staring in fascination at him, obvious wonder on his face. Arcene's mouth was agape, looking at Marcus as if he were a god. Letje was crying.

"That's so sad Marcus, how do you cope with it all?"

"Sad? Why Letje, you have the wrong impression entirely my dear. It's glorious. So much of life is hidden from those not Awoken, it's like you're missing the best bits. Yes, you see the depth of sadness and sorrow that is part of the natural cycle, but you see the beauty shining forth, you see the amazing way that all things interconnect, and you understand the absolute miracle that is life. It's infinitesimally rare you know? The chances of everything coming together to allow life to flourish? Such a thing is basically impossible. Yet here we are. Here are the plants and animals and insects. The air we breathe, the oceans with their teeming life, the skies with the birds and the clouds and the rain and thunder, all an impossibility for such diversity to come together to make it a reality. Seeing it all working is like a dream. An impossible dream.

To understand the depths of human despair is to revel in the beauty of a smile and see the lights ping into existence as your brain flares orange and your aura shines like a beacon in the night. Being Awoken to just one aspect of the potential we have within is a thing to be grateful for. Most people never see what I see. It is not within most to Awaken to all potentials, yet you can Letje, if you want. Do you want that?"

"I don't know, what if I can't cope with it all? What if it gets too much and I collapse under the weight of seeing into the souls of other people?"

"It is not without great responsibility Letje, and great sorrow. Hard choices must be made and I won't pretend your life will ever be the same again. But think of the beauty, and the truth you will see."

"Can you cope with it Marcus? Does it make you happy?"

"Sometimes Letje, sometimes. And other times I lay on top of mountains of bones and I cry until I am empty inside. That is the price you pay, that and more."

"And if I don't want that for myself? Is that bad?"

"Of course not Letje. What is more beautiful than just being alive and knowing yourself to be a Whole person? That is more than enough, more than most have now. A gift. And besides, you can always just turn it all off if you wish. With true Awakening comes much more than what I have just described. Your inner self is open to you, you may do what you wish, know what you wish." Marcus paused, then whispered, "You can even forget parts if you wish — if you really want to."

"Marcus?"

"Yes? I think I probably am Letje. Mad, that's what you were going to ask isn't it? Am I mad?"

"It was."

Marcus sighed deeply. "Letje, the things I have done, still do, and the life I have led, I expect I am rather mad. I don't know. Who's sane any longer anyway? But the choice is always there, and we can be what we want to be. My life has been so long, I am probably well past what should have been allowed. With age comes problems even I cannot overcome. And sometimes I am tired, oh so tired. But I don't regret it.

Without me, without the things I have done, then I am sorry to say I very much doubt there would be anyone left, certainly nobody in the UK would be alive by now. Responsibility always comes at a price Letje. Don't ever forget it."

Arcene got to her knees and bowed before Marcus. He bent forward in his chair, grabbed her by the shoulders and lifted her to her feet. "Don't be silly. I'm not a god Arcene, I just Awoke to the potential we all have within us, that's all."

Arcene remained quiet, staring at Marcus as if aliens had landed and asked if they could have a cup of tea.

~~~

"Is he a god Letje? He must be. You heard him, people can't do those things, can they?"

Letje looked at the young girl, now so different to the last time she saw her. It was as if she had aged much more than a year in the intervening period.

"No Arcene, he isn't a god, he just sees and feels a lot more than we do. I just didn't realize quite how much. Treat him like normal, well, as normal as you can. He is a little odd, but I do like him. Just be aware that he is very old, even though he doesn't look it. And don't let what he said make you think he is God, he is just a man who has Awoken to what a lot of us could become — if we want to."

"Do you want to? It seems kinda scary to me. I don't want to cry on top of a pile of bones. Ugh!" Arcene shuddered at the thought, her long hair dancing in the sunshine. She glanced around nervously, suddenly afraid Marcus could hear her.

"Don't worry, Sy and Marcus went inside. The boys are tired and I told them to use the bedrooms for a nap. Oh, and George is there." Letje pointed over to an old rusty wheelbarrow, the wheel now a simple wooden circle her father had made. George was asleep in it, curled up like a little baby in its bassinet.

"Phew. Well? You didn't answer my question. Do you want to be Awoken like that? It all sounds crazy to me anyway."

"I'm not sure yet. I want to be Awoken, I want to be sure if I have a family they don't get The Lethargy, but as to the rest... it's a lot to think about. There is more than I ever thought possible, it's a bit scary."

"Don't be scared, you have me now," said Arcene brightly.

Letje had the distinct impression that the girl had grown up a lot, and as far as Letje could tell Arcene had decided that she was now staying with her. How that was going to work out she had no idea. Especially as The Eventuals were still after them; there was going to be a lot of trouble to come yet. Would Arcene be safer on her own? Letje wasn't sure. They were certainly on the rampage at the moment, a young Whole girl would be at serious risk.

The arrival back at the house had opened up a whole load of extra concern for Letje. Not only had the last few days turned out nothing like she had expected, not that she had really known what to expect, but hearing about Marcus' view of the world had come as something of a surprise too. It seemed like the issue of having a young girl in her company meant that there was a lot to think about. What should she do? Did she really want that kind of life? To know so much, to feel so deeply? What was Arcene expecting of her?

And what about her father?

For a minute she had actually forgotten about Constantine, if she should still call him that at all.

"Wow, life is strange. I've had nothing but myself for company for years and now I have all these things happen at once."

"Huh? What was that?" asked Arcene, who seemed to be dropping off to sleep where she sat.

"Nothing, just thinking out loud is all. Go back to sleep."

Arcene began to nod off, and pretty soon her snores were regular and amazingly loud. Letje looked down at Constantine/Daddy, and asked for his advice. "Well Daddy, what do you make of all that? What do you think your daughter, of seventeen years I might add," Letje frowned at the tortoise for holding back her age from her, "should do? It's not like you can ever be the same again once you experience the kinds of things Marcus has."

Don't ask me, I'm just a tortoise.

Letje got the distinct impression her father was not feeling quite himself. Maybe he needed a nap too. The boys did seem to get sleepy an awful lot.

No stamina, that's their problem. Now, if a woman were ruling The Commorancy... Letje's thoughts drifted, imagining herself with the powers of Marcus. Soon, she too was asleep in her chair, the waning sun giving up its last warmth of the day.

Being Arcene

After Arcene first met Letje she found it rather lonely when she was on her own once more. She had insisted she would be fine when Letje left after staying a week and cleaning what she called her filthy home. Arcene had never given the state of herself or her house much consideration. She had known nothing else, but once Letje had gone she thought about a lot of things, and cleaning and keeping a tidy home unfortunately happened to be only a few of them.

This wasn't all Letje had introduced her to though, there was so much more. Things she had never heard of: The Commorancy, The Noise, Eventuals, men out to kidnap pretty girls (and worse), and the danger of even talking to strangers. Let alone robbing them then acting like nothing was wrong. Letje had introduced her to books, reading and writing and so many other things. Arcene wondered if she wouldn't have just been better off never knowing about any of it. Now there were a million and one things she was missing out on because she had never been taught about them in her ten years. And anyway, quite a lot of her time on the planet had been spent trying to feed her mother, who died anyway, never having taught Arcene very much of anything at all.

Still, at least now she knew a little of what was possible in her world, and she decided to learn all that she could. To her own surprise she also decided that she would like to stay clean and relatively tidy. It wasn't easy, that was the one thing Letje had omitted.

Finding soap, sorting out running water, shampoo, combing her hair every day, brushing her teeth, trying to fold clean clothes neatly and wash the dirty ones, and not mix the two up were all chores she found not only very time consuming but also excruciatingly boring, not to mention mostly energy sapping and pointless. Still, she had promised, so she did her best, and although when she returned to the house every now and then she did make a bit of a mess, it didn't translate to her own personal cleanliness.

She loved the feeling of running her hands through her hair, liked to see her skin unblemished by food detritus and dirt, and actually enjoyed wearing pretty clothes that fit her properly, rather than anything she just grabbed whether it was her size or was way too large for her slender child's frame. She liked that Letje said she was pretty — it made her feel good, so she did her utmost to make certain that she did look presentable, even if it meant having to brush her hair every single day!

It was only a couple of days after Letje left that Arcene realized that she actually did miss the company. She thought about going to her home, Letje had drawn her a map, but was actually proud of herself for remembering that she had said she was very busy trying to get to The Commorancy, so Arcene decided not only to not visit, but to be sure she was out when Letje came to visit her — if she did as she had promised. That way Letje could do her work without worrying about her.

Arcene felt it was very grown up of her to be so considerate a girl.

After moping around her impossibly tidy house for a few days, finding it increasingly frustrating to find anything as it was all put in different places, and was becoming really annoying, Arcene decided that she would once again leave home, but this time vowed not to get lost. She made up her mind to go and learn about the world Letje had only had the time to hint at.

Things got very scary very quickly.

To begin with everything was going great. Arcene managed to make her way to a small town that had quite a big library, and what was even better was that there were still lots of books there! She stayed for days, sitting cross-legged on the floor flicking through the picture books, frowning at the thick tomes filled with nothing but words that made no sense to her at all. But the pictures, oh how cool were the pictures. She never knew there were so many things in the world, and it was only after finding books with actual photographs that she began to realize lots of the animals she had seen as drawings were actually real live creatures, not just made up by clever people who could draw really well.

She wondered if all the buildings that people drew were real as well, but most of the ones she saw in the comics — that was what Letje had called them — she couldn't find as photographs so had her doubts. It was still a wonderful time. The only reason she left was the fact that she saw a group of men walking past on her second day and began to grow nervous. Previously she would have thought little of following them and trying to steal anything that looked useful, or she could eat, but Letje had told her that was wrong, and besides, they didn't look like they had anything, not even a rabbit between them — losers.

She tried to go back to the books, to see just how much she could learn, even finding a nice clean little room where she closed the door and almost felt safe. But Letje's words played on her mind, she couldn't settle. The strangers left her feeling uneasy, so a few hours later she packed up her rucksack and left the building.

Everything felt different all of a sudden, like she was living in the real world, not a bubble where she believed herself to be an invincible young girl where things would always turn out for the best — now she felt exposed and part of her blamed Letje for this rude awakening to the dangers of the world. Arcene headed back in the direction she had come from, away from the group of men, and decided to stay home and wait for the visit that was due soon from her one and only friend.

~~~

"I wish I had a little tortoise friend like Letje did, I wouldn't be all alone now if I did. I wonder where you get them from?" Arcene was brooding in the still relatively tidy living room, finally admitting to herself that she did prefer to have some company than to be all alone with nobody to talk to. But she had to go, she wanted to explore and do things, and she needed food anyway. She would go fishing, Letje had taught her how to do it with a lot more success than she had previously. Plus she had changed her mind and decided that she didn't want to be here when Letje arrived. She sniffed away a tear that threatened to turn into a full on cry-fest, knowing that if she saw her she would cling to her like a little baby and beg her not to leave her on her own.

"Ugh, stop being silly Arcene, you did fine on your own before, and besides, you wouldn't want to be bossed around all the time being told to wash your face and brush your teeth." Arcene pulled a face, knowing she was lying to herself. "Do this Arcene, do that Arcene," she shouted out loud, doing her best bossy woman impression, but it didn't make her feel any better, she really was feeling alone, and a little scared too.

But being the independent young woman that she was, she gathered together a few pieces of equipment, some clothes and the like, and went to go fishing at her favorite spot. There was gear stored there for the actual fishing and for camping out, she was clever enough — after lugging it back and forth a few items — to realize that it made more sense to simply leave it all hidden where she would actually need it.

As she was about to close the door behind her Arcene let out a mumbled, "Fine, alright." She turned back to the living room and tidied up a bit, just so Letje wouldn't think she couldn't cope. "Perfect," she said, oblivious to the mess that had began to infiltrate the space again somehow.

She spent a few nice quiet days fishing and gorging on succulent flesh of the freshly caught fish, then the lure of knowledge called her once again. How she wished she could read. It sounded magnificent to be able to just pick up a book and learn what secrets it held within those tiny squiggles. She had never thought about it before, but now she wished to discover all the secrets the ancient books kept locked away from the likes of her. But she could still learn, still discover new things, so felt that visiting another town would be a good idea.

Arcene ended up traveling from small village to small village, from town to town and going back and forth, criss-crossing routes that she became familiar with, often backtracking so she could be sure where she was and wouldn't get lost. She taught herself to read maps, marking out the routes she took, where she was, where she had been, although the roads on them were often nothing more than grassy walkways, or blocked, and she had to go cross-country before finally joining them again.

Then the inevitable happened: she found other people. But it wasn't a group of bloodthirsty cannibals, or a pack of half wild men on the hunt. From what she could tell it was just a nice little family, a man and a woman with a young boy, maybe just a year or two older than she was. She hid in the house she had been rummaging through for anything interesting, peeking from behind a broken pane of glass, trying to remain invisible, staying as quiet as a mouse.

They seemed harmless enough, maybe just doing what she herself was: scavenging for goodies. As she watched from across the street she followed their progress. In and out of houses they went, the man or woman keeping guard outside with the boy while the other went in and came out with some little trinket or other, nothing very interesting though by the looks of it.

Arcene soon lost interest in the people, apart from the little boy that was, he was mean.

No, it was the little dog that caught her attention, and the more she watched it, and how it was treated, the more she hated the little boy. She hated him more than anything in the whole world. The dog kept yipping, pawing at the legs of the people, wanting attention, wanting to play. The man and woman would hush it, patting its head and trying to keep it quiet. But if nobody was looking the mean little boy would kick it, or smack its head. The little dog responded by dropping its tail between its legs and wagging nervously. The boy seemed to delight in this, so Arcene made it her mission to save the doggie and get herself a new friend at the same time. It would be happier with her, and she would have company. What could be wrong with that?

It turned out to be a very bad idea indeed.

My Doggie

"Don't worry little doggie, I will save you." Arcene was deep in concentration, her hair hanging in front of her face keeping her extra hidden. She watched the family intently, and had moved house herself to keep up with them. She almost had to leave as soon as she crept into the room at the front of the house as sat in chairs were the remains of two bodies, little more than bone, tissue and skin, long dead but still in one piece. Not to be turned from her mission she summoned up her courage, walked gingerly between the resting corpses of those consumed by The Lethargy, and crept to the window.

Her hand went to her mouth in horror as the little dog yelped pitifully. It rolled over and lay still, apart from a feeble waggle of its fluffy tail. Arcene was resolute now, she would save the creature and it would be her new best friend.

Through the rest of the day and into the early evening Arcene followed the family's progress as they made their way to the end of the street, then headed out of the village and into the countryside. It got harder and harder to follow them, the darkening sky and the sporadic places to hide meant she risked either being seen or losing them. In the end the choice was taken out of her hands. As she peered from behind a tree she felt a sharp tug at her leg, then a *yip, yip, yip,* before she was grabbed from behind in a choke-hold that was impossible to escape from, however much she kicked and scratched and tried to bite the arm of her attacker.

"Hold still, hold still," yelled the man. "Gosh, you're a feisty one aren't you? Don't worry, I'm not going to hurt you, but you have been following us all day now, that's not polite." Arcene felt the grip loosen and wriggled free. She stepped back, wary of the man — he smelled kind of funky to her.

Cautiously Arcene asked, "You knew I had been following you?" She thought she had been super stealthy.

"Of course, you were peeking through the windows back in the village, banging about, making all kinds of noise. And I think I've heard about a hundred twigs break since we got into the country. You aren't exactly a little ninja lady that's for sure." The man smiled at her, he seemed nice, and the dog was sniffing at her leg now, tail wagging furiously.

Arcene was forlorn, she thought she had been so careful too. She bent and stroked the little dog, it felt so soft and warm. "What's his name? He's lovely."

"That's Ruffles, he's pretty young. We would keep him at home but you can never be too careful these days, people will steal anything."

Arcene felt rather uncomfortable and shifted from one leg to another, pulling at her bottom lip, unaware how guilty she looked. "Really, that's awful, who would want to steal a little doggie?"

"You'd be surprised," said the man. He gestured through the trees. "You hungry? Want to come and get something to eat? Where are you from anyway?"

"Oh, I'm from a long way away. And, um, I'm not sure, I shouldn't really..."

"Oh, come on, I bet you're starving, a young thing like you out here all alone. Why would you be following us if it wasn't for some food and somebody to talk to? I know how lonely it can get out here by yourself."

Arcene stared at the man, then the woman and boy standing some distance away, seemingly impatient to get going before darkness truly descended. The dog yapped repeatedly. "Hush now Ruffles, be quiet naughty dog."

Arcene glanced down at the animal and after weighing up the warnings of Letje versus the rumblings in her belly, plus the thought of maybe stealing the lovely dog afterward, she nodded her head. "Thank you, that would be lovely. I am a little bit hungry now that you mention it."

Although Arcene was very wary of the young boy, choosing to ignore him for the most part, she did find the adults very friendly. They seemed more than happy to feed her — a lovely stew that evening with real bread that had been cooling since the early morning. Arcene wolfed it all down and didn't refuse seconds. Or thirds.

She ended up staying the night. They were nice, apart from the horrid boy. She was full and it was dark outside, so she snuggled up on the sofa with lots of blankets and the plumpest pillow she had ever lay her head on in her whole life.

~~~

Clack, clack, clack, came the noise from the kitchen. "Up and at 'em, breakfast's ready."

Arcene emerged from under the blankets to the most delightful smell in the whole wide world. Forgetting all about brushing her teeth and washing her face, she pushed her matted hair away from her face and staggered into the kitchen to find the woman — Aileene, that was her name — dishing up crispy strips of meat that she called bacon, eggs that were runny, toast, and there was even what looked like proper butter. She tried not to drool on the well mopped floor.

Arcene went to grab a piece of the meat only to have the back of her hand smacked. "Ow. Waddya do that for?" It really stung.

"Manners young lady. We eat at the table and we eat with knives and forks from plates. What we don't do is go sticking our hands into pans and stealing. Didn't anybody ever teach you manners? Tsk."

"I'm sorry. I was just hungry. My mummy died years ago, I guess I don't think too much about manners."

The woman hugged Arcene, whispering that it was alright, that she understood. Then directed her to help set the table for breakfast. Arcene found the whole situation rather overwhelming. She had never had a family life, just her and her increasingly distant mother ever since she could remember. Even though she didn't like the boy she still felt the warm cocoon of close family wrapping her in its embrace.

Arcene chatted away happily over breakfast, talking about the things she had done, the places she had been and the life she lived. Even to her young ears it sounded rather lonely and pathetic. Words just didn't quite come out right.

Yet for all that she liked the comfort of the house, and of the people, she also felt somewhat claustrophobic — there were rules to obey, others to think of, and when she saw just how often the little boy was ordered to do this, and do that, she knew that such a life was not for her. She was a free spirit, wanted to explore and see new things, learn new things, not just struggle from day to day.

After breakfast she helped with the washing up and then offered to go do some chores before she left. Her offer was accepted gratefully, although the man and woman both said she was welcome to stay as long as she wished. Arcene said her thanks politely, but insisted that she had places to go, then wanted to meet her friend who came visiting on Sundays who she hadn't seen for a long time. It was only a half truth. She actually did miss Letje and planned on going straight home to wait for her — she didn't want to miss her on the weekend. And staying in another family's home made her realize how much she wanted to go back to her own, even if only for a short spell.

Once the dishes were put away there was a flurry of activity. There were a lot of chores at the house as well as the upkeep of the land and the tending to animals. Arcene offered to help in any way that she could.

"I can go and look after the animals, feed them. What about the dog, does he need a walk?"

"Oh, no, no Arcene I wouldn't dream of it," said Betlic. "The animals are very messy. Maybe you could help Timon with the vegetable garden? It's terribly weedy and that's not the way to get the best out of the soil. Vegetables don't like to have competition at all. Timon, you be sure to show Arcene how we do things around here, okay?" The boy stared at Betlic intently, as if his orders were of the utmost importance.

"Okay dad, I will." Timon moped off sullenly, beckoning Arcene to follow.

Arcene skipped after him, enjoying her morning, looking forward to going home. She was feeling content with a full stomach, and actually rather excited about doing something physical, even if it was with the horrid little boy. She felt it was important to pay back the hospitality of the family, then she could be on her way knowing she had done the right thing. Letje would be proud.

"Not like that, like this, see?" Timon tilted the mattock slightly, dragging the rich soil to the sides, expertly making ridges where seeds were to be planted now that they had got rid of the weeds.

"Fine," said Arcene, grabbing the mattock back and trying to make her ridges as neat as his. She kept at it, and after a few more ridges found that she was getting the hang of it. But when she stood up, her back aching, and looked at her handiwork she realized that she really wasn't very good at making straight lines at all. She waited for the laughter, but none came. She glanced over at the boy only to find he was fast asleep leaning back in a large wheelbarrow.

"Typical," said Arcene, "leaving me to do all the work." She needed a rest though, so decided to go for a wander around the rest of the place, maybe take a look at the animals, see if she could be of use there. She also secretly wondered if she could go play with the dog for a while — she hadn't seen it since the night before.

Although Arcene tried not to admit it to herself, she also thought that maybe, just maybe, if it happened to really want to come with her it wouldn't hurt to know where it liked to play so she could maybe, just maybe, go and get it when it was time to leave.

She went to investigate, just on the off chance of course. Really all she wanted to do was help with the chores before she left to go home.

Letje Was Right

"Letje was right," screamed Arcene, face bright red, eyes clouded by tears, her hands clenched tightly by her sides, then pulling at her hair as the horror just built and built. "There are bad people in the world, really bad people."

Betlic turned at the screams, interrupted from his butchery. "Arcene! What are you doing here? I thought you were with Timon?"

"He's asleep," sobbed Arcene. "You, you murderer, you horrible man. How could you?" But Arcene had seen enough and she didn't wait for an answer. The vision in the small cramped brick shed was enough to send her running for her life. She didn't care where she went. Just away, she had to get away.

She ran.

As she ran the vision of the nightmare space threatened to overpower her, and running was hard with the tears pouring down her face. Betlic was bare from the waist up apart from a thick leather apron, stained dark from blood. In his hands he held huge knives, razor sharp and terrifying. And on the table in front of him was Ruffles, belly sliced open, innards in a large bucket beneath the wooden butcher's block. She knew it was Ruffles, he hadn't been cut up by the evil butcher yet, he still had his fur, was still mostly whole.

But that wasn't the case for many other poor dogs that were skinned, gutted and currently hanging from hooks along one short wall. Arcene didn't even think that was the worst of it though. Along the opposing wall were cages, tiny cages stacked floor to ceiling with countless dogs, from tiny puppies to mothers trying to feed their young in the confined space. Not a one of them was making much more sound than a whimper. Their fate all too apparent to them, supposed Arcene, knowing if they were noisy then they would be first to face the evil butcher.

How could he? How could they? She thought the young boy was cruel to their pet, but it seems that was nothing in comparison to what the father did. Arcene stopped to retch violently onto the grass.

Was that what I ate for breakfast? Did I eat dog with my eggs?

She retched again, bent double and unable to find the strength to right herself. Then it was too late.

"Get off of me!" It was beginning to become a habit, being grabbed from behind by this foul man.

"Arcene, Arcene, you have to let me explain. Please, it's not what you think," pleaded Betlic.

"I think it's exactly what I think. You cage those poor dogs and then you let them watch the others be butchered and then you eat them!" Arcene was beside herself, screaming hysterically, kicking and biting, until he eventually pinned her arms by her side, slung her over his shoulder and unable to resist she found herself carried back to the house and dumped unceremoniously onto the squishy couch in the living room. He towered over her, eyes dark, face like thunder as he scowled at the cuts and the bite marks all over his forearms.

"Stay there, don't you move one muscle little girl." He edged to the doorway and shouted for his wife until she came inside.

"What's going on? Betlic? What happened? Arcene, are you alright?"

"Alright? YOU EAT DOGS!" Arcene broke down sobbing. How could they?

"Oh honey, is that what's got you so upset? Can I at least explain? It's not as bad as it seems you know? It's not ideal, but please, just listen okay?"

"I don't want to," sobbed Arcene, "you are bad people."

"We don't have to explain ourselves to the likes of —" Betlic was cut off mid-sentence by the steely glare of his wife.

"Arcene, we have to eat. It's not easy finding food you know? All our other animals were stolen a couple of years ago. The chickens? Well, we managed to round up a few of them, but the pigs, goats, even a cow were all stolen from us. What were we supposed to do to feed ourselves?"

"You have them in little cages." Arcene wasn't about to be treated like a child when it was obvious they were cruel.

"For their own protection honey, so they don't get stolen. We take them out every day for a walk, and we look after them real good. You saw how much fun Ruffles had didn't you? He had a good life."

Arcene still had her doubts. She told of Timon being mean to the dog. "What!" Betlic was furious. "I'll have his hide for that. I've told him to not hit the dogs, it's like beating on your own food."

A churning in her stomach told Arcene it was time to go. Something was just not right about these people. They were 'off' somehow. She was only just coming to realize it, but there was simply something that she couldn't quite place that she didn't like but didn't know what it was.

"Okay, fine. I'm sorry. I just got a little upset I guess. Dogs are so lovely, I don't want to eat them."

"That's okay honey, I understand. We understand, don't we Betlic?"

"Sure we do."

"Sorry for the trouble then," said Arcene, trying to remain calm and say what she thought they wanted to hear. "I think it best I go now. Thank you so much for the food and for letting me stay last night, but I'll get out of your way now — go home, wait for my friend."

There was a long silence and something icy gripped her insides, squeezing tight. An unconscious warning that there was something seriously amiss that she was as yet unaware of.

"Oh honey, you aren't going anywhere. You're part of the family now, just like Timon is. You will stay with us and you will grow older and when you children are of the correct age you will marry and have children of your own and we will have grandchildren to care for us all. It will be grand." Aileene smiled beatifically, looking off into space, lost in her dreams of an extended family gathered around her.

"I'm going home," said Arcene, getting to her feet and squaring her shoulders.

Betlic blocked the doorway. "We can't let you do that Arcene. We can't let such a young girl leave here and go live on her own, it wouldn't be right. We are your parents now, just like we are Timon's parents now too."

If Arcene was feeling out of her depth before she now felt well and truly scared. "Wha... what do you mean? I thought you were his parents?"

"We are, but it took a little while for him to adjust to it is all."

Arcene was locked in with the dogs for a week to 'teach her some respect for her new parents' as they put it, then she was allowed back into the house as long as she promised to behave. She didn't have a lot of choice. She may have been strong-willed but they were a lot bigger and a lot more clever than she thought. She tried to escape as soon as possible but they tracked her down within the hour and the punishment was truly terrible: they stripped her naked and threw the innards of the butchered dogs right over her, then made her sit outside all day as the flies buzzed and the stench made her vomit over, and over, and over again.

She behaved after that.

Or so her new parents thought.

~~~

Arcene was not a girl to give up easily, and she vowed they would not break her. So she bade her time and she learned all she could of them and the young boy that was now a part of her unwanted family.

It turned out the boy wasn't so bad after all. His violence toward the animals was understandable even to Arcene once she knew of the circumstances. It was nothing but pent up fury that had to find a release somewhere, and once she got to know him she found he was truly sorry for the way he had treated Ruffles — it had been a day that had seen him having to help with one macabre chore after another earlier in the morning, and his frustrations boiled over. As he told Arcene that, after she confronted him about it, they grew closer and she got to know him quite well over the coming days.

He had been stolen away from his own parents, who were both still alive as far as he knew, but the memory of them was fading fast. He had been a reluctant son to Betlic and Aileene for over a year now and had given up hope of ever seeing his real family again. Arcene interrogated him for all information she could possibly think of, and got quite a lot of background detail on both him and her hideous new parents. It seemed that a few years ago they had a family of their own, a real one. Then The Lethargy had taken their young children from them, and their hopes and dreams were shattered. It warped and twisted their minds and with the theft of their livestock combined with other robberies led them down the path of the thievery that had been inflicted upon them. Being Whole they thought it their right to have a family, so they went and stole Timon, believing, at least this is what they told him, that they would be better equipped to raise him as they knew they were both Whole adults. They felt it was their right and their duty to raise children, and now Arcene was to be their second child.

"Well, we'll see about that," said Arcene, with steely determination. "I'm not letting anybody tell me what to do, and I'm not living here with them, they're horrible. And those poor dogs."

Timon was in tears. "But we can't get away, they will catch us, and you know what will happen then. It's no good getting your hopes up Arcene, it just makes you more depressed."

"Have faith, I'll get us out of here, don't you worry."

So they plotted and they planned, and Arcene finalized her vengeance on the kidnappers of reluctant children. In the meantime they were both on their best behavior, doing nothing to get into trouble and be punished, although sometimes Betlic would fly into a rage and beat them even when they had done nothing wrong. Arcene took her punishment silently, apologizing, acting meek and even called him Daddy, which seemed to gain her more trust and thus more freedom to move about without constant supervision.

~~~

"Mmpf." Arcene kept her hand over Timon's mouth until he stopped struggling and realized it was her. Arcene put her finger to her lips as she removed her hand.

"Come on, we're going. And be quiet. Get dressed, quickly." Arcene was already wearing as many clothes as she could — it was cold out and she knew trying to carry bags would just slow her down.

"Turn around," whispered Timon, as he tried to get dressed while Arcene stared at him, vibing him to hurry up.

"Fine, just hurry up."

Minutes later they were panting heavily and rubbing at their hands as if it would make the rope burns disappear. It hadn't been easy, but Arcene had managed to sneak in a few lengths of rope. Tied together then secured to the window frame they were just long enough to reach the ground with a little drop at the end. Their bedroom door was bolted from the outside — it seems that their new parents only trusted them so far.

"What now?" asked Timon, his hands already beginning to blister.

"Now we get our revenge," said Arcene. "But first we let the dogs out. The poor things deserve their freedom. Come on, we need to be quick, and don't make a sound."

They made their way over to the grim room where the dogs were kept. Most never got to go outside, regardless of what her would-be parents had said. Although now and then a young pup was lucky enough to be taken out when some form of early warning was needed while they were scavenging, most never got to enjoy any form of freedom. As they entered the room the dogs became silent. They knew better than to bark when the door opened — punishment was always swift, often deadly.

Arcene turned the light on and motioned to Timon to unlock the cages. The dogs wasted no time in making their escape, although many were reluctant to leave as they had young pups.

"What are we going to do with the young ones? The mums won't leave their puppies behind." Timon was getting edgier by the minute, his indoctrination, and fear of reprisal was obvious in his jittery manner and the nervous twitching of his cheek.

"They won't have to, they can stay. We just need to get rid of our 'parents' so they can live here and be happy."

"Get rid of...?" Timon looked at Arcene, sensing he wasn't going to like this one bit.

Arcene nodded grimly, her hair bobbing around her face, exaggerating the movement. "Yup, we need to get rid of them. Look what they've done to us. Waddya think they'll do to the next kids they find? They can't be allowed to get away with it and we need to protect others too. Come on, to the workshop."

A reluctant Timon trailed behind Arcene, wanting nothing more than to get away, rather than confront his kidnappers. But Arcene was so determined, and had taken charge of their actions, so he followed behind, taking her lead. Inside the workshop Arcene searched until she found what she wanted, a tightly sealed drum that held the most precious of materials: gasoline.

"Grab that container," Arcene instructed, pointing to a metal jerry can in a corner. Once he brought it over she filled it up and grabbed the handle in one hand and the hand of the boy in the other.

"Arcene, what are we doing? We should run, they might wake up."

"Don't worry, it'll be over in a minute."

They rushed outside only to be confronted with a number of dogs howling. "Damn, the moon." The dogs, never having been outside, were howling at the moon, a bright partial orb in the sky that they couldn't understand. Arcene let go of Timon and rushed to the house. She uncapped the can and poured the fuel all around the front door. Then she trailed it back along the ground and away from the building.

As the dogs continued their barking Arcene's worst nightmare came to life — the front door opened.

"What the hell's going on out here?" shouted Betlic. "Arcene? Timon? What on earth are you doing? Did you let the dogs out?"

His wife joined him at the front door. "What's going on? It's freezing. Arcene, what have you been up to?"

"Saying goodbye, that's what. And good riddance." Arcene bent to the ground, pulled a flint and tinder from her pocket and struck it repeatedly.

Whoosh.

A spark caught and fire streaked across the ground, the front door exploding into flame in an instant. The couple went up in flames immediately. The flammable liquid that had pooled all around their feet licked up their bare legs, caught the thick woolen dressing gowns alight in a flash and before they even had the chance to run they were batting at their hair and rolling on the ground trying to put out the flames. It was no good, the fire was fierce and eager to consume all in its path. It licked at their faces, dancing into their mouths and nostrils as they tried to breathe, searing their lungs as it melted the flesh from their faces. The house was now ablaze, the whole front burning bright, lighting up the night as flames curled ever higher and higher.

Vengeance.

Arcene grabbed a terrified Timon by the hand and turned away from the pyromaniac's delight. They walked into the night. She felt no guilt, no sense of having done something wrong, it was right, she was sure of it.

She headed back in the direction of home, her home. Where she could feel safe, do what she wanted, and answer to nobody.

~~~

"And what about Timon? Where is he?" asked Letje, not sure what to think of her young friend, apart from that she was glad she was safe, but sorry that she had felt compelled to carry out such an extreme act of violence.

"Oh, a few days later I took him home. Silly boy was rubbish at reading maps, he would have got lost on his own."

"Did you see his parents then? They were okay?" asked Marcus, standing to stretch his legs. After listening to Arcene's tale for so long he was feeling a little stiff in the unfamiliar chair. He really missed furniture he was more intimate with — there was simply nothing like the comfort of a seat you had used for hundreds of years.

"I saw them and they looked fine. I didn't go to the house though. I'd kind of had enough of adults at that point, I just wanted to go home. But I saw them hug him. His mum was crying, his dad was swinging him around. They looked happy." Arcene trailed off, lost in thoughts of a life that would never be hers.

"Well, thank goodness you're safe. And now here we are. All together, all here."

"Yes, and, um..." Arcene began to cry.

Letje got up and hugged her tight. "What is it? It's okay, you're safe now, don't worry."

Arcene drew back from Letje and with tears in her eyes said, "Can I stay with you now? I don't want to be on my own any more Letje. I forget sometimes but I'm just a little girl. I'm not a grown up yet, and I want to have people to talk to and even be the adults now and then. I don't want to have to decide everything for myself, do everything myself."

"Of course, of course, we're a family now, a proper one. A family that wants to stay together, not one that is made to." Letje hugged her tight, looking over her shoulder at the nodding heads of Marcus and Sy, telling Letje that it was alright, that Arcene was better off with them.

"I'll put the kettle on," said Marcus, happy to have something to do so they could stay locked together for a little while longer.

Six Soul Crushing Words

Marcus was getting a little stressed out. Why had nobody told him that it would be somewhat foolhardy to embark on the construction of the grandest project in history when he had a young child to raise?

That was exactly the issue though — there wasn't anybody. Everyone was dead or uninterested in his problems, or his insane ambitions. So he mustered energy from as yet untapped reserves, and consuming thousands upon thousands of calories a day he looked after his son, manically built his new home and controlled countless Lethargic at the same time. He was lucky there were two of him, otherwise it really would have been beyond stressful. Even with both of him it was exhausting — his abilities were still somewhat raw and as he honed his new skills, controlling energy levels, doing without sleep and maintaining his grip over the unfortunate souls lost from their own realities, he found himself slowly sinking into a funk, losing himself in a warped reality of his own creation.

The years went by, The Commorancy grew wilder and more extravagant by the day, and his son grew from a babe into a toddler into a teenager.

Then the problems really started.

With guests now arriving, and Rooms needing to be carefully considered and amended, let alone invitations sent, Orientations to attend and the constant running of the sprawling expanse of the impossibly convoluted Commorancy to maintain, the last thing he needed on top of everything else was to find his son moping around saying he was bored.

"Bored! How can you be bored? This is The Commorancy. It's the one greatest single achievement in terms of construction that the world has ever seen. With countless Rooms, impossibly complex systems to learn, endless views from no end of really cool walkways, bridges and tunnels. We have animals and grounds that are vast, and you are bored?" Marcus couldn't believe it, it was simply not possible.

Oliver just shrugged and wandered off before Marcus could list any more reasons why The Commorancy was such a mind-blowingly brilliant place to be.

One day he just left, no warning, he was just gone.

There was a note: "I don't think this is normal," read Marcus, the paper sopping wet from tears before he had even finished reading the single line. That was it, nothing more. No farewell, no long explanation, no signature, no sorry, no 'I love you Dad'. Just six words that ripped out Marcus' heart and left him emptier than he had ever felt in his life.

The last of the old Marcus was gone, the one thing that held him steadfast and kept him even slightly grounded.

Marcus knew it was the beginnings of a long, slow descent into other-worldly madness.

~~~

"Which one are you then?"

"Does it really matter," sighed Marcus, hoping for a better greeting from the son he hadn't seen for years.

"I don't suppose so, no. Hello Dad, I've missed you. A lot."

Before Marcus could reply in kind his son ran to him and wrapped his no longer scrawny arms around him tight, like he didn't ever want to let go. Marcus didn't want him to.

Contact had been sporadic at best, and always conducted through The Noise. Oliver didn't want to see Marcus, felt he would be drawn back to a place that he simply felt wasn't normal, wasn't where his future lay. He knew that if he returned before he had forged his own path through life then The Commorancy would be his future, and only The Commorancy.

He was right. Marcus had seen that future, and knew his son was correct. But still, he missed him dearly, and missed, for selfish reasons, his one tie to a life now long buried.

Marcus broke the embrace eventually, holding his son at arms length. "Let me look at you. You've grown, you're older. Stronger too."

Oliver smiled back at him. "Well, you look the same, as always. No surprise there. I'm still trying to find my perfect age — externally. It's hard to know when is best to stop looking older. I don't know how I will look in the future, so I think I'll just carry on getting a few more wrinkles for now." He smiled, and the corners of his eyes did show signs of crows-feet.

"Well, I think you look very handsome. Very manly. It's so good to see you, I can't tell you how much I've missed you. Are you ever coming home?"

"Dad, please. You know I can't. You know the future I have if I do. I'm not like you. The Commorancy, that madness, it isn't where my path lies. You know that."

"I know, sorry. But I had to ask."

"Fancy a cuppa? I have tea."

"Real tea?" asked Marcus suspiciously.

Oliver smiled, some things never changed. "Yes Dad, real tea, out of a bag and everything."

They walked back to his house, arms on each other's shoulders, two grown men talking as if the intervening years had never happened.

Such a reunion was never to be repeated. After his visit Marcus returned to The Commorancy and a few years later he felt his son drop out of The Noise altogether.

He was gone.

He had eschewed the knowledge he had been given, and allowed himself to age naturally. Marcus assumed he was dead, and wept for a decade for the loss of his son as a part of his life through the years. It was the biggest price he paid for living how he did, for making the saving of humanity his main goal in life. He often wondered whether he had made the right decision, but it was too late now, some things could never be changed — put right.

~~~

Hello father.

Marcus jolted out of his reverie, wondering if it was just wishful thinking as he was missing his son more than ever now he was back on the mainland with some distance from The Commorancy.

Is that really you? It can't be, you died didn't you? Years ago.

There was a pause, then the reply he hoped against hope he would hear. *No father, I didn't die. I'm here, on the mainland, still going strong... sort of anyway. You want to meet up? It's been a while.*

Marcus wiped away the tears. *Haha, a while? More like two and a half centuries. You got any tea?*

There was a smile in The Noise. *Some things really do never change do they? Sorry, no tea.*

That's okay, I have some. Can I bring a few friends?

There was a longer pause. *Friends? Now this I have to see. Sure thing Dad, bring them... and the tea. It's been ages. Got any sugar?*

You betcha. Right, where are you, I'll be there in a jiffy.

Marcus was happy, truly happy. Maybe there had been more than he had first seen in his reasons for leaving his home behind. Some things even he couldn't see in his future. He was going to meet the most important part of his life again, it was like a dream come true.

No, The Other One

Soon enough it was time to leave the relative comfort of her home. Letje wished they could stay for longer, but she was as aware as Marcus and Sy that the longer they stayed the more chance there was of her home being discovered. She didn't want that any more than the others did.

What the final solution was to be she had no idea — Marcus was continually evasive when asked about the ultimate plan for dealing with Varik and his devoted Eventuals. He insisted that he had seen the future and knew that their fates lay well away from their current location, but would never give too much away. She was always left to guess from cryptic hints and odd glimpses of fragmented futures she herself was beginning to see — tiny revelations as to what was possible once you were truly Awoken and had mastered The Noise.

"So where are we going to now? I assume that you know?"

"Let's just say that I had a rather unexpected surprise conversation this morning and I can't wait to get going."

Letje looked at Marcus closely, now that she thought about it there was definitely something different about him. He seemed... he seemed rather manic, over-excited, strangely perky. "Hmm. You going to tell me what's going on? Who did you talk to?"

"Haha, you will just have to wait and see. What I can tell you is that I am very excited, and a little nervous too. But enough of that, let's get ready. We can leave this evening and travel through the night. Once we get packed up we can have a little doze this afternoon so everyone's rested enough to put in a fair few miles. It's best to put some good distance between us and your home just so Varik won't find out where it is. Okay?"

"Okay," said Letje warily, catching the smile that Marcus seemed incapable of losing since she had see him earlier that morning. "By the way, have you seen Arcene? Normally she would be in the kitchen trying to eat anything that isn't nailed down, but I can't find her."

"I think she's outside with Sy. They said they were going to go and pull up what vegetables are ready. She's a really nice girl Letje, and I can tell she loves you very much. You're doing the right thing you know, she belongs with you now — your sister."

"She is great isn't she? If a little naughty. I'm just sorry about what happened to her, it must have been terrifying."

"She's a strong girl, and although I can't say I approve of ten year olds burning people to death it's not as if they didn't have it coming. But things like that leave permanent mental scars, so look out for her, and be patient. She is still only a child after all."

"I know, and trust me, I think that Arcene is always going to be a handful. I'm positive she was born with an extra naughty gene or something."

"You may be right," smiled Marcus, who went off to check his packing, whistling as he did so.

Definitely up to something, thought Letje, as she went to find Arcene and Sy, dismissing an image of him working in the garden with his shirt off, sweat dripping down his chest... Letje flushed, and tried to think about practical matters instead, but she got that feeling in her stomach again and found herself rushing out the door into the sunshine.

~~~

"Oh my god, what happened?"

"It was his fault."

"It was her fault."

Arcene and Sy shouted out their accusations at the same time, both almost helpless with laughter.

"Look at the state of you two, you're filthy." Letje tried to keep a straight face but couldn't, and burst out laughing at the sight that now confronted her.

Sy and Arcene were caught red-handed, each of them standing there holding on to great clumps of mud, caked in it from head to toe. What had started as a bit of gardening had quickly turned into a full on mud fight when Arcene got a little over zealous with the hoe and 'accidentally' flicked soil at Sy, just after he had washed his thick unruly hair too.

The end result was a manic five minutes of mud flinging that left them both out of breath, wet and filthy, but happy, all worries forgotten for a few brief minutes.

"Wanna join us," beamed Sy, pulling his arm back, ready to fire the messy missile.

Letje stared him down. "Don't you dare, do you know how long it takes me to wash my hair?"

"Hey, it takes me ages too, you don't see me complaining," shouted Arcene, ready to join the fight again.

"Yes, but the difference is Arcene that I don't really enjoy being dirty, but you do. And look at your clothes, you'll have to get changed now, and get washed again."

"Spoilsport," pouted Arcene, dropping her hand to the side.

Sy winked at Arcene. "Yeah, you'll have to go and get clean Arcene. In a minute. Haha." Before she knew what had hit her Letje found herself battling for survival against an onslaught of sloppy missiles flung from two very enthusiastic dirty warriors. There was nothing else for it...

"Right, that's it, you two better look out." Letje bent and grabbed herself large handfuls of the wet soil, and tried to return fire before the next barrage.

It was carnage and by the end of the battle they were all reduced to tears, too tired to continue, all in serious need of a good clean.

"I surrender. I think it's time we all got cleaned up, right Letje?" said Sy.

"Absolutely. Then try to get some rest, as we're on the move again this evening."

"Spoilsports," said Arcene, grinning manically, but visibly wilting after the frenzy of battle.

George peeked out from behind the bushes, checking if the coast was clear. He sidled up close to Arcene, but kept enough distance so she couldn't touch him with her filthy fingers.

"Letje?"

"Mm?"

"I think I've changed my mind," said Arcene coyly. "I don't want you to be my sister now."

"What? Oh," said a disappointed Letje.

"No no, I don't mean it in a bad way. I think... I think I want you and Sy to be my mum and dad instead." With that Arcene stood on tiptoe, kissed Sy on the cheek, gave a kiss to Letje too, and skipped off happily, with George, for once, actually playing catch-up to somebody. He seemed rather enamored with

Arcene, having taken to following her about and stealing attention whenever he could.

"Oh," was all Letje managed to say before Sy grabbed her hand, the drying mud squishing into her hand — she didn't care.

"Well, I don't see that we have much choice in the matter, do you." He smiled at Letje, his large strong hand giving comfort. It was as if that firm grip solidified the future of a ready-made family that promised to hold a rather interesting, definitely never mundane future, for them all.

"I don't think we do. Once she makes up her mind there's not a lot that will change it. I just hope she doesn't think it includes George too." Letje smiled after Arcene, who seemed happier than ever now she had a little mud covering her pretty face.

"Thank you Sy."

"For what?"

"For being so good with Arcene. It's what she needs."

"Hey, no problem. She's a great girl, and to be honest I think I enjoyed it more than she did."

Letje smiled. "Yes, it was fun, if a little on the muddy side."

Showdown

Bishop was about as annoyed as he had ever been in his life, and he had never been what you would call the jolliest of men. Countless years as a part of the church of The Eventuals had done nothing to improve his demeanor, and now here he was, out in the rain, wandering around the damn dirty countryside looking for Marcus and whatever remained of the small group of people that had followed him to the mainland.

It had been going on for way too long now, and he was getting angrier and angrier by the day. He didn't fight and claw his way to the position of Bishop (even if Varik insisted all Bishops be referred to as just that — Bishop) to then be degraded by doing work the novice acolytes should be doing. He had grown used to a rather luxurious lifestyle over the decades, yet now here he was, traipsing about the place half starved. Plus half his Ward had already either run off or fallen foul to the wild people that seemed intent on destroying anything with a red face.

He scowled at the backs of the idiots in front of him, somehow still able to muster enough enthusiasm to carry their heavy loads without grumbling constantly. He longed for his own bed, his meals brought to him every day, a warm fire and even the occasional bedfellow when a new acolyte seemed eager to please his or her new Bishop.

He had had none of that for a long time now, and was seriously wondering why he hadn't run off himself.

"Because Varik will find me and flay me alive, that's why," he muttered to himself under his breath.

He looked around nervously, aware that merely thinking such thoughts was enough for serious punishment. Even now it was easy to forget that anyone adept in The Noise could theoretically read some of his thoughts if they were powerful enough. He put such sentiments aside, instead focusing on the task at hand. Maybe this would be the breakthrough he hoped for? It certainly seemed like the lead he had been given was genuine. But then, so had countless others since they began to trail Marcus and his fellow castaways from The Commorancy.

Marcus had been tracked and lost countless times since the chase first began. Each time he seemed to vanish from the face of the planet just as his trail seemed to be getting warmer, maybe this time it would be different? Bishop was assured by one of his more competent acolytes, a relatively newly Inked young man, that he had caught sight of Marcus along with two women and a man. Oh, and a goat as well.

They were heading east and as far as he could tell were traveling with nothing more than rudimentary precautions. He had trailed them through the night then left them as they entered a building to rest for the day. It seemed like they were cautious enough to travel when it was dark, a simple way to cut down on the chance of being spotted. The acolyte had not attempted anything himself, so he was at least smart enough to obey instructions. Which was more than could be said for Bishop.

Rather than reporting his findings up the chain of command, Bishop recalled the members of his Ward, instructing them to convene a mile away from where Marcus had been spotted. As he approached the rendezvous point it was more than obvious that a number of acolytes had not obeyed. Now that a confrontation with Marcus was appearing likely almost half had run off in the opposite direction, happy to be a part of something until there was a significant chance it would be the last thing they ever did. Bishop regretted not reporting that he had in all likelihood found Marcus. He had wanted the victory as his own, to make a report once Marcus was dead, but now the odds were not so greatly stacked in his favor and he was beginning to get nervous.

"Stupid, shouldn't have been so keen for the glory," muttered Bishop, as he surveyed the sorry remains of his once large Ward. The members looked worn out, undernourished, edgy and nervous, but most worrying of all was that they were obviously completely demoralized. He had never been good at motivating others, it wasn't as if he had joined to be any kind of army commander. He had joined for the comfort of the church and the opportunity to rise in rank and thus power. He wanted all the trappings that came with it. Well, it looked like he had finally got his just reward, and it weighed heavily on his fat shoulders.

Guess I will have to make-do with what I've got, thought Bishop, mentally tallying up the numbers, trying to come up with an appropriate plan.

He approached the tent that was always erected when they made camp, and without acknowledging his guards he entered the relative comfort of the canvas lined room. He sat on a chair and thought, expertly entering The Noise then tracking countless scenarios simultaneously, following their progress and possible future outcomes, until he found something that actually might succeed — he even surprised himself with the beauty of the plan. He smiled for the first time in weeks, shaking his head in wonder, his gray jowls wobbling as the mirth shook his extensive frame.

~~~

As daylight broke Bishop was still in a rather good mood; it was infectious. The confidence with which he had given his instructions and walked through the camp early that morning had given the acolytes a much needed boost in morale. He wondered if he wasn't actually a rather good leader of men after all.

Then again maybe it was just the fact that they were eating well? Knowing Marcus' location meant that for once Bishop had allowed the lighting of small, but intensely hot fires. Meat was roasting, pieces cut off the instant they were cooked enough to stuff into eager mouths. That alone was enough to lift the spirits of his men. Combine that with a possible end to the relentless marching across the countryside, pursuing a man they all hated so much it actually ached, and he believed he was on to a winning formula.

He suspected that he was probably one of the least interested in Marcus out of all the men present. He may have been in charge, and supposedly deeper into The Eventual's doctrine than the rest, but the fact of the matter was that he cared little for the religion or for what it stood for. He was a fatalist, and did see the end of humanity as the most likely outcome of The Lethargy, but he was mostly interested in just leading a comfortable life while he had the chance — something he kept well hidden from anybody else, as the punishment for such a blasphemy would be harsh indeed.

But if he could pull this off? Eliminate Marcus and lead the way by example? Well, the rewards would be glorious, his position greatly increased within Varik's church. His future would be as secure as it possibly could be for the time he had remaining on the planet — which he hoped would be substantial.

It was assumed that their prey would have moved through the night, so Bishop sent a small group ahead to check on their location. Not finding them where they had been spotted the previous day, Bishop ordered the men to stay put and wait for the rest of them to catch up.

Once the camp site was packed up and the men finished eating then doused the flames, they caught up with the forward party quickly. Bishop now knew that they could cover the ground they needed to through the day, as Marcus and his party were in all likelihood resting and waiting for evening to fall before setting off once more. Maybe this would be the last day of having to walk through the damn drizzle and the mud and he could finally get back to the life he had been rather enjoying?

One more day, just one more day.

As they walked he daydreamed and finalized his plan. By the afternoon the scouting party reported that Marcus was but a few miles ahead. Orders were flashed via The Noise that all members of the Ward were to stay out of The Noise from now on. They were absolutely not to drop the guard that prevented them from being discovered by those who were as adept as Marcus.

Here we go then. Showdown.

Another One Bites The Dust

Marcus shook his head in wonder. Who did they think he was, some amateur? Didn't they know that their presence shone like bright stars on a clear night for somebody as proficient in The Noise as him? Were they forgetting what he had built, how long he had been Awoken?

"Idiots!"

"What's that?" asked Sy, startled by the sudden outburst.

"Oh, nothing. Just thinking out loud. But listen, all of you," said Marcus, gesturing for Letje and Arcene to join him. "We have company, and they may be rather stupid but it is best never to underestimate your enemy. What this means is that we need to act to defend ourselves, and I'm afraid it is going to mean some rather, um, how shall I put this...?" Marcus scratched his head.

"It's going to get all deathy isn't it? You're going to kill people that want to kill us?"

"Well, yes. Thank you Arcene. I was trying to be a little more diplomatic as you are so young, but yes, it's going to get somewhat 'deathy', if that is an actual word?"

"Of course it is," said Arcene, "everyone says it."

Letje nudged Arcene in the ribs. "Everyone who? You don't know anyone."

Arcene smiled back unperturbed. "Well, I say it, and Marcus says it, so there." She stuck out her tongue at Letje, pleased to be proved right.

"Good, now we have our nomenclature sorted out, I think it best that we move. We've had a good rest and this is certainly a nice, if somewhat cramped place, but it's better to be out in the open if we are to defend ourselves properly. There's no need to panic unduly, I can take care of them easily enough, but Sy?"

"Yes?"

"We will be better off working together, it will go a lot more smoothly and there will be less undue risk. So, here's the plan..."

Ten minutes later everybody knew what they were to do. It was to be simple but very effective. They just had to be sure to execute their part as Marcus had instructed. Nobody argued. Arcene stayed quiet even though it was obvious she was very excited, and Letje interrupted only to state that she felt it unfair that she didn't have a more important role to play.

"Letje," said Sy, "you and Arcene need to be protected. If Marcus and me can deal with this small group on our own easily enough then why put yourself at risk? It's all going to go a lot smoother if you can keep an eye on Arcene, and I will feel a lot happier knowing that you are both safe. The same goes for Marcus. Right Marcus?"

"Absolutely. This will all be over a lot quicker if you let us deal with it. And no offense to our beautiful young girl here," said Marcus, smiling at Arcene, "but I know how excited you get and I don't want to have to be worried about you being in the way when things get a little 'deathy'. Okay?" Marcus winked at Arcene who was trying her best to look shocked that she could be seen as anything other than a huge help in any and all circumstances.

"Okay, but please be careful."

Arcene saluted smartly, although the effect was ruined somewhat by her yelping and grabbing her ankles as she banged them together too hard.

~~~

Bishop may have been used to his home comforts and a life of relative luxury, but he was no fool. Regardless of motivation and personal life preferences you didn't rise high in Varik's church unless you were intelligent and willing to do what needed to be done when instructed. There was no space for those that didn't obey orders, and Bishop was more than aware of the repercussions for anybody not performing to the best of their ability.

He almost pitied the Eventuals that had deserted — if they were found the punishment would be lengthy, as well as extremely unpleasant.

He knew that there was a strong risk of Marcus simply shutting down his men before they even got a chance to attack, so had taken effective measures to ensure that his most trusted acolytes were concealed. He was actually quite pleased with the plan he had designed. He smiled to himself slyly as he thought of the punishment Marcus was soon to dish out to those Bishop knew were borderline deserters — he would use them to his own ends before they left, thinking they were free from the faith they had decided no longer served their purpose.

Bishop's men spread out, taking various paths until they formed a circle with Marcus and his group at the center. They had their position fixed so kept out of The Noise and converged on the center once they were evenly spaced a half mile from their quarry.

They began to close in. Some following the orders they assumed had been issued to them all, the trusted men following a different set of instructions entirely.

~~~

Marcus was sweating slightly, but at least it was almost over. The presence of the would-be attackers was easy to detect in The Noise, even if they tried to conceal themselves by ceasing their communication. Their hatred made them even easier to find. Their fear, their desire to flee and not get involved made it even easier still. Strong emotions made them light up in The Noise and they were a cinch to pinpoint. Even their scent was easy to detect — Marcus' virtual Jacobson's organ once again proving just how useful a modification it had been.

Marcus and Sy stood at the center of an invisible battle, one that was waged well in advance of physical contact. Marcus reached out, aiding Sy as best he could, and together they focused on the approaching Eventuals. It took a great deal of concentration and both of them were breathing deeply, Sy feeling the pressure of such focus much more than Marcus.

One by one the attackers were taken over, then simply shut down. It was no easy thing, Marcus and Sy dealt with Whole without too much issue, but those on the cusp of Awakening, or those that were Awoken, were not going to be dealt with so easily.

Then the real assault began.

Sneaky Creepy

abu made his way through the trees — sure-footed and feeling heavy yet full of energy. He knew he was one of the most trusted of all in his Bishop's Ward and planned on proving himself this day. He would be a part of the last major event in history: the killing of Marcus, then the bringing about of the true End. For a brief moment his name — albeit just a random collection of letters — would be known by all in the church of The Eventuals. He planned on being the one to eliminate Marcus and the rest of the small group he still had with him. Then he would hunt down the rest before he took his rightful place in The Void when the time came.

The physical body of abu was still a half mile from Marcus, slumped in a seated position with its back leaning against the thick stump of a once virile tree — dead long ago.

The boar, extinct for seven hundred years but accidentally re-introduced only a few years before The

Lethargy, was part of a large family unit that had fed the men well — the rest came in useful in an opportune but unforeseen way. abu had unwrapped the cloth tied around its snout to keep it quiet and then went quickly deep into The Noise to enter its mind before it got out of range — he was surprised by just how fast the creature actually was. Once inside its mind he found it to be a rather barren place, with little going on apart from a rather grating repetitive obsession with grubbing for food with even the concern for its lost family receding quickly. The mind was still somewhat immature however. Though currently still part of the large matriarchal sounder it would not be welcome to stay once it grew to adulthood — then it would lead a solitary life. Or it would have if the hunger of The Eventuals had not caught up with it and its family.

Now having compete control of the boar abu ran fast on short stocky legs, heading directly for Marcus as he knew others were doing. He already felt the disturbance in The Noise of men with The Ink rapidly winking out of existence; it was as if they had never been. He faltered as yet another presence disappeared, recognition of the power of Marcus finally realized. Still, he had surprise on his side, and while the sacrificial acolytes paid the ultimate price for their less than total devotion, abu knew that he had a very good chance of succeeding.

He regained his footing, concentrating hard as the poor eyesight of the boar made it hard to progress when the ground became uneven. A slight nagging at the back of his mind had to be constantly suppressed: the urge to stop and root around in the loose loam with his large snout was almost overwhelming. He ignored it best he could as he tried to make good speed but also avoid the low hanging branches that would give warning of his presence long before he arrived at his prey's location.

Suddenly the thinning trees gave way to open ground and he spied two figures. He had no option but to attack the person nearest to him.

Damn, it's not Marcus. I'll deal with him next.

Two hundred pounds of solid muscle bounded toward its prey at close to twenty five miles an hour. As he felt the heat emanating from the man, abu bent his familiar's head down and slammed the top, on its short thick neck, against the kneecap of the man. He heard a satisfying crunch and the body crumpled to the floor. In an instant abu felt the mind of the boar occupied by the man's presence: Sy was his name, but not for long. Before Sy could orient himself and take control, for abu became instantly aware that his victim was much more powerful than him, he shook his head furiously and speared Sy repeatedly in the midsection with his tusks.

It wasn't working, the tusks were still not fully grown and were not long enough to inflict serious damage unless he got really lucky.

He bit down hard on soft flesh, as giving as if he were biting into butter. The huge lower canines of the boar pierced the skin easily and abu rooted deeply inside the jagged opening he had made. He snuffled and chewed and ripped and shook his head again wildly, the juvenile tusks causing irreparable damage to the man this time.

Then it was over. He was pushed out of the boar's body, Sy's waning life still strong enough to dismiss abu's presence like blowing dust from his hand.

As he faded from the mind of the boar he heard a satisfying gurgle and with eyesight clouding over he saw bubbles of blood popping rhythmically from the dying man's mouth.

~~~

"Sy, Sy. SY!"

"Stay back, I told you to stay back," shouted Marcus, already snuffing out the life of abu as he felt the opportune attacker's presence leave the boar and return back into a body some half a mile away.

Damn, I should have been more careful. Too busy focusing on the people to take a proper look at the animals.

Marcus spun in a circle as he felt bodies of various animals emerge into the clearing, or make their way through the woods on all sides. Letje was already beside Sy, with Arcene not far behind.

They didn't listen, I told them to stay put. But it was understandable, Letje and Sy had planned to marry, and no matter what he felt about that, or the fact that he knew that somehow Sy would be dead before long, he had to admit he hadn't seen it coming yet, or in this way. Fate was a funny thing, and once again it had proved that even if you knew the future it could still come as a surprise. Now it could change at any instant if he wasn't careful.

Marcus had to stay focused, he couldn't let his attention focus on Sy. He had to protect Letje and Arcene.

Don't forget about me, came a voice through The Noise.

How could I? Tortoises are always at the fore of my concerns, quipped Marcus.

Well, that's alright then.

Marcus didn't know how he did it but Yabis managed a virtual wink that was felt not seen.

Keeping control of the boar, Marcus sent it hurtling at the mature female that was at this very minute rushing toward them with her head down and some very large tusks poised to rip Letje's kidneys to shreds. The immature male slammed its head into the side of the female, sending them both flying. Marcus directed the boar to its feet in an instant, then took control of both, shunting the Eventual out of the mind of the female and back into his own body half a mile away.

Then an owl came diving like a dagger toward him, its wide eyes asking for release even as its talons threatened to rip his skin to shreds.

It was easy to enter the small mind and fill the space with his own presence, then release it. The bird flew off startled, unknowing of the damage it had nearly caused. Then there was nothing but silence, no more animals, the only Eventuals still alive now over half a mile away and too powerful for Marcus to eliminate all at once. He would deal with them soon, but first he had to check on Sy, make his dying moments as comfortable as possible.

Just as he approached he felt a strong ripple in The Noise, a familiar presence from what seemed like a lifetime ago. There was a flash of wild hair, as if with a life of its own, as the tendrils wound their way around the naked body of a man that went from Eventual to Eventual, killing them as easily as if they were nothing but fish in a barrel.

Marcus heard the death-rattle of Sy as his pierced and mangled lungs gave up the last of their air.

All that was left was the sobbing of Letje. Leaves rustled quietly in the wind.

Ooh

Sy was dead.

What had been Sy and countless other lifeforms throughout space and time went back to The Void that spawned all existence in a universe that held not only hundreds of billions of galaxies but thousands upon thousands of billions of stars within each one, all with infinite realities.

The impossibly unimportant mote of energy entered the timelessness once more and if such a thing as time had existed in The Void then it would have been re-birthed ten million years previously onto a small moon circling a dark red planet that had been abandoned by its dominant life-form over a million years before.

As the newborn came into the world in a small room surrounded by curious faces and a still screaming mother, it drew its first breath just as its mother drew her last.

Minutes later the child was cleaned and dressed in the ceremonial garb that was only fitting for the future leader of the tiny population that remained Whole.

The child's mother was incinerated a few hours later, just another victim of The Lethargy. Her ashes were shuttled out into space along with the rest of that week's victims, where they added to the emptiness as tiny motes that could never live or die, just transform from one form of energy to another.

The child finally opened its eyes and looked out at the great hall that contained all that was left of a once proud race numbering in their trillions. A species that had once occupied countless planets in the center of their galaxy, now nothing more than a myth the remains of the diaspora found impossible to believe.

Is It Love?

Letje felt empty.

Sy was dead.

How could he be dead when she was going to marry him? It didn't seem possible. But it was true, another person taken from her life, gone to The Void, never to return. Sy had been a good man, not at all how you would imagine somebody that had lived for hundreds of years to be — he just seemed, well, normal. He wasn't condescending, didn't act like he knew everything because of his age, and certainly acted like a young man of twenty one years, not somebody who had been alive for countless generations. Letje wondered if time in The Commorancy was so warped that all those centuries counted for mere years rather than how the rest of the world experienced time. It was certainly a possibility, the one thing she had learned since meeting Marcus was that anything could happen.

But so what, he was dead!

She was going to have a husband, have children, be happy.

I'm sorry Letje, said Yabis. *I know how much you liked Sy, he was a nice boy.*

Liked? I loved him Daddy, he was going to be my husband.

There was a long pause before Yabis replied. *Letje, there is a big difference between liking somebody and loving them with your very being. I don't want to upset you, that would never be my intention, but you must learn to understand your feelings, and maybe not be quite as impetuous with boys, I mean men, that you meet.*

I don't want to talk to you at the moment father, you don't know what I'm feeling, what it was like. I thought I had found somebody I could live my life with, be happy, have a chance at a family, like you and Mummy had with me.

I know darling, I know, and I am sorry.

Letje walked behind Marcus and Arcene, lost in her own thoughts, not wanting to be disturbed. She felt she was owed that much, and really didn't think she could stand talking to anyone. It was all getting too much, had gotten too much. She had met too many people and lost too many people too suddenly. It was overwhelming and the grief threatened to pull her into a state of giving up and just going home and staying put which she knew would be all too easy. Life just wasn't fair. How could people just die so easily when they had so much to offer, so much more life to live?

Letje kicked at a stone in the path, sending it off into the bushes. Marcus turned at the sound, but saw Letje kicking at the dirt and turned to face forward once again.

Then he hesitated and whispered something to Arcene. She nodded and walked over to a tree where she happily sat back resting against the damp bark. George joined her and she talked nonsense to him while Marcus walked back and took Letje by the arm.

"Let's take a little walk, just you and me."

"Fine, just don't try to make me feel better, I'm not in the mood."

"Oh, don't worry, I won't," said Marcus, a look of grim determination on his face.

~~~

"You've got no right to say that! Who are you to say what is meant to happen and what isn't?"

Marcus shifted uncomfortably, he really wasn't used to such confrontations, he felt rather out of his depth. He knew there would be tears soon, maybe he had made a mistake?

"Some things have to happen Letje, otherwise the future won't play out as it should. There's no getting away from that."

"You mean what you want to happen, don't you? You said yourself that there are countless possible futures. You are just picking the one you think is best for you," shouted Letje accusingly. The tears began to pour down her cheeks uncontrollably, the numbness wearing off.

Marcus knew it was coming but still carried on talking, he had to. Letje had to understand what was at stake. "It's not about what is best for me Letje, I wish that was all I had to think about. It's about what is best for you, for Arcene, for Umeko with her husband and her future family, for everybody still in their Rooms at The Commorancy, for everyone sinking into Lethargy on that hillside, for all the Whole on the planet and for the future of everything. You think that doesn't weigh heavily? You think I don't want to run around shouting how unfair it all is and let madness take me away from such responsibilities? You don't know what it's like, you can't even begin to understand yet how it feels to see your own future, your own death, and try your best to make sure it happens."

"Your own death? You saw it?"

"I did. I have seen it in countless futures. After all, nothing lasts forever, we all die."

Letje's anger surfaced again. "But you have still chosen, haven't you? Decided to let things happen, so that the future you want will come to pass?"

"Yes, I have. I take that responsibility. I do it for you, but more than that I do it for everybody else."

"And what if I don't want the future you have decided on?"

"Then it will be up to you to decide, nothing is certain. You have free will and soon you will have the power, be truly Awoken. You can make your own mind up then about what will happen in your life, but you will see that what has already happened was for the best. Even if it meant Sy dying."

Letje found it too much, it was like Marcus had known from the beginning, before any of the madness since she had set foot in The Commorancy began, that most of their group would either leave or perish.

"You knew ages ago didn't you?" accused Letje. "You saw it all and you allowed it."

Marcus said nothing, just stared at her with his unfathomable green eyes. Eyes that were full of grim determination yet a sadness that hinted at unimaginable responsibility, and maybe even doubt, maybe even madness.

"You knew Sy would die and you let him."

"Let me ask you a question, answer honestly. What do you think Sy would have wanted?"

"To be married to me and have a family. Be happy."

"And if the only way you could survive, and countless others, if not everyone, was for him to die, then what do you think he would have chosen?"

"He would have chosen to die," whispered Letje. "He would have died and been happy that he had made a difference."

"Then you have your answer."

"It doesn't make it any easier though, does it? He's still dead."

"Oh yes, very much so."

"Well, don't be too nice about about it," sulked Letje.

"I'm sorry, I'm not good at this kind of thing. Please, forgive me. I known it hurts, trust me, I know better than anyone, but Sy lived for a long time, had a better life than most, and in the end he found happiness, even if just for a short while. But it was with you Letje, you made him happy, and that counts — a lot."

Letje thought for a moment, regained her composure somewhat. "You're right, he was happy wasn't he? Can I ask you a question?"

"You can ask."

"What were Sy's... you know, powers? What did he get out of being in his Room for so long? I know he was Awoken, but what exactly does that mean for everyone? For him really, what did it change?"

"Sy didn't get any special 'powers' as you call it. Not that they really are powers, they are just potentials that are waiting to be Awoken in some people. Sy could enter The Noise, feel things like all Awoken can, more sensitivity to other minds, even maybe a bit of what seems to be mind reading, but is just being very attuned to human reactions on a minute scale, and he could control his body to a surprisingly high degree, although he actually chose not to. I'm not sure I should tell you what Sy gained from being in his Room Letje, I don't think he would mind, not now, but I don't know..." Marcus thought for a while, actually lay on the ground and closed his eyes while Letje grew ever more impatient until she finally thought he must have fallen asleep.

"Okay, I'll tell you," said Marcus from the ground, without opening his eyes. "But you have to understand the context, the reasons. At least, the reason Sy gave some two hundred and what, fifty years ago? He was a young man then, a young man who just wanted to forget and didn't know how. He had no idea, just knew he couldn't stand it any longer."

"Now you have me worried Marcus. What do you mean, he came to The Commorancy to forget? Not to Awaken and gain the benefits of it?"

"No, that was just a side-effect of Sy forgetting that he had been married and had a baby boy."

"Oh." Letje didn't know what to say, what to think. How could he have not told her?

"He didn't tell you because he didn't know. It's why he came and it's what he got. As far as Sy was concerned he had only ever kissed a girl once when he was very young. He died having no knowledge of the wife he had or the baby he lost. It almost broke him, and he made up his own backstory, a history that he dreamed up to replace what happened to him — to his family. Much of his life was a lie, a replacement for what really happened, at least in the few years prior to entering The Commorancy. I think that for maybe the last two years there was just fabrication, replacement memories of roaming the country, finally deciding to enter The Commorancy to Awaken, when really his last years before he came to me were full of unbearable sorrow, desperation, and a frenzied hunt for access to a Room. He very nearly went completely mad — he was as close to the edge as I have ever seen anyone."

"Tell me. Tell me the story. Please." Letje couldn't imagine what could have been so bad that Sy purposely decided to forget a wife and a baby, but she wanted to know more about the man she thought she would have spent her future with.

"Okay, but you won't like it, there is no happy ending, as you know."

~~~

Sy's life up until he was a little over nineteen years old had been one of independence, early sorrow when his parents died when he was thirteen, loneliness, a longing for company, and a few encounters with individuals or groups of people that he found it impossible to relate to properly or they to him. That or they were outright hostile and he was lucky to escape with his life.

He had roamed extensively, and had grown into a strong and resourceful young man. But he had not been as buoyant and mostly happy with his solitary life as he believed after the first few years within his Room. It was then that he began to be able to alter his own memories, making them into what he knew he needed them to be if he weren't to simply give up and fall into a form of self-induced Lethargy.

Sy was intelligent enough, and caring enough, to understand what a waste of a precious human life that would be. He wanted to change himself so he could go back out into the world and make a difference, help humanity flourish, do something, anything to help rather than waste his precious gift of existence.

Above all else Sy wanted to forget.

He wanted to put his past behind him and start again — something he knew he couldn't do in his current mental state. But it wasn't just that, not just that he didn't want to feel alternately suicidal or manic, he just wanted to be happier; he wanted to eradicate the memories of the cruelty of existence. Often, he feared he could succumb to the lure of The Eventuals, he regularly felt his life to be pointless — nothing more than a punishment for unknown crimes.

All Sy had wanted since he could remember was a return to the happy times when he had his mother and father alive. He wanted to be able to support a family of his own, but it was just impossible to find anybody — not just a wife, but people in general. Then it had all changed in an instant, and he was head over heels in love. He knew it was love, knew it was the real deal. How else could he explain the fact that he couldn't breathe properly and his stomach practically jumped out of his mouth when he saw her?

He felt no shyness as he approached the raven-haired woman, for that was what she was, this was no girl. She lived alone in a small house on the outskirts of what was once suburbia, where she had resolutely refused to move from even though there was added danger living so close to the remnants of the city. It was as though she didn't realize she was surely a great prize for any man that encountered her.

Sy had seen her cutting the lawn of all things, using a contraption that cut as it was forcefully pushed. It was surreal. There he was, cautiously walking down the street, dodging overgrown hedges and trying not to trip on the cracked paving slabs that were shifted by the ever growing trees that had once been kept so orderly.

He stopped in his tracks.

Here was The One. His wife, he knew it. Hair that reflected the light yet was as black as the darkest night. Short denim shorts that showed a shapely figure and a loose blouse that hinted at curves underneath. When she turned to mow in the opposite direction, and he saw her face, he knew he was lost forever and would do anything she wished. Her eyes were almost as black as her hair, her skin was lightly tanned and her lips were full and as red as a cherry.

Then she smiled at him, obviously amused by the man that was gawking at her with his mouth hanging open and his hands limp by his sides.

Yet Sy felt no embarrassment, wasn't tongue-tied or worried about what to say, for he knew that this was to be his wife, the mother of his child. He was right.

Massassi watched as he approached, head cocked to one side — fearless. She told him months later that she had known the minute she saw him that he was a good man, and that she thought she could love him. She told him that she did love him, that she was going to now call herself his wife, and him her husband. Sy was so happy he thought he must be in heaven. When she told him that she was to have a child Sy knew that he truly was in heaven.

"He told me all of this Letje, when he first came to The Commorancy. He told me of the woman, Massassi, and his love for her. He wept as he told of their time together, and their beautiful baby child. He sobbed his heart out when he whispered of the deep ache he had inside as his love threatened to overwhelm him. He slammed his fists into the walls and screamed like a madman as he told me of what happened to his family and the wreck of a man he became. He wanted to forget it. He knew he had to, he couldn't go on knowing what he knew."

"Wha... what happened to them? Was it truly horrible?"

"Yes Letje it was. He came home one day and his baby was dead, smashed like an unwanted doll, and his wife was gone: taken. He lost himself to madness. Fury consumed him. He tracked down the people that had taken his wife, killed his child because it would have been an inconvenience to them.

Two men were responsible. They had abused his wife and beaten her, doing it over and over again — until she was too broken to abuse again in ways you do not want to know, or you will dream of such things for ever more, just as Sy did until it finally was forgotten.

They had left her dead, dumped with the trash when they moved their camp. They didn't want Whole, or Lethargic women, they just wanted to be evil. There was nothing to stop them. Apart from Sy. He told me what he did to them, the time it took, and that he could never forgive them for the man they turned him into. So, I ask you Letje, did you love Sy? Did you love him like he loved his wife, like she loved him?"

"No, no I didn't," sobbed Letje. "Poor Sy, that poor woman, that poor baby."

"I'm sorry, so sorry that he is dead, that you had to hear that. But part of growing up is accepting responsibility for your emotions, for your honesty. Above all else you must at least be honest to yourself Letje, and that means looking deep inside and knowing what is true, and what you merely wish to be true. Sy found true love once upon a time, and he may have found it again with you, but it wasn't to be. Life is not fair and not everybody comes out a winner. I'm sorry." Marcus left Letje and went back to Arcene and George. She needed time alone, time to come to terms with the realities of being alive and the responsibility that you must have for your own words and actions.

I'm sorry Daddy, you were right. I don't know that I could ever feel like that about somebody else.

Oh, you will my dear, you will. You know, when I first met your mother I actually thought I'd had a heart attack? She stole my breath away.

You mean because she hit you with a frying pan as she thought you were a thief trying to steal her chickens? Letje couldn't help but smile at the story her mother had told her about meeting her father.

Oh! She told you that story did she? Whoops.

Life as a Tortoise

Yabis was getting more frustrated by the day. He didn't show it to Letje, or even to Marcus, but being a tortoise was actually beginning to really get on his nerves. Apart from the constant need to re-adjust his expectations, as he continually forgot that without hormones from a human body feelings and emotions simply couldn't function in the same way, he also just found it really annoying.

It was like being a tiny baby again but with self-awareness. He couldn't just decide to do something then physically go do it. He felt like an invalid but without even the comfort of being able to look down at your own body and have a permanent sense of self — Yabis knew that it would be all too easy to slip into madness, and a crushing terror of being trapped inside an alien body was always *tap, tap, tapping* at his consciousness. A constant reminder that he was not meant to be a tortoise, he should either be a human being or nothing at all.

Dead, that's what he was supposed to be.

Dead.

Day after day Yabis had to endure nothing but darkness, or a dimmed light that came when the duffel bag he was carried around in was open to the sky. It was always dull and depressing inside and he was either being knocked constantly, even though Letje did her best to be careful, or he was put on the ground somewhere and often totally forgotten about. In the beginning he would get angry at his daughter for forgetting him, but soon settled into a state of acceptance, knowing in his alien heart that it was perfectly understandable; after all, Letje hardly expected to be having to carry around the mind of her father in the form of a tortoise.

He grew to accept his new life reluctantly. What had seemed like a perfect solution to be there for Letje at first had switched to a nightmare the more they traveled and the more a burden he became. He switched from being glad he could talk with his daughter to wondering if she would be better off without him, to counting his blessings for still being alive and given the chance to maybe help Letje now and then and to be there for her when she needed him.

But what could he offer really? All he could do was talk to her through The Noise. There was no physical help he could offer, only emotional. And how had that gone? Not very well was the answer more often than he would have liked. He knew he had approached the death of Sy in the wrong way, and felt that maybe Marcus had too — maybe she didn't need to know about Sy's forgotten life? Maybe Letje should not have been made to confront the issue of love so soon? Didn't most people go through their whole lives never thinking about such things? Should a young girl with minimal life experience be put through that level of turmoil? Maybe she would have been better off if simply left to grieve for him without the added burden of having to confront her own depth of emotions.

Yabis felt the true burden of what he had done, what he had become.

It had been one thing watching silently as Letje went about her search for The Commorancy, but it had become something entirely different once all the recent madness had begun. He had thought that he could offer sage advice or at the very least be a comfort for her in times of stress, but he now wondered whether all he was in the end was a responsibility and a burden that she would have been better off without. Doubts crept continually into his mind, then receded as he reassured himself that she was pleased to have him to talk to, and wasn't it always like this for families? Didn't kids get annoyed with their dads, and didn't dads always doubt that they were doing the right thing, that they were anything but a burden holding their children back? He just didn't know, and maybe that was the point: life was complicated.

But human life, not this abomination of a life he had stolen from poor Constantine. The tiny tortoise mind was, after all, still entirely present, and had been most gracious accommodating Yabis into his cramped carapace.

Now Letje had to deal with too much too quickly. There had been event after event since finally reaching The Commorancy. Yabis knew that it wasn't about to let up any time soon.

Ah, but the future? Yes, that was why he stayed, why he didn't just give up and let his mind drift gently into The Void. Yabis had seen the most likely future for his daughter — it was one of immeasurable burden, but not without its own beauty.

He found it fascinating that Letje, his daughter, would be the woman he saw in the destiny that waited for her. To think that his little girl would change so dramatically and become something so wondrous. It was hard to grasp the full scope of such a thing, it turned on its head everything he had ever hoped for her, everything he had dreamed his daughter could be. All he had wanted was for her to be Whole, maybe Awoken, not for the future he saw; it constantly astounded him.

So he stayed.

She needed him.

She would definitely need him more in the future, meaning he would simply have to get accustomed to being a tortoise. After all, it wasn't that bad — not really.

As long as you liked lettuce. He must have words with Letje about that, a bit of variety would be very welcome.

This is Confusing

The pace slowed somewhat after the death of Sy, too much had happened too soon for them all — it was draining. Marcus felt split in two, felt himself sliding in and out of time, irreparable and lost. His sense of what was real, what was happening, what had and what would come to pass was becoming obfuscated by impossible slithers of memories of things yet to be that hadn't happened to him.

He had a vision of the birth of a child in a vast underground cave, the child held up to rapturous clicking of alien appendages heralding their future leader — it all got too much for him and he found himself stumbling more and more, his sense of self ebbing and flowing as everything got mixed up like ice melting into water.

Marcus knew he was a hair's breadth from losing his mind, his visions of alien lifeforms a sure sign that he had probably already gone well over the edge of sanity. He may have been accustomed to The Noise, but seeing things on other planets, probably in other timelines, didn't seem like something he would have access to, so it must be his brain losing its grip on sanity and plunging him into hallucinations. He had seen glimpses of such bizarre things before, usually when somebody died, but this was different. He was there, seeing it all, feeling it, and that shouldn't, couldn't happen. It was as if he could simply slip away from his own body and become something entirely alien if he so wished, the pull was that strong. He felt certain he could do it if he wanted, which led him to the conclusion he really was lost to some form of age related insanity.

Either that or there was a lot more to the infinite Noise than he thought possible.

Arcene was out of her depth and knew it, surrounded by things so strange she felt like a plaything for the gods.

Letje was in a funk and distraught about Sy, as well as trying to come to terms with her true feelings for him. Trying to get to grips with understanding that a lot of her emotions were part of the hormonal changes in her body as well as being over-exaggerated because of her lack of experience.

"Marcus, couldn't you have just taken it from him?"

"Taken what from who?"

"The memories, from Sy? You could have done that couldn't you, made him forget?"

"Made him? Yes, I could. But there is a real danger in such things, and neither Sy nor I thought it was a good idea. He was a clever man underneath the soppy hair and big grin on that handsome square face you know. Quite an astute young man. Ugh."

"Marcus, are you okay," shouted Arcene, running up then peering down at him.

"Fine, fine, just lost my footing there for a minute. I felt something, something in The Noise."

"What was it? Something bad? When can I go to The Noise? I want to see what it's—"

"Not now Arcene, let's help Marcus up."

Arcene pouted as only a ten year old could, and spoke through a closed mouth. "Fine, just asking. Didn't want to go to the stupid Noise anyway, I bet it's—"

"Arcene!"

"Alright. Keep your knickers on."

"Haha, where did you hear that? Haven't heard that saying for a very long time."

"My mum used to say it to me — quite a lot," beamed Arcene. "I was a little bit of a handful apparently. Can't see it myself."

"No, me neither," snickered Letje, trying not to look at Marcus who was going to make her burst out laughing if she did.

"No, nor can I. I wonder what gave her such a crazy idea. Here, help me up will you?"

Arcene and Letje grabbed an arm each and pulled Marcus to his feet. Suddenly he grew serious, the smile fading. "Over there," pointed Marcus, "let's go and sit and talk for a while. It's been a sad time lately, and I know that both of you are finding it a little overwhelming. I know I am so I can't imagine what it must be like for you both. Come on."

As they walked George brushed against Marcus, his old friend being surprisingly considerate for his feelings. The goat seemed to know how much life away from The Commorancy was draining Marcus. Marcus smiled down at his companion, pleased to see a familiar face amid the never-ending changing landscape and encounters with people he wished would just leave him alone. Wishful thinking, he knew.

They made themselves comfortable on the strange contraption, what Marcus explained was a combine harvester, or what was left of it — a very common sight when he was a young boy.

"But that's not important right now, what I am more concerned about is how you both are. Letje?"

"I'm alright, I guess."

Marcus stared at her, then just kept staring some more. He knew the truth, wanted Letje to admit it.

"Okay, fine," said Letje, giving in to the silent treatment. "I'm not alright, not at all. Sy is dead, I don't know how I really felt about him apart from that he was lovely and we would have been happy and now he's dead. My dad is a tortoise, people are chasing us, I'm scared for Arcene, scared for myself, and scared that you know a lot more than you are telling us — telling me."

"Well, that's good Letje, that's normal. Don't bottle it all up, I know it's hard. I'm so sorry about Sy, I truly am. He was such a nice man, a true gentleman. I'm sorry I told you about his past, but I thought it fair you knew. And Arcene, how are you my dear?"

"Hungry, and tired. Mostly hungry."

Marcus ruffled the child's head playfully. "Well, I'm glad some things never change. Haha, where on earth does all that food go? Now, please listen. It's just us now, for a while at least. Let's stick together, and keep alert. I know this is all exhausting but next we are going to meet somebody very special, and soon all of this will be over. It won't last forever."

"So, who's so special then?"

Marcus smiled broadly, green eyes twinkling with excitement. "You'll just have to wait and see, now won't you? So, onward and upward, let's get moving, I'm sure there will be more people after us soon enough, so let's enjoy the peace while we can."

~~~

"Well, this is confusing," said Arcene, trying, and failing, to come to grips with the parent and son combo before her. "How are you his son if you are older than him?"

"Ssh, don't be rude," said Letje, jabbing her in the ribs, trying to allow them some time to greet each other properly.

"What? Just sayin', it's all the wrong way around."

Marcus had explained on the way that he had no idea how old his son would look, hoping that Arcene would be able to understand that things could get a little confusing when Awoken could halt the aging process at any point they chose, or slow it down at the very least. But confronted with the reality of Marcus calling an old man with gray hair and beard his son simply didn't make sense now she was witnessing it firsthand.

Letje was having a hard time dealing with the bizarre situation too, and Marcus, if he would only admit it, found the whole thing rather disconcerting as well.

Marcus and Oliver had hugged tightly, no words spoken, just feeling the closeness that neither of them thought they would ever have again.

"Why didn't you tell me?" asked Marcus. "All these years, all these long years. I thought you were dead. You dropped out of The Noise so I assumed the worst."

"Sorry Dad, I just wanted to try to get back to some kind of normality. Live a life without all the baggage. Not just you, but the whole Awoken thing too. It's great and all, don't get me wrong, but it's not normal is it? Not how people are really meant to be."

"Well, I don't see it like that, but I understand. Still, you could have done all that and maybe let me know you were alright. I mourned your death, for a long time."

"I know, I'm sorry. But I had to do it, had to just live without all the... oh, I don't know, just live a normal life. Have a wife, kids, that kind of thing."

"You did that?" Marcus' face lit up with delight. Grandchildren, a daughter-in-law. A family. He couldn't wait to meet them. Then it dawned on him. "They passed?"

"Yes Dad, a long time ago. There was no Awakening for them, no extended life like mine, for my sins. They died a long time ago. Mary, my wife, she succumbed to The Lethargy eventually, but we lived together for almost fifty years. Then the children, two of them, they lived to a ripe old age, it's why I let this happen," Oliver tugged at his beard, ruffled his thinning hair. "I didn't want them to have to deal with the strangeness of looking older than their father. So I grew old with them. They were good kids, they had long, but normal lives."

"They never had children of their own?" Marcus felt so deflated. Let down by his own choices, realizing more than ever what he had given up to try to halt the decline or possible extinction of humanity.

"No Dad, it just didn't work out. So few people now, so hard to find a partner. Neither of them found somebody to spend their life with, so we all lived here,"

Oliver indicated the rather beautiful house that he had called home for centuries. "It was nice, comfortable. More than that, it was humbling and it was a dream that I find hard to get past. Such a life Dad, a family, no craziness, no mad Rooms, no Orientations, no cheating time or getting lost in The Noise, just normal life."

"Son, I'm sorry. You know I don't understand, not really. When The Noise is there it seems to me that it is a part of the natural order of things now, but we all make our choices, yours sounds like a fine one. A life with your children... what I wouldn't have given for that."

"Apart from The Commorancy though, right? You wouldn't have given *that* up, would you?"

"Let's not talk of such things," said Marcus hurriedly, knowing as well as his son did that Marcus had made some hard, but for him necessary choices so long ago.

"Okay Dad, and anyway, how do you happen to be in the company of such beautiful and shy young women that are hanging back as if I somehow may infect them with my old age?" Oliver smiled at Letje and Arcene, who had, until now, been ignored after a brief introduction. When they smiled back he beckoned them closer. "Let's have a proper chat shall we? Dad?" Oliver held out his hand, and Marcus rummaged around then produced his tin of teabags, and the sugar.

Marcus was ecstatic just to see his son's face light up in delight, eyeing the gifts greedily, obviously itching to make the tea. "It's been a while, quite a while."

"I bet. So, you going to make it or not?"

"Okay, definitely. If you would all like to follow me, we can sit at the table, have a cuppa, and get to know each other. I think it's well past time, don't you Dad?"

"Definitely. I can't tell you how pleased I am to see you Son, we have quite a lot to catch up on, quite a lot."

As they followed the father and son up to the house, Arcene tugged at Letje's sleeve insistently. "Are you sure? It seems like the old man should be the dad, not the other way around. It's all back to front, it makes your head hurt."

"I'm sure, it's what happens when you are the likes of Marcus. Things get a little confused and topsy-turvy. It's the same for others who are adept in The Noise — they can stay looking whatever age they want. You could do it too, me too I think."

Arcene's eyes were saucer big. "Cool. What age would you be then Letje, I would be..." Arcene chewed at a nail while she thought about it. "Um, I would be twenty seven I think, that sounds like a good age. And as I'm so young it means I'll have a chance to learn everything and be a proper grown up woman first."

Letje looked at her young friend. She had matured a lot since she last saw her. "That's a very good choice Arcene. You are a clever girl, you know that? As for me? Well, I don't know, it's quite a big decision to make, and I guess there is no hurry."

They followed Oliver and Marcus through a side door and into a large and comfortable looking kitchen. A room that screamed family home, a comfortable place where there had once been a happy family, now just a man who had outlived them all, alone and living an extended life that even he believed should never have been.

Marcus thought it was the best cup of tea he had ever tasted in his life.

~~~

"Do you wish you had never built The Commorancy Marcus? I mean, just had a life with your son?" Letje could see the sadness in Marcus as they left early the next day.

"I wish I could have had both Letje. But I made my decision, and he made his. He could have stayed, helped with what I was, um, am doing, what I have done. But no, I made the right decision. The only one for me really. It was meant to be, things are as they should be. He had his life, I had mine."

"Had? You mean have?"

"All things come to an end," mumbled Marcus cryptically.

They continued in silence, each lost in their own thoughts.

Marcus wanted to rip out his heart and throw it to the ground and stomp it to mush. It hurt too much, he thought it would surely have broken in two by now anyway.

What's Eck Lips?

"Eck lips? I've never heard of it." Letje, wondered if Marcus was just making it up.

"Eclipse," said Marcus, spelling out the word slowly. "Ones like this don't happen very often. It can be hundreds of years between them."

"Well I don't like it," said Arcene, shading her eyes and looking at the sky suspiciously.

"Let's just wait for it to pass, and then we can be on our way. It's nothing to be afraid of, perfectly natural."

"But how, how can it actually work?" Letje simply couldn't believe that the sun was actually going to disappear in the middle of a cold, but startlingly bright autumn day.

As the moon began to hide the sun and the light faded, Marcus explained, while Arcene huddled up to Letje and Letje had to pretend to be brave for the younger girls' sake.

"Well, although the sun and moon are very different sizes, every now and then, like today, the moon is the right distance from the sun and the earth so that when it passes in front of the sun it hides it perfectly. Arcene, you do know that the earth goes around the sun and the moon goes around the earth, right?"

"Duh," said Arcene, trying to look knowledgeable, glancing left and right, then down to the ground.

Marcus smiled. "Well, anyway, right now, as the moon passes in front of the sun the moon is in perigee, or the closest to the earth that it gets. And although the sun is four hundred times larger than the moon the moon is right now four hundred times closer to the sun than the earth so they fit together perfectly."

"So there is a God then? There has to be."

Marcus looked at Arcene. "Why? What do you mean?" Marcus noticed wavy lines all around, going from light to dark to light again, an effect of the eclipse.

"Stands to reason doesn't it? There is no way stuff like this can just be an accident. Someone must have designed it that way. Right?" Arcene glanced up at Letje then to Marcus. "I mean, how can it fit perfectly? Look!" Arcene pointed up to the sky. The moon had totally eclipsed the sun, a dazzling corona around a perfectly dark orb was all there was to see.

"Wow."

"It's pretty impressive alright. As to God? Maybe you are right Arcene, it is a kind of crazy coincidence otherwise. Now, just a few minutes and it will be day again."

They stood in silence, deadly silence. No birds were chirping, no insects made a sound. Night had descended in an instant as confusion reigned for the life of the British Isles for a few minutes.

"Let's go, it's getting lighter already. We need to pick up the pace, Varik is getting close and I don't fancy meeting him somewhere like this."

Without more time to ponder the design plan of God, Arcene and Letje picked up their gear and followed Marcus and George. The proud goat didn't seem at all perturbed by the sudden vanishing light, but then, he had already seen a lifetime's worth of bizarre things — this was tame in comparison to some of the happenings in his longed for home.

Marcus felt his heart lift as the sun slowly took its rightful place in the sky, some natural events really did make you question the whole premise of life being some kind of impossible accident — even with his knowledge of The Void he still felt uncomfortable when his beliefs were questioned. The birds began their chatter, the last few remaining bees buzzed about, trying to gather the last of the nectar before winter encroached, and his spirits lifted somewhat. Marcus was lost in his own thoughts, awareness focused inward rather than where it should be: on those he needed to protect.

"Well, well, well, what have we here then?"

Marcus came out of his reverie with a start. What was wrong with him? How could he lose focus at a time like this? Staring at the group of men in front of them he was just glad it wasn't Varik or his Inked acolytes that had taken him by surprise.

"Hey. Hey, Dad!" Before Letje knew what was happening her duffel had been ripped from her shoulder and even as she had the antique weapon pointed at her face the young boy was running off with Constantine/Yabis. Letje went to run, thinking only of getting her father back. A loud *crack* stopped her dead in her tracks.

"Next one will be making a mess of your pretty little head, so be still and shut your mouth. Hey guys, guess I finally have me a nice little wifey. Seems like it comes with a ready made replacement too for when this one wears out." The man leered at Arcene greedily, sending a tremor through her body. This was what Letje had warned her about; men were dangerous creatures and now she was encountering the dark side of desperation for the second time.

"I'm not going to be you wife, and neither is Letje. You are going to die if you don't let us go."

"Haha, is that right little missy? And do pray tell exactly how that is going to happen when we are the ones with the guns, and you," the man pointed at Letje, "what's all this about 'Dad' then? In that bag my little boy has is he? Got his ashes, or his head in there eh? Do you?"

Letje just glared at him, trying to put into practice what Marcus had taught her about staying calm, when all she wanted to do was scream and try to make a mad dash for it.

"I asked you a question." The man approached Letje, a deep scowl on his dirty, creased face.

"She's just shy, it was just her pet tortoise, she calls him dad. She's a little simple in the head." Marcus winked at Letje, and she felt him goading her to play along via The Noise.

"I love my dad I do," said Letje, trying to act simple. It didn't help that Arcene began to snigger. Letje nudged her with her elbow.

"Ow."

Letje just glared at her.

Marcus had had enough. Obviously there was no way that any of them were going anywhere with these sorry excuses for men, it simply wasn't an option. Already he knew where the little boy was, and although Yabis was very concerned, Marcus understood there was still time before he was in any serious danger — he hoped.

Timelines were getting jumbled again, and he fought to stay in the present, rather than lost in the futures that would never happen unless he acted correctly in the here and now.

"Nobody is being anyone's wife, not today at least. And certainly not to any of you."

"Shut your mouth. What, they yours are they? Well, finders keepers I'm afraid." The man sneered at Marcus, looking him up and down, sizing him up but itching to waste a bullet and get back to camp with the girls.

"No, they aren't mine," sighed Marcus. "They are free to do as they please, but they are currently under my care and if you think that pathetic creatures like you are going to just walk away with them then you have sorely underestimated me. Drop the gun."

"Drop the gun? Oh, okay, is there anything else you would like for me to do before I blow your fu—"

Marcus was as surprised as the man was. Before Marcus had a chance to finalize his command through The Noise the man was splayed out on the floor, a naked man sat on top of him, strangling him with thick rope that was curled all around his scrawny body. Marcus frowned deeply, he knew this man, he had felt this presence before — twice now. It felt like the presence that had helped when they had been attacked and Sy was killed, but more notably he had been out on the water, in the lead vessel with Varik. This was the mind that had contaminated The Lethargic, that had caused so much disruption and what Marcus was sure would have been deep sorrow for the him that was still in The Commorancy.

But why was he here? What purpose did attacking these would-be captors serve him? There were questions to be answered. Marcus sprang into action — a sharp spike in The Noise sent the two remaining men to their knees, their weapons dropped. He tore their minds from them, leaving them drooling and splayed out in the wet leaves, all memory of who they were mere seconds ago stripped from them, for the time being or for good Marcus had yet to decide.

"That man's got no clothes on," giggled Arcene. "Look Letje, you can see his willy and everything." Arcene couldn't stop giggling, she had never seen a naked man before and was bemused to see how wobbly and dangly the bits between their legs were.

"Ssh, don't be rude. And now is not exactly the time you know. He looks dangerous, and that boy still has Father."

The naked man rose from his position on top of the now dead man, untangling his hair from around the throat as he did so. The man had a dark red line across his neck where he had just experienced death by dreadlocks.

"Hi, I'm, Fasolt. I believe I owe you an apology."

"I think you owe me a little more than that, don't you?" said Marcus.

Fasolt hung his head in shame, nodding vigorously, hair swinging manically with a life of its own. He hauled it back in and coiled it around his shoulders. "You're right, I do. It's why I'm here. I think we need to talk."

"So let's talk. Fasolt is it?"

"Yes. I'm Varik's father."

Time to Apologize

Fasolt had picked up their trail some days ago, always holding back from introducing himself, trying to find just the right time, never quite sure how to approach Marcus without risking simply being attacked. He knew Marcus was powerful, more than him, yet wasn't afraid. He just didn't want their first face to face encounter to be one of violence between the two of them.

He observed from a distance, occasionally looking down from a tree through the eyes of owls, sparrows, even a squirrel now and then. It was easy to stay ahead of them even though his physical body was well back and out of range of being spotted. He was adept at such things, and was confident his presence in the small creatures would go unnoticed even by the likes of Marcus. Fasolt intruded minimally and left not a mark on The Noise that could be picked up.

He had helped them already, even though it was obvious Marcus would have dealt with the killers of one his group on his own. Then he went back to keeping a safe distance once more.

He watched them make their progress, felt the presence of others closing in as the eclipse came and went just as quickly. Fasolt marveled at the perfection of the orbs, each fitting perfectly. It couldn't be mere chance, surely? Yet how was it so marvelous when you compared it to life itself? To The Void, The Noise, the minds of the creatures he inhabited, now subtly rather than with brute force? Once again he lamented the man he had been, the things he had done, and faltered, almost falling from the tree, before he released the owl back to its dreams, and continued his gentle pace on foot. He no longer needed to rush now he had found Marcus and what was left of the group he had started with so little time ago.

Fasolt's feet had blistered, peeled and torn, but were now hard and calloused. His hair seemed to grow lighter and wilder as he allowed the sense of freedom and affinity with his surroundings to consume him. He became a part of the natural environment, a creature that was accepted and welcomed. He regretted for the millionth time the centuries he had locked himself away in dark, dank places underground, away from life and all that made being human a delight rather than a punishment.

So much had been missed out on, so much time confined to a room rather than exploring his world, enjoying the sun and rain and snow and sheer beauty of all that being alive had to offer.

But at least he had found his true self eventually. He could have exited the world without ever coming to realize just how beautiful the simple things in life really were.

He felt so alive it was almost painful. How could he have squandered the gifts that were offered to his impossibly precious life?

He stepped lightly, no longer making a sound as he progressed through the thickets, crossed streams and slept on the ground with a small fire for comfort rather than for a warmth he didn't need. Each morning he awoke to new wonders. What kind of man locks himself away from all this beauty? A once bad one, that's what kind. Now he was reborn and every day brought forth more delights. He actually found himself laughing out loud at the antics of the creatures all around him, marveling at the purity of life, unsullied by a sense of self, just an instinctual existence that was as pure as The Void itself.

Part of things — that's what he had become, after centuries of willful denial of what it was to be a human being. Flawed, yet trying to do what he had always known was morally right, just, and the way things were meant to be. No more trying to impose his will, a will he knew deep down had always been evil, just like his son. He hoped more than anything he could convince Varik that his self-made religion and philosophy was wrong, a blasphemy against the natural order of things on so many levels.

He had his doubts. He would try nonetheless.

Now he could begin to make things right. As he watched from the small squirrel's keen eyes, hidden in a hole high up in the almost bare beech tree, he simultaneously crept forward silently, a part of the surroundings, no more out of place than the trees themselves.

As he approached he returned fully to his own body, lowering his core temperature just for the sheer joy of feeling the icy air dance across his bare skin. The eclipse had passed, the creatures of the woods resuming their business, the darkness forgotten for more immediate matters. Fasolt followed suit, but with the distinct advantage of being aware quite how much he was enjoying feeling truly alive.

With life comes death — a natural cycle. Who was he to interfere with the order of things? Fasolt went to make his kill — something he no longer enjoyed doing since he had been reborn as something pure, and righteous.

~~~

"Why are you laughing little one?" Fasolt was perplexed by the young girl with silver hair. Surely witnessing a killing should see one so young scared rather than laughing.

"I can see your man bits," mumbled Arcene, pointing between his legs just in case he wasn't sure where they were.

"Oh," said Fasolt, glancing down. "Is it so very funny? It is rather chilly you know." He turned to Marcus as he spoke, as if for backup from another male.

"Um, true," said Marcus, unsure how else to approach the situation.

"Hey. Is that your real hair, it looks like it's dancing. Can it do anything else apart from kill people?" Arcene, seemingly unable to keep any kind of curiosity at bay for more than a second, lunged forward and grabbed a huge matted dreadlock from off the ground and peered at it curiously. She put it to her mouth instinctively.

"What are you, like two or something?" said Letje, grabbing the hair off Arcene, dropping it to the ground hurriedly.

Fasolt wasn't sure what to expect once he revealed himself, but this certainly wasn't it. The young girl seemed inured to fear, and was more curious than anything else. Marcus and Letje were understandably more wary, but he could see that his appearance had more to do with that than anything else.

He held up a hand, knowing what Marcus was about to say. "Yes it was me, I was the one in control of those you had, and if you don't mind me saying so, rather foolishly hoped you could revive at some point. I apologize, and I want to try to make things right. I want to help my son, and I want to help you as well. If you will let me?"

"It's not as easy as that though is it? We need to talk." Marcus felt the man's honesty, understood this was no evil person. Whatever he had been, whatever he had done, he had undergone a total metamorphosis. This man was something altogether purer, even if he had just committed murder with his very own hair.

"Marcus, before any of that we have to get Constantine, Daddy, back. They could be eating him for all we know. Do you sense where he is?"

"I do," said Fasolt. "Don't worry, they haven't eaten him yet, but we shouldn't dawdle. I can help. I want to help." Fasolt saw the glances between Marcus and Letje, yet knew that they would not dismiss his offer. He knew the strange way he looked gave cause for concern, but also knew that he projected the truth of what he had become as a person. Even Marcus couldn't deny that he posed no immediate threat to them. If Marcus was as powerful as he assumed then he would know no dangerous intent was there in their futures from Fasolt's hand.

"Just keep that hair tied up will you? It's dangerous." Marcus rubbed George's head absentmindedly, then had to pull open his jaws and prize out a mangled dreadlock.

"Deal," said Fasolt, sad to lose the end of one of his favorites.

They went to save Letje's father from a fate that made him re-consider the wiseness of inhabiting such a small and defenseless body, even if it was for the sake of his daughter.

Tortoise Stew

Yabis was rather worried. In fact it was more than that — he was terrified if he admitted the truth, but was trying to stick with worried as it made him feel slightly less constrained and constricted. Being a tortoise meant that high emotions were best kept buried, whenever extreme feelings surfaced it felt like his brain was trying to push out of its tiny enclosure.

The whole emotion thing was a bizarre issue anyway. Without a human body it was really rather difficult to feel in the same way any more. The longer he lived as a tortoise the more he had to fight to remain who he was. There were different hormones in a tortoise to a human, so being sure about his own feelings was hard to judge at times, and when he knew he should feel a certain way, so tried his best to let those emotions surface, it all got a bit fuzzy around the edges. He was never quite certain if he was an emotional tortoise or an unemotional reincarnated man.

Yabis shook his scaled head. Now wasn't the time for philosophical debates anyway, he was about to be tortoise stew and was all out of ideas. There was no cunning plan or ingenious means of escape he could devise, not when he could just be picked up and stuffed into a large pocket. It wasn't like he could make a run for it, or fight his way out. His best line of defense was to pull his head and feet into his shell and hope it all just turned out all right in the end.

Wishful thinking was not going to work this time though, not when the pot was beginning to boil, hanging from a tripod over the coals of the campfire. The noise was deafening, even in the dark confines of his hard shell. He was going to be scooped out and boiled some time soon.

Being a tortoise had some serious drawbacks, this was probably the worst of them so far.

Where was Letje? And Marcus? And that crazy young girl Arcene?

Surely they would come for him? Well, it was getting a bit late for that. Yabis' only consolation was that he had company, if of the rather sedate kind. Constantine was, if truth be told, far from a great conversationalist.

Yabis opened his eyes as he poked his head out from his shell. He was being picked up. *Here we go,* he thought. *I'm going to die by being somebody's damn supper. What a way to go.*

Kicking his feet ineffectually Yabis was held by the shell and carried over toward the fire. A pair of dark eyes greeted his. He was held up high and the boy was peering at him, a big smile on his face.

"Right then, how do we get you out of this shell then? Hey, should we just whack the shell with a rock and break him out or what? Not sure how you go about cooking these things. Maybe it will add more flavor if we leave it in the shell until after it's cooked? Waddya think?"

"Just bung it in as it is, but give it a rinse first. It might spoil the taste if it's all dirty. Who knows what's stuck to that shell over the years."

"Good idea, let's give the little fella a bath before he gets cooking. I wonder when Dad will get back? You think they're okay?"

"Your old man hasn't let us down yet has he? And if what you say is true," said Malik, glaring at the boy until he squirmed, "then they won't be having any bother. Your dad and the others won't be worried by a couple of girls and one other bloke will they? Hey, maybe you will have yourself a nice little girlfriend, the young one sounds pretty tasty."

Gregor reddened beneath his dirty face. "Ugh, I'm not interested in girls. She had weird hair anyway. But Dad said that the older one would be his wife, so I guess that means I will have a mum again. I miss her, and she looked after us didn't she?"

"Yeah, I remember, she was a fine lady your mum, very nice. But your dad's done alright by you, he's looked after you hasn't he? Done his best anyway. Hey, be careful with it, you don't wanna drop it and get it all dirty now that it's clean."

"I'm being careful, sheesh."

Yabis was now sat on the thief's lap. The boy kept rapping the shell, poking fingers at his head and generally making it very uncomfortable to be a tortoise. What if what they said was true and Letje and the others genuinely were captured? Surely Marcus would be able to use his power to get them out of the situation? He hoped so, he didn't want to meet The Void as supper.

Yabis stared around him while the old man and the young boy continued their chatter. Their conversation just went around in circles about getting more anxious about when the others would return and if they should start boiling the meat yet or wait for them.

They meant him by meat! Yabis' stomach somersaulted again and again as he tried to focus on his surroundings, looking for even a hint of what he could do to get out from the sorry situation he found himself in. He also sent a message through The Noise, and was gratified when Marcus answered that they were on their way. Letje was still not in tune enough to pick up his broadcasts when they were separated by any significant distance.

Just hold on a few more minutes Yabis, they are coming to help you. You won't be anyone's supper this day. Yabis repeated the mantra as he looked around from his position on the boy's lap. It was a sorry excuse for a camp if ever he saw one. Apart from the fire, which was contained haphazardly with rocks in a crazy approximation of a circle, everything else seemed to be in total disarray. There were random bags strewn carelessly around, cooking utensils, pots, pans and buckets abandoned where they were thrown, and even the heavy canvas tents didn't seem to be pitched or tethered correctly.

Yabis assumed that this was a group of men that had, until recently, had women to tend to such matters, and they were at a bit of a loss as to how to stay organized without a helping hand or two. Still, that was no excuse for the way they had treated him, for the way they had treated his daughter and the others before he was whisked away by this poor young boy. He hoped that when they arrived Marcus and the others wouldn't be too rash with how they treated the youngster, he didn't know any better after all.

~~~

Marcus kept George close to his side and Letje and Arcene even closer as they trailed behind Fasolt, constantly trying not to trip over his hair which danced wildly and refused to stay wrapped around the scrawny torso of its owner. Their brief conversation after they had tied up the two remaining assailants was necessarily rushed as Letje would have run off on her own otherwise, but Marcus couldn't deny that however he delved into the man it was obvious that he was reborn and honest in his intentions. So although he still felt somewhat uneasy about his company, there was no actual reason not to let him help for now, then reassess later at his leisure.

As they hastily followed the very vivid trail left by the boys presence Marcus kept getting a repeatedly funny sensation up and down his thighs. They began to tingle then itch, then the same happened to his arms. He found he had to consciously stop them from pointing out to the sides or up in the air.

Of course, no change of clothes!

So accustomed to wearing different outfits for different occasions was Marcus that his body was automatically getting into the positions for dressing or undressing — it was an involuntary reaction as his body assumed there would be some form of outfit change and Marcus would be right now dressing in appropriate rescue clothes.

He couldn't help but smile at his own self. He had to admit that he really did miss his home now that he had been away from it for so long. Yet the draw of the outside world, especially the freedom it had to offer, was tempting at the same time, and he was still unsure about what his final decision would be. Not the what, but the when. He knew that one life was over for him. New adventures were to be had, The Commorancy was no longer his true home, other things called. Called strongly.

A tug at his sleeve pulled Marcus from his musings, something that he knew he was doing more and more of recently. He looked down at the top of a silver head, then into eyes that were as startlingly large as always. "Yes Arcene, what can I do for you?"

Arcene frowned and pursed her lips tight in disapproval. She pointed ahead. Marcus looked and all he could think of was that she was pointing at Fasolt's behind. "What? His bum?"

"I don't like it. It's bony. Can't you tell him to cover it up?"

"You can hardly see it," smiled Marcus. "His hair covers it most of the time. Watch your step by the way." Arcene skipped away from thick coils that threatened to trip her if she wasn't careful.

"I know, but it keeps catching my eye. I don't want to see a man's bum, it's gross."

"Haha, don't be silly. We all have them you know, even me." Marcus smiled down at the concerned child, knowing she would be a force to be reckoned with a few years from now.

"I know we all have them but it doesn't mean we have to go around looking at them all the time does it? I mean, I know I have a bum but I haven't actually ever seen it, you know, like up close." Arcene paused, thinking. "Well, I haven't seen it from far away either. I haven't seen it at all."

"Um, well, okay then." Marcus distracted himself by patting George again, then subtly picked up the pace so they all caught up with Fasolt.

Marcus felt a tug at his sleeve, and turned to see a pale finger pointing at Fasolt once again. This time the frown was replaced with a hand over a mouth that obviously wanted to snigger like a... well, like the young child she was. "Stop staring, and pointing. It's rude."

Marcus smiled as he heard the giggles escape like a balloon deflating as Arcene could control herself no longer.

Talk about inappropriate timing. Doesn't she know we are on an important tortoise saving mission? Marcus smiled to himself at that. What a funny old world it was, never a dull moment it seemed.

My Beautiful Face

Tears poured down Marcus' face, mixing with snot and saliva, blood and sweat. He was finding it hard to see — for that, at least, he was thankful. He couldn't stop. He hooked out with a right, completely missing, momentum sending him past the now dead flesh.

He spun wildly, anger unstoppable, sorrow unquenchable, despair a totality.

Marcus didn't even know how he got to The Fighting Room (Simulated Meat) let alone when he had hooked up the body to the machine usually containing a very lifelike approximation of human flesh and bone. Well, he had something better now didn't he? A real body, made of real flesh and bone, not to mention blood and spinal fluid, all of which covered his naked body as he kicked, punched, bit and clawed at the body held upright by the still perfectly functional pneumatics.

Marcus had pulverized his own flesh. His face was no longer recognizable, the kneecaps were hanging out of the legs, the spine was broken, synovial fluid turning dark blood a sickly cream like gone-off milk. Cheekbones were smashed, nose flattened, eyes gouged and hair pulled. The torso of the enslaved body was almost black where lethal blows had made contact and the blood had pooled instantly. The shins were poking out, ribs threatened to rip through the flesh, and one arm hung limp, the radius and ulna fractured in multiple places, shards offering up their obvious surrender to an assailant that seemed incapable of stopping the ruthless punishment he doled out on his very own body.

Wiping his face with the back of his hand, vision returned. A curse as Marcus was confronted with the totally broken body as his reward. And it was him, his body, the way he had looked for centuries, never changing, always the same, always Marcus the invincible — the man that ruled The Commorancy.

There was no memory of bringing the body here from The Body Room, no memory of hooking it up to the machine. Not a hint of when he might have done such a thing, a gap where there should have been decision making and consideration for what was surely now nothing but the act of a true madman.

Had he finally gone too far? Lost what it was that made him almost unique? Was this the final blasphemy against all that was natural and right in the world?

He suspected the answer was yes.

But he was thinking again, at least that was something. He knew he shouldn't be doing what he was doing, knew how wrong it was, how depraved it was to take out his frustrations, his sorrow, maybe his madness, on one of the countless bodies waiting in the dark for if they were needed. Well, this one would never contain Marcus now, it was damaged beyond repair, and cold. No tubes entered the body any longer, no fluids pulsed back and forth. No liquid surrounded the already shriveling skin, exposed so abruptly to the air before its punishment began in earnest.

Marcus stopped, keenly aware of his own damaged knuckles, the wetness of his face, the bruised forearms and shins he had used to beat the flesh that was his own. He was covered in bodily fluids of all description, his and *his*, and he felt sick to his stomach.

"I'm going out. I can't take this for one minute more."

Marcus went to pack a bag, his home could look after itself for a while, he needed some fresh air. He needed to find peace. But more than anything else he needed to find his sanity — it had left him, and he didn't like what had taken its place.

~~~

Click.

The door closed behind Marcus, quietly and efficiently. The non-Marcus body, damaged and impossible to actually place as a genuine Marcus, opened a swollen eye, the other was gone, squashed to nothing but goo on the floor. It crunched neck bones as it swiveled its head, rattled as it sighed deeply, and moaned with a throat full of blood.

It began to unstrap itself from the pneumatics, but eventually just gave up and embraced The Void with mangled open arms.

~~~

"Marcus, are you alright? You went so pale I thought you were dead."

Marcus stared up from the floor with eyes so intensely green Letje took a step backward. "I'm fine," he gasped. "Just had a bit of a situation is all. It's over now, well, for a little bit. But we need to get going, finish what we started. I'm afraid that we, um, may be getting some company soon, and I'm not so sure that um, he, is exactly in his normal frame of mind."

Marcus stood, brushed down his clothes, and calmed himself. The ferocious shine in his eyes dimmed back to normal intensity and he entered The Noise.

Nothing.

What was going on? He had no idea what just happened, what was real or merely a dream. Sometimes funny things happened being two people, and now he wasn't sure if the loss of the connection between the two hims was leading to tricks of the mind, or he was getting genuine flashbacks as to what was happening in The Commorancy.

But what was the body? Was that real? Obviously not all of it, it was certainly dead when Marcus left after giving such a ferocious beating. Wasn't it?

Marcus wished he could remember exactly how there were two of him, the one pact he had made with himself he wished had never happened.

But there was no point crying over spilled milk, those memories were gone forever as far as he was aware. Unless the other him...

Agree to Disagree

"So we are agreed then?"

Marcus sighed deeply. "Why do you have to ask? You agreed, right?"

"Yes."

"Well then, so did I."

"Look, no need to get funny about it. I was just asking. This is all new to me you know. It's alright for you, you've been around for ages."

"What! What are you talking about? It's me that is new to this, not you."

"What? No. Is it? Really?"

"I, um, well, that is... It's happening already isn't it? We really are both you, me, us?"

"I guess so. Well, it must be. What do you remember from the last five minutes?"

Marcus took a moment to think. "I can remember waking up, suddenly knowing everything you know. But I can also remember.... Oh, wow! I can remember helping me off some kind of pedestal, and I can remember feeling nervous about going to meet me, wondering if I was doing the right thing. If I would be alright. If the connection would be there. I guess it works then. We swap everything back and forth, updating each other through The Noise?"

"Same for me, so yes, that's it. Everything is working. I remember being you, and being me. I don't know which one I am, not that it matters. I don't think it does anyway."

"But am I actually me any longer? I mean, is what I experience actually happening to me, or to both of us?"

"Well, as far as I can tell what happens is what happens, me, you, however it works then almost instantly we update ourselves... um, so... I guess it happens to us as individuals for a short time then it gets mixed up with the other's experience, so in the end it doesn't matter."

"That's what I was thinking, and all I know is that this is damn cool, and clever. It's going to make life a lot easier, we can get so much more done. I just hope it doesn't send us over the edge."

"Look, we have each other to ensure that we don't lose control. Although, actually, that won't work will it?"

"No. Because if one of us loses the plot or can't handle a duplicated life then the other will be just as ill-equipped too, right?"

"We're doing it again you know? Asking each other questions like we are talking to a different person. Damn, I just did it too."

"Hey, it's all new, we're allowed to have some time to get used to the idea. But anyway, let's get the final bit of business done with shall we?"

"Yes. As long as you are sure? Well, of course you are. Gosh, this is really confusing, I think we need to keep conversations with each other brief in the future. Already I am remembering this conversation from both points of view and it's getting weird. It's like I am just talking to myself, it's enough to drive you bonkers."

"I know. Which is why I thought long and hard about doing it before I did, and why the next step is so important."

"Yes, I knew it would be weird so let's both get this over with."

"Agreed."

Marcus entered The Noise, making a connection between each other that left no room for error. As an invisible timer counted down to zero in their imagined space they got ready. As it hit zero they simultaneously wiped certain memories from themselves, memories that could never be retrieved.

Gone was any concept of just how they managed to reach such duplicity.

Gone was the memory of just where the Room was that held the secrets to their twin life — even the memory of the name of the Room was wiped.

Gone was the knowledge of how there was a duplicate body for Marcus, how it was grown, animated and how Marcus' memory — his very being — was copied so perfectly into what even now they assumed was a cloned body, but weren't quite sure.

Maybe it was a real twin? Maybe it was somehow a body that looked exactly like him? Or maybe insanity had taken hold and there really was only him, talking to himself like a crazy person with nobody there to correct his madness.

All details concerning Marcus' new double life were irreversibly wiped from the history of Marcus. He no longer knew how it was achieved or where in the still only partially constructed Commorancy the twinning had been done. Even the memory of agreeing to wipe the memory was erased, just the knowledge that it had been erased.

Marcus was now truly just Marcus.

There was no difference between the two, they were as one and would be for centuries to come.

Save That Tortoise

Marcus felt less than useless. He was still reeling from the sudden connection to events at The Commorancy, if what he had seen was a real event. He tried to clear his head but the vision kept returning. Had he really gone truly insane — both of him?

He was sure, positive, that there really were two of him, but what he had just seen made a mockery of the whole thing. But then, if there were two Marcus' then why would it be odd that there were other, yet to be animated versions of him hanging around? Maybe thousands of them.

He staggered into the clearing, Fasolt, Letje and Arcene already ahead, George trotting along excitedly, wondering what the buzz was about.

Arcene was the first to the fire, and shouted out rather dramatically, "Drop the tortoise or the old man gets it!"

Marcus was amazed to see the wild child with a gleaming dagger in her hand, now held tight against the soot and sun blackened old man's neck. She glared at the boy who was nervously holding Yabis in his hands. The young boy stared around wildly, aware of the absence of his father and his uncles, unsure what to do. The old man nodded slightly, careful not to get cut in the process.

Everything went into slow motion as the boy, taking Arcene's word at face value, simply let go of Yabis. The tortoise head retracted and the legs wiggled wildly as he fell upside down toward the rocks at the edge of the fire. He would be cracked open like a walnut in a split second.

Marcus stopped time.

He never even knew he could do it.

There was a serious drawback to it though: just as the flames no longer flickered and the leaves were stationary on the trees and Yabis was frozen in mid-air, so Marcus was unable to move either, not even to bat an eyelid, let alone rush to rescue Yabis.

Think Marcus, you can still do that can't you?

Marcus thought for a long time, it may have been an hour, it may have been a day or a year, time meant little when you were as deep in The Noise as he was. He descended, to try to save not only Yabis but the only remaining family Letje had. He knew that losing her father like this would be too much for her after the loss of Sy and the gradual dwindling of the group since the leaving of The Commorancy.

He simply had to come up with a solution.

~~~

"Daddy!" yelled Letje as she saw the boy's hands open and the tortoise begin to twist and fall to the blackened rocks around the fire.

Shmm.

Bird grabbed the tortoise in a single huge four-taloned foot and swept over the fire, his enormous wings fanning the flames as he passed, sending them high above the pot that boiled over in an instant. His wings beat lazily as he spiraled high up into the air, circled the shoddy camp twice, then plummeted back to earth with dizzying speed.

Less than a second after the boy let go of the tortoise Bird was perched on Letje's right shoulder, tortoise safely dropped into the open duffel, blood already pouring down Letje's arm from the talons embedded deeply into her flesh.

She didn't mind, she was sure she would get used to it in time.

Hello my friend, thank you, thank you so much.

Bird turned his head to stare into the eyes of the woman. He blinked rapidly, intelligent eyes saying all that needed to be said. His dark orange beak opened, the curve as viscous as a knife. His pink tongue poked out before he let out a loud *screeee* and with a gentle nibble of Letje's ear he took to the sky, heading back to the remains of his family, knowing at the same time that he had found a kindred spirit. She felt right somehow. He was certain that they would meet again in the near future, just not now, not yet. His family needed feeding, his Master needed dealing with.

"Argh, help, help me please."

The old man, taking the opportunity to stagger from Arcene who was distracted by Bird, had caught the full force of the oxygenated fire as he tried to get away. Bird's forward momentum had sent the flames licking toward the old man and he was running around, flapping at his clothes, fanning the flames just as Bird had done, turning a containable fire into a roaring conflagration that consumed him in seconds.

A faint ripple in The Noise told Marcus that Fasolt had ended the man's life, an act of compassion — nobody should have to die like that. Well, hardly anyone.

Marcus nodded at Fasolt, who acknowledged the gesture as they turned to make certain the young boy did nothing stupid, both knowing he was little risk. Marcus stared into the scared and confused eyes of the child before the boy took off as fast as his legs could carry him. Fasolt looked at Marcus quizzically. "Leave him be, we can't take him with us, he's too unstable, but he'll be alright."

"Agreed," said Fasolt, heaving a handful of hair over his shoulder, looking worryingly at the still roaring fire that was making the area uncomfortably warm.

"Letje, are you okay?" Marcus looked at her shoulder, noting the holes in her clothes, the blood already dripping to the floor. It had soaked through her sleeve and was falling off her fingers.

"Huh? Um, yes, I think so. What just happened? Was that Varik's Bird?" Letje peered into the duffel bag, gingerly taking out her father, checking that he was all right. They communed silently, the reassurance calming them both — the family bond stronger than ever.

Thank you Marcus, that was you wasn't it?

Up to a point yes, but Bird, that's what he calls himself, was under his own volition. He offered. I don't think he is too happy with Varik any longer.

Either way, I have to say I didn't see that one coming. Very dramatic. Yabis sent an approximation of a smile through The Noise.

Me neither.

"That was indeed Varik's Bird Letje, although don't ever call him that, he wouldn't appreciate it. Is your shoulder okay? Those talons are deadly."

"And big," said Arcene excitedly, running over and ignoring the fact there was a smoldering man she had to jump over. "Did you see that? Wow! What a cool Bird. Is it coming back? Is it our friend now? Hey, how's the funny tortoise?"

"Let's just calm down a little Arcene, I think that was a bit of a shock for us all wasn't it? Let's get away from here somewhere a little less... untidy." Marcus glanced at the burning body, then nodded to Fasolt, who came over and tried to guide Letje and Arcene away into the woods without exposing more flesh than he had to.

"Come, let's be gone from this bad place. It is no sight for such beautiful young women as you two."

Arcene nudged Letje and stifled a giggle as she pointed at Fasolt's bum as he led the way. He had a sooty handprint on his left cheek. It stopped him looking quite as imposing a figure and Letje had to turn away before she burst out laughing. It wouldn't do to set such a bad example in front of Arcene.

Marcus sidled up to Arcene and pointed at Fasolt's behind.

Well, so much for trying to be grown up, thought Letje.

They all burst out laughing.

Fasolt kept staring straight ahead, smiling to himself. He thought it would take the seriousness of what had just happened out of the situation. His new-found humbleness meant he wasn't above being the butt of the joke.

He laughed at his own wit. *Haha, butt of the joke, very funny Fasolt.*

Sweeties

The Room That Dentists Love was almost overpowering with its intoxicating smell. As Marcus opened the glass paneled wooden door and the bell jangled, the sweet aromas rushed at him eagerly; he almost had to exit immediately so mouth-wateringly scrumptious was the smell.

Marcus entered, the whole place a scavenged copy of a childhood sweet shop that had never been. Marcus never had a traditional sweet shop such as this — he missed such delights by a decade or two. Still, it brought back childhood memories of when he was genuinely happy with his home life, and he stepped inside eagerly.

The black and white linoleum floor was scuffed and tattered around the edges — as it should be, as was right. The dark wooden shelves lined every available piece of wall in the tiny store, more a closet than a place to lose yourself in. On the gleaming wooden counter was an old till, but no money had even been taken here, it was all for show. All props in a fake store in a fake building in a fake life.

The jars and jars of sweets had long since lost their luster, the once shining individual sweets had stuck together, making giant clumps of sugary goodness that would forever remain contained — no children would ever come here and drool over the choices on offer.

Even for free the sugary substances would never be eagerly devoured with tiny hands stuffing them hungrily into mouths smiling in delight.

Marcus was alone — again.

He hadn't come for the sweets though, he had come for a different reason entirely.

Marcus was shutting up shop.

He took a few steps back to the door, flipped over the sign hanging on a nail by a piece of string, from the outside of the door the sign now read 'Gone to Lunch'. Marcus didn't know when he would return, didn't want to think about it, and knew deep down that the chances were good this would be one of the last Rooms he ever visited.

Lifting a part of the counter Marcus walked behind it, then through a bead curtain to the back of the Room. He entered a storage locker and pulled the metal door shut. The space was cramped and pitch black. As he stood there, the sensation of movement barely perceptible, he wondered at the folly of such antics.

It had all amused him so much once upon a time: the Rooms, the fun to be had playing in such a home.

Now the edge was gone, a blunt numbness had replaced it all, and it was down to Varik and the things he had been made to do, the people he had killed in such numbers it could never be forgiven.

He felt like a fool in his own home, felt like he had lost the spark of life that it normally gave him. The entertainment, the joy of discovering new things, the wonder of the human imagination, all of it seemed to have gone.

Poof. Just like that.

Was it just The Contamination though? Or was it that he was alone? Marcus had gone, so had George, and he was at a loss as to what was happening to them. He felt that the fate of The Commorancy had been stripped from him: he was no longer guiding its future, it was the other him that was doing that.

Letje. It was because the other Marcus was with Letje.

He knew her future was inextricably tied up with The Commorancy and he felt out of the loop. He should be there with her, guiding the future, making sure the right things happened at the right time, not standing in a locker waiting to reach his destination.

Get a grip Marcus, you're just feeling depressed because of what you did. It will pass.

He shook, trying to dispel the funk. A good talking to was what he needed so he tried to jolly himself up. He opened the locker, walked across a gleaming floor, then opened another door and stood outside, the wind whipping at his hair as a hat he never even remembered putting on blew off his head and tumbled over the side of the narrow circular ledge he was stood upon. No matter, he had plenty more.

Marcus walked over to the landing circle, marked out by a white rifle scope symbol that was desperately in need of re-painting. He cracked his knuckles and felt the old familiar nervousness rise from his belly.

"Right. Let's hope I can remember how to fly this damn thing."

Marcus got into the small, insect-like helicopter, adjusted his seat, flicked switches, checked displays and then got back out and sighed heavily.

"Fuel, best fill it right up to the top. Who knows where they are, it might take a while to find them."

Twenty minutes later Marcus was looking down on his home, marveling at what can be accomplished when you are young and full of the joy of being alive rather than wasting away like the rest of the planet.

He knew he would never be able to accomplish such feats of wonder now, unsure if that was a good thing or not. With age comes wisdom, and such epic accomplishments could easily be put down to nothing but the folly of youth. Marcus banked sharply and headed for the mainland, leaving The Commorancy behind to fend for itself for... He had no idea how long for.

He smiled as he ventured into the unknown.

~~~

Marcus opened his eyes suddenly, the helicopter veering wildly. He grabbed the controls and righted it slowly — acting too hastily would only make things worse. He had blacked out for a second, the connection and ensuing memories too overwhelming for him to deal with all at once. There had been too much of a lag between updates, and this much new information was hard to process. But it was there now, it was there and he felt his spirits lift, felt his life regain meaning. Things were right again, all the missing pieces had been returned and it was as if a missing limb had been re-attached, not realizing until it was back just how much a part of him it truly was.

Marcus dropped altitude and looked for somewhere to land.

He was excited about meeting himself again.

Was that wrong? He suspected it was ever so slightly the sign of complete megalomania.

Oh well, everyone had their flaws.

Decisions, Decisions

Marcus put the key in the battered wooden door and turned it until he heard a satisfying *snick*.

Hidden bolts retracted from within the reinforced walls, circuits broke, and toxic weaponry slid back into holes no larger than the head of a pin.

Marcus took off his muddy boots and placed them to the side of the door on the silver planks of the wooden veranda.

He entered The Room Of Permanent Decisions.

The cabin that contained the Room — for that was all that was behind the large wooden construction — was set deep into the woods, untouched for hundreds of years if the state of the grounds around it were anything to go by. The building itself was in good condition — Marcus chose materials carefully for such buildings to ensure they would be there if he needed them.

The problem was he wasn't entirely sure he should have come, this was not a Room to trifle with. It was, after all, a Room for Permanent Decisions. There would be no going back once a choice was made within its walls.

Marcus closed the door behind him.

Once inside he stripped naked and hung his clothes up on the hooks on the wall just to the right of the door. He then carefully dressed in the vacuum sealed outfit still pristine in its wrapping. After checking for creases and feeling satisfied, Marcus walked over to the chair and sat. The thick chain extended upward into the rafters of the single story building. Wrapped tightly around the cross-beam it creaked slightly as it took his weight. Marcus let the chair swing gently, spiraling in circles as he shifted slightly to make himself more comfortable. He had a lot to think about, but didn't really know where to start.

Should he just make the decision and be done with it? Or should he allow himself the luxury of remembering the totality of his life first and make the decision after being informed of all relevant details?

Marcus hesitated. He wasn't sure if such total recall would even fit in his mind any longer. For so many years now he had allowed certain memories to slip away. Sometimes they were retrievable, but often he had to refer to documentation within The Commorancy to recall events, even years, of his blasphemy of a life.

He made up his mind, and resolute he entered The Noise.

Skwee, skwee... Skwee, skwee.

Marcus came out of The Noise abruptly, a deep frown on his face. This was a sure sign he was not himself as normally he could ignore external stimuli without even thinking about it. He stared up at the chain where it was wrapped around the beam, the source of his interruption sending dust floating down to coat his face. Marcus jumped and grabbed the chain then climbed to the top, hand over hand in effortless and graceful movement. He sat on the beam and released the carabiner. The chair clattered to the floor with the chain following loudly.

Marcus swung from the beam and landed back on the floorboards.

He opened the door and pulled the chair outside. Flinging it off the porch he slammed the door shut behind him.

"Wow, I really am in a bad way. I don't think I've ever lost my temper with a chair before. I've got annoyed by them, but never actually treated one badly. Hmm."

Marcus dusted himself down, annoyed his Decision Making Clothes were now a little less than pristine. He sat on the floor in the space freed up by the absence of the offending chair, and entered The Noise once again. He let out a sigh as the endless wonders of The Noise engulfed him and took away all the pain of being a man that should no longer exist.

~~~

He got what he had wanted — his answer.

Marcus walked over to the long console at the far end of the Room, marveling at his own work. He sure was meticulous back then, obsessively so. Each Permanent Decision was labeled neatly, a small printed sticker stuck fast beneath each switch, as if he had placed them there just yesterday.

Marcus' finger hovered above the 'DIE NOW' switch, knowing that he had come close to making it his Permanent Decision. It was understandable, and he didn't think anybody would judge him badly if he decided to flip the simple brittle plastic toggle. Deep in The Noise he had followed timelines back and forth, watching as his decisions played out in countless variations. He knew they could never be totally accurate — the future didn't work like that — but he played in The Noise until he was satisfied.

His death would have serious repercussions for sure, but for him personally it finally seemed like a waste of an opportunity. Why go back to The Void when he had the chance to do so much more than he had done so far?

There were countless opportunities available to him, and he had finally chosen a different path.

Marcus knew that a part of him had died inside with the severing of the connection from himself. Not severed, but so intangible that the silver strand was almost broken, finer than a length of cotton. He was unsure if he would ever get it back, be able to claim the lost parts of himself that had dealt with The Contamination. He had looked into the futures and many saw him alone, sat upon a chair on a raised dais as a man millennia old, dealing out punishment to those that still came to take his life and power away from him. He knew he couldn't be that man, even if the other Marcus could.

The years spread out in front of him like a trail of broken promises, the gift of extended life never quite living up to the expectations, the slow days and years flowing into the future like a death slower than the worst The Creeping Lethargy had to offer.

It would be annihilation by change of character. Slowly morphing from the person he was as memories faded and history lost all meaning. He would become a different man, unable to remember his youth, the things he had done, the person he had been. He would forget his loves, his child, the joy and the sorrow, he would gradually meld into something else, an ancient man unknowing of who he really was.

Marcus knew that a sliver of such an existence was already upon him, his life extension coming at a price he sometimes thought impossible to bear. Yet on he went, in his own rather bizarre way.

But a thousand years?

More?

He was not the man who could do such a thing and retain his link to humanity — the very reason he had done what he had in the first place.

No, it was time. This dream was over and he would begin another in a reality that suited his promise of a long life if he so wished.

Marcus pushed the 'CHANGE' button.

His Permanent Decision had been made.

The timer began to count down in his head. There was no turning back now. Once it reached zero he would die if he hadn't completed the bargain he had just made with his very soul. There was no changing his mind, it was out of his hands and he felt a lifting of his spirits like nothing he had ever known before.

The chance to be reborn. How beautiful it was to be one of The Awoken.

But what a price there was to pay for such opportunities.

Marcus wept for a while, then changed back into his regular clothes and closed the door behind him on his way out.

As he walked away the building collapsed in on itself. It's function complete it was no longer needed. In seconds the whole artificial edifice was nothing more than a flat-pack kicking up dust. Delicate circuitry still working after centuries performed a final function and gases that were once deadly were nullified through nozzles protruding from internal holes. As Marcus stood staring in the opposite direction a blue spark lit up the center of the building and moments later it was nothing but ash.

Marcus had other things on his mind. There was work to be done, adventures to be had, company to enjoy and a student, his first genuine hands-on student, to teach.

Was he doing the right thing? Priming such a young girl to take over his role? And would Marcus agree to the decision he had come to? He'd have to of course, for it was him the decision had been made for after all.

Wasn't it?

He shouldn't have to ask, of course he would agree with what he decided, there should never be a question of their viewpoints differing. But they had drifted, the initial blocked reception from Varik and his church had infected them, Marcus deciding that the sense of freedom was to his liking, and now, when he wanted the comfort of his own self, he found it lacking. But he still hoped he would agree to what he had decided, and if not?

Well, he didn't need to ask permission of anyone, he was Marcus, he had the right to choose his own fate.

Snap!

"I guess you know what I've decided then?"

"I know what I have decided, and I guess it's the same thing isn't it? We just came to the decision in different ways. As soon as I landed I felt what you were doing. I already updated on the rest of it. But I know what was decided in the Room, I know what you want to do, what I want to do too. I missed you."

"I missed you too. Although I enjoyed being really truly me I must admit."

"I did too, for a bit. But then... all the killing Marcus, it was too much. I felt so alone, like I never have before, not really, truly alone."

Marcus began to cry. Not gently, not quietly, not trying to hold back the tears, but really cry. The depth of sadness and loneliness of centuries bubbled to the surface and spilled over in huge shaking sobs that sent him clinging to Marcus for comfort. When it was over they knew that things could never go back to being the same again.

"We aren't the same any more are we?"

"No, this has changed us, forever. It shouldn't make a difference, it shouldn't matter now which one of us dealt with The Contamination and which one was out here drawing away Varik, but it does."

"How? We both have the same memories now. We should be the same person again, with the same experiences, the same life. But I can feel it, feel that we are no longer identical. I should leave."

"I know, I can't explain it, but yes, you should leave. I'm sorry. Sorry it couldn't have been different. I didn't know it would be like this. I wouldn't have put me, well it isn't just me now, I wouldn't have put anyone through this if I thought it would end like this. Forgive me?"

"There's nothing to forgive is there? The decision was mine, we were me back then. But now I am different, I'm no longer you, you are no longer me. I don't get it, I have the memories of what has happened here, and at The Commorancy. Everything is right up to date. I don't know which one of us it was that did what, do you?"

"No," said Marcus shaking his head sorrowfully.

"So, how can we be different?"

"I don't know, but we are. This is the end isn't it? Time to let the future in, let what we, as individuals now, know is what should happen. What will happen if we do as we are supposed to. Time to cut the connection for good."

"And say goodbye?"

Marcus just nodded his head, he wasn't sure if he could find the words.

It was all over too quickly, too easily. Two men named Marcus entered The Noise, finding each other there, the connection there, the thread that bound them was strong again now, after having almost broken completely. Soon it would be broken for good. There would be no return to being Marcus, they would forever be Marcus' once the deed was done.

They connected one last time in The Noise, a familiarity so close it was frightening in its intensity. A love, not narcissistic, but a closeness that went beyond the bounds of what any other human being had ever felt.

Then it was gone.

Marcus and Marcus were alone.

"Goodbye Marcus."

"Goodbye Marcus, and good luck. My friend."

Marcus smiled. "My friend. I like that. We haven't really had any for a long time, have we?"

"No."

Marcus patted George fondly, who nuzzled in tight, rubbing his head on Marcus' leg. "Goodbye George, you be good you hear me?"

Marcus walked to the helicopter, cracked his knuckles, got in and adjusted the seat. Adventure awaited, a true adventure. One he would experience through only one pair of eyes. His own.

Marcus waved as the helicopter rose, then walked back into the woods, back to Letje, and Arcene. And Fasolt too. There was still a lot to be done before this adventure was over, and he knew that the future he had seen was not a foregone conclusion unless he played his part.

Marcus, alone, truly alone, with no chance of ever knowing the life the other Marcus would lead, wondered at the life, lives, he had led so far, musing about the madness that had consumed him for centuries, already wondering as he walked alone if any of it had ever been real.

Could there really have been two of him? Was it all just a dream? The visions of a madman who had lived too long, gone insane in a home that should have been vacated a long time ago.

Did it matter?

He was genuinely alone now. Whether he had cut a real tie with himself, and was right now off experiencing life as a true individual, or had merely cut a mental connection that brought him back to his sanity he felt it didn't matter. He only hoped and prayed it had all been real, not the delusions of a madman who was supposed to be the salvation of what was left of humanity. A tiny pocket of life battling extinction with nothing but him and his home between a final entry into The Void for the scattered remains of a mostly Lethargic species.

Hmm

Arcene eyed Marcus suspiciously as he appeared out of the woods stepping into the clearing. "Hmm. You look different. Doesn't he Letje? Look at him, what's he been up to? What have you been up to Marcus? Did you bring us anything? Is there any food?"

Marcus smiled, staring past Arcene at the remains of the meal not long consumed, the bones of at least three rabbits waiting to be cleared away. "Where do you put it all? Your legs must be hollow. No, I'm afraid I didn't bring you anything Arcene, I had some rather sad business to attend to. But it's over now, no point dwelling on it. C'mon, we need to clear up and then be on our way. We have our destiny to meet."

Letje and Arcene stared after Marcus as he walked over to the compact but warm fire and stood there, his back to them, trying to find comfort in the flames. They watched him, confused and worried. He wasn't acting normal, not even normal for him.

Marcus turned to them, tears tumbling down his cheeks like an avalanche, and the two girls ran to him, hugging him tight, trying to do their best to comfort the man who was almost a god on earth, but now seemed more human than ever.

Marcus hugged them tight, never wanting to let them go. "Thank you," whispered Marcus. "Thank you so very much. It's lonely, oh so lonely at times."

They stayed like that until Fasolt returned, two more rabbits for the ever-hungry little girl that must have hollow legs.

"Run," shouted Marcus. "Now. That way, over there, toward Fasolt. Fasolt, FASOLT! Take them away, quickly, I'll catch up." Marcus wiped his eyes, pushed the girls toward Fasolt, and sprinted off in the opposite direction. He glanced back quickly, pleased to see the girls doing what he told them, hoping Fasolt really was the new man he seemed to be. He really needed to get that hair cut though, how could the man hold his head up with all that weight?

Marcus sensed the death that was approaching through the trees, there were quite a few of those with The Ink, and some that were mere pre-acolytes, but still more than happy to do the bidding of Varik and his chain of command. Well, no time for tears now, lives were at stake, important lives — the future of humanity important.

As Marcus ran he let the pressure inside build. The deepest, most primitive and base instincts to fight were growing, waiting to be unleashed, waiting to spend energy pent up for centuries on a real, physical, energizing battle against those that would destroy the rightful future of mankind, and Marcus and his friends. He smiled, tears forgotten, a sense of freedom taking its place. A sense of The Now, and the basic emotions men since the beginning of time had experienced as they fought to protect their loved ones.

Marcus roared at the top of his lungs.

Birds scattered from the trees and men with red faces paused as the true power of a man they thought was a mere mortal reverberated through their skulls. They found the strength gone from their legs as their stomachs began churning with dread at the fight they were too late to back away from.

Marcus was a devil without care, a beast that fought like an animal and gave no quarter. He ran at his attackers, easily dodging missiles from guns, bows and other weapons the motley crew felt would make them invincible against a single man.

They were wrong.

Marcus sliced and diced and chopped like he was back in the butchery room, each movement honed over centuries, each cut given effortlessly, fluid motion directed perfectly to cause maximum damage. He knew his anatomy, had practiced on the meat he ate — his cuts always perfect. Now was no different and in less than a minute Marcus was the bringer of death to all but one of the attackers. Body parts lay where they were dissected from their hosts, gobbets of flesh slid down the trunks of trees, scalps lay on the wet leaves, a prize for the mice getting ready to hibernate and looking for suitable nesting material to keep them warm through the encroaching cold months.

It was all over practically before it began. Marcus was back in control. He felt different, sad, even lonely, but he felt more like himself than he could ever remember. All that he had learned felt like it was his and his alone — he saw everything more clearly than ever before. He felt invincible.

Marcus marched over to the remaining attacker with confident strides, weapons hanging by his sides. He was immersed in the present yet also deep within The Noise — there were no others in the vicinity to be concerned about, but he knew it wouldn't be long before Varik sent re-enforcements on a large scale now he knew where minds had gone dark.

"Please, please don't hurt me. I don't want to die. I'm sorry, I'm sorry." The attacker was nothing but a boy, only just into puberty. Marcus looked into his mind, stripped back the layers of indoctrination, and found a child mourning the loss of his parents, a Bishop taking advantage of his weakness and turning him to ideas of martyrdom, a glorious afterlife where there was no suffering, and a wish for oblivion, an end to his sadness. This child was no threat, didn't deserve to be at the sharp end of his wrath.

"Promise me something," said Marcus, only slightly out of breath, feeling the buzz of life emanating from the air, the ground — everything. Truly wondrous.

"Anything."

"Don't go back to them. Go make your own way in the world. It's beautiful out here if you only open your eyes to it. There are adventures to be had, great tales to tell your children. Even fun to be had." Marcus stared down at the kneeling boy, eyes as green as emeralds sparkling with the energy of life he only just realized had been missing when linked to the other Marcus. "Well? I'm waiting."

The boy was confused, he didn't understand. His life had held no joy or chance to marvel at the beauty of the world until now. "I... I promise."

"Good, now go."

The boy got to his feet and went to run off. "Wait. Not that way, *that* way." Marcus pointed through the trees, knowing the family a few miles distant were grieving for the loss of their son, knowing that this child would be given a home by strangers desperate to remain a family unit. The boy looked confused, but obeyed, amazed his life had been spared by the man he had been taught was one of the foulest creatures on the planet.

He ran.

He didn't stop until he found himself staring at a woman clutching a handful of eggs, talking to a few chickens pecking at the ground next to a small coop a short distance away from a basic looking but obviously comfortable family home.

She looked up as she felt the boy's presence. "Hello. Are you hungry?"

The boy smiled, the simple gesture of kindness filling his heart with something he thought lost to the world: love.

~~~

"Is everything alright? You look different," said Fasolt, staring deeply into Marcus' eyes, seeing more than was on obvious show.

"Everything's fine. I dealt with the problem, but we should move away from here, get some distance between us and what just happened. I had to... um, have words with some Eventuals, so you can bet that Varik, sorry, your son Fasolt, is going to be after us in no time. I guess it's not going to be long before you confront him the same way I will have to?"

"Yes, it won't be long. But the timing needs to be right, and I need to talk to him alone. I want all of this to end."

"You aren't crying now," said Arcene.

"No, I'm not. And I want to thank you for the cuddles Arcene, and you too Letje. I can't tell you what it means to me, but I'm sorry if I upset you. Are you two alright?"

"We're fine Marcus, and you know we love you, right? But what just happened, you seem different?"

"I'll tell you all about it later, let's just say I feel better now, more myself than I have in a long time. Free. I'm not exactly sure, but there were men in the woods out to get us, and I had to deal with them, so it isn't safe here. Let's move."

They began to walk, away from the forest. Marcus leading them out into the weak sunshine. He tried not to think of the other him — it was already becoming a distant dream, an impossibility. He wondered how he was doing, what it was like for him. Did he feel the same as he did? It was a new start for both of them.

Life would be personal, a secret, and that was odd. Nobody to share things with on such an intimate level, yet it felt right, the past somehow unreal. He made a conscious decision not to dwell on it, to live in the moment, fully awake and in The Now. He took pleasure in the walk, each step firmer, more solid, energy sucked up through the soles of his feet, giving him power and increased drive.

They walked on, each lost in their own world, until darkness began to descend. The skyline was marred by dark shapes of all description, the remains of a once world-famous capital silhouetted behind the setting sun.

"Is that a city?" asked Arcene, her hair shining orange in the fading sunlight.

"It is, yes. And that is where we are going Arcene. Into the heart of what used to be where most people in the country lived. To a city where buildings block the light and most paths are man-made. Back to the past to a time and place mostly forgotten by all."

"But not by you and I Marcus," said Fasolt. "I remember, I remember the way it was, the chaos, the din, the way it all seemed so normal — before I found The Noise." Fasolt fell silent, unable to stop remembering the man he had become soon after The Lethargy descended, the bad father and husband he had been even before that time.

Marcus turned to Fasolt. "That man is gone now Fasolt, you are not him any longer. I can see it, let it be. Focus on who you are now, the righting of the wrongs you are attempting. Be happy." Marcus beamed at him. He wondered if he was becoming somewhat crazed with happiness. Was such a thing even possible?

Did he even care?

~~~

The outskirts of the city were almost gone, grasses of all description, trees huge and small, and plants once the pride and joy of vigilant and proud weekend gardeners had flourished, seeding and taking root in any crevice available. The result was that the lesser roads into the city, the cul-de-sacs and streets leading to once well kept suburban homes, were a mass of color even as autumn sent the plants back into stasis, ready to spring forth with renewed vigor the following year.

The two story houses that made up the bulk of suburbia in all parts of the country were mostly still standing. Raging fires had ravaged only relatively small sections of the numerous districts that made up the city as a whole. The gardens spilled over into the verges, grassy parks and front lawns of the better off, ivy creeping over the roofs and penetrating the windows. A virulent strain of ornamental bamboo, once a pot-bound prized plant for the owners of 26 Leebold Street, had spread like wildfire once left to its own devices, and nearly every patch of ground for miles around had anything from a small clump to a bamboo forest making passing an impossible task.

It was beautiful.

As they walked by the houses, net curtains and satellite dishes often still intact, it was hard to imagine what it had all once been like. Marcus had lived on such a street, remembered that all the grass underfoot was still eaten up tarmac just below the surface. The road would once have been continually busy with traffic, fumes spilling out, staining the brickwork of the now empty houses. How things had changed.

They passed through the suburbs. The wider roads were still clogged with vehicles of all description: trucks, buses and cars. Now they were little more than huge mounds of plant and animal life, many even now with patches of dead spreading out from them like a cancer where the fuel tanks had finally rusted through, their contents fouling the ground.

Buildings became more unstable the closer they got to the main hub. Odd noises stalked them as their passage sent subtle tremors through the hardly ever interrupted streets — timbers and brick crashing down on either side of the patchy roads.

It was an alien environment, yet there were still a few people that made it their home. Not many, for scavenging was a hard way to maintain life. Almost everything of use had been stripped — food was no longer to be found, stores had been ransacked centuries ago. But the low numbers of survivors even back when The Lethargy began meant that for a long time it was possible to go from house to house and one large superstore to another and live for generations. Now those that made the city their home lived on the edge, feral and wild, hunting and being hunted, uncaring about the lives around them, just trying to survive, waiting for The Lethargy to overtake them.

Most lived away from such ruin, in the clean countryside where crops and animals could be tended with ease, where the water was clean and you could see for miles without man-made obstacles being a constant reminder of what life was once like and how it had all gone so horribly wrong.

"I don't like it." Arcene was looking unwell, almost green. This was not the life she had ever known, not a place she had ever ventured. At the most she had gone to small villages so the scale of the city was overwhelming. There was nothing to put it into context for her. "Its ugly and stupid and why would anyone build such things and then live in them? It's not right."

"Arcene, don't think of it that way," said Marcus. "Remember, things were different. People liked to live differently, and it's all a matter of taste. You should see The Commorancy, it puts this place to shame, but still, it has big buildings too."

"I don't think I would like it then. I want to leave this place." Arcene stopped, refusing to go forward, the large empty office blocks towered on either side of the road like sentries from the past, guarding the repetitive chain coffee shops that flooded the city further on, mirrored on each side of the street so busy workers didn't have to cross in the traffic to spend the money they had just earned. Marcus had to admit that he found it none too comforting a place either, but this was where they were supposed to be, where things would begin, or end.

"Um, hello...

...is anybody there?"

Prader waited — nothing. What was going on? Had he come out too soon? He didn't think so, it felt right, felt like this was the time. He'd used the right door hadn't he? He turned and checked. Yep, couldn't really miss the huge EXIT sign in neon red. Unmistakably the right door.

"Well, what now?" he muttered to nobody in particular. "What do I do?" Prader shifted from one foot to another, then took a hold of himself.

"C'mon dude, what's the matter with you? Fifty years you have been in here, you're a changed man now, no need to worry, this is The Commorancy." Prader let the unease pass, let his body and mind settle into strength, a relaxed confidence. He had learned a lot in his Room, couldn't really still believe he was the same person that went in all those years ago. He had mastered The Noise, fully Awoken, and was ready to go home to ensure the continuation of his line.

It was what he wanted more than anything, why he had come in the first place. His body was under his control, his genetic makeup shifted just enough to be sure that his offspring would remain Whole. It was why many people came to The Commorancy, not only for themselves but to try to ensure that children had the best possible chance of making it in the world too. Awoken could do such things, make such changes, and for some it took a few years, others centuries, but much more was learned than could ever be wished for. Prader was no exception.

He took stock of his surroundings, noted the lines of power — seen through the walls as clear as if they were actually on the outside. It was like being in a different world, one where half of it had been hidden before. But it wasn't the power circuits that interested him, it was seeing his Room from the outside that captivated him. On the inside he had spent many years investigating much of it, never finding the time to see it all, and now he understood why: it was vast.

He began to walk, to try to understand better the construction of such a strange place that had intrigued him for nigh on fifty years now. As there didn't seem like there was anything else to do at the moment he figured why not?

In truth the floor was not a floor and the walls were not truly walls, at least not in any conventional sense. They were alive, they breathed. As the years passed in his Room Prader began to see it all for what it truly was, and it changed, it grew, the Room actually expanding during his occupancy, morphing and shifting over time to be ever more beautiful, growing physically just as he did mentally. He felt connected to it. Now he had the chance to take a good look at what he felt was an old friend, as if they had grown up together.

As he stepped away from the exit the first thing he noted was that there was no roof, he was outside. Taking a few more steps back he shielded his eyes to take in the glory that was his living Room.

"Oh boy, wow. You are one strange looking tree, that's for sure." He craned his neck but was too close to truly understand the scale of the tree that had been subtly directed via The Noise to grow in a certain way. Over the years it had strayed from its initial instructions, deciding for itself just what shape it would finally be, but always keeping the empty inner space for its honored guest.

A leaf landed on his nose as if to welcome him to the world of sunshine and rain. "Well, hello my old friend, and how are you?" Prader felt the tree's happiness through The Noise. That was good enough for him, he carried on walking. It took some time to make his way all around the strange tree, but he made it back to his starting point eventually. The trunk was huge, wide, gnarled and knotted, home to creatures of all kinds. Its canopy was dense, so it was actually rather dark this close to the trunk. Prader decided to take a stroll away from his friend to get a better view of it in all its glory.

Things started to get weird then.

It wasn't until he was some distance away that the situation he found himself in truly became apparent. He could see from the exit that he was in a large open space, but it wasn't until he got out from under the shade of the tree that the scale of it all revealed itself.

"Oh, wow. Damn, I need to stop saying that, but wowee. How on earth did Marcus build all of this?" Prader wandered down a rough walkway, flagstones bordering it on either side, complex patterns swirling in the polished cobbles. Mosses and grass reveled in the damp conditions between the various forms of paving, before joining with huge swathes of well maintained lawns that spread out in all directions. Prader's home of fifty years was but one of many living Rooms that dotted the perfectly flat vista, but there were plenty of other strange constructions to draw the eye. It wasn't merely the buildings themselves, everything was just so... so well designed. Along the edges of the numerous walkways were ancient stone aqueducts, taking water run-off down the imperceptible slope, nothing going to waste. Prader followed one and found himself peering down into a cavernous space in the floor, at the moment mostly empty, it was a huge excavated cistern that must be able to contain hundreds of thousands of gallons of water.

Wandering over to a particularly shiny piece of what could only be described as 'nothing' Prader was surprised to find himself smacking his nose hard. It was a solid, not quite invisible wall now he was up so close. It was hard to make sense of it. It was see-through, as clear as day, yet if he squinted right up close to the glass then he could just about make out things inside what must have been a Room.

It all got weirder and weirder.

Coming to the end of a particularly maze-like path he found himself walking along a bridge — he hadn't been on the ground at all. He had been on top of yet another building, and the view from the rather wobbly bridge was not only magnificent, but was terrifying too.

"I have a very bad feeling about this, I really wish Marcus was here to greet me. Heck, even George would be better than nothing at the moment." He looked down, then back where he had come from, at the massive stone construction that his Room and countless others sat upon, but there wasn't a person in sight, at least not a living one. "Hello? Hello?" Prader was getting uncomfortable, nervous of the silence, even more nervous of what he was sure were bodies, or body parts, littering the ground beneath him. It was hard to be sure, he was up so high, the wind gusting strong, whipping his hair around his slender, still young face.

Well, only one way to find out the truth, he thought, giving up talking out loud as there was obviously nobody to hear him.

Down on what he assumed really was the ground, the genuine ground, the scope of The Commorancy dominated the view in all directions, and it was hard to not feel insignificant in comparison. Prader decided to stick to the grassy areas — the connection made him feel a lot less uncomfortable. He wandered under a series of huge stone arches, their purpose impossible to guess at. He approached the body gingerly, what was left of it. No doubt about it, it was definitely a body, and one of The Eventuals too. He didn't linger, he kept on walking, heading in a certain direction although he didn't really understand why. It felt like he was being drawn toward something, as if the ground, the buildings, everything were conspiring to steer him somewhere specific.

There were more bodies, and there were also chunks of not very much. And there were lots of bones, tattered clothes and scuffed grass where the only obvious explanation was that animals had feasted well — not very long ago either. Prader increased his pace, no longer as interested in the marvels of The Commorancy as he was in getting to the end of wherever he was now certain he was being directed.

~~~

As the sky darkened and evening fell, Prader found himself edging cautiously through a narrow ravine, sheer stone walls towering high above him. He had to sidle sideways as the space had now got so narrow, but at least there was light at the end.

"You have got to be kidding me," laughed Prader, picking up the note and sitting on the ancient Raleigh Chopper bicycle in fire engine red. He rang the bell and smiled. "I have to hand it to you Marcus, you are definitely one odd dude." He shook his head, but finally managed to relax. Prader read the note out loud, just to break the silence. It echoed back down the ravine, carried up the rock face and repeated over and over as he spoke.

"Dear Prader, my apologies for not meeting you in person after your stay at The Commorancy, but as you are probably aware by now something came up. Rest assured that The Contamination has been dealt with, but pressing issues have taken me away from my home, I do hope that you understand.

You will have been safe, all Eventuals have been dealt with, and all ferocious animals (Grr) have been kept away from where you may have realized you were being subtly guided.

Anyway, I hope you enjoyed your stay, I know that you got what you came for, and I am happy to have obliged. Enjoy the bike ride, and don't forget to close the door on your way out if you would be so kind.

Marcus Wolfe."

Prader rang the bell again, pushed off with his feet, and free-wheeled down the smooth as glass slope. He came to a huge wooden door, larger than any he had ever seen in his life, and as he approached, finding the brakes weren't working — one of Marcus' jokes no doubt — the door opened just in time.

It closed just as quickly behind him and Prader found himself exiting The Commorancy the same way almost all other guests did. It wasn't at all what he had been expecting, and he wondered just how Marcus had managed to automate such a complex way to get back to the mainland, for it was now obvious he was on an island somewhere.

"Oh well, this looks like it will be fun." Prader came to a rolling stop, dismounted and flipped down the kick-stand. He stepped up into the strange contraption and before long found himself holding his breath as he made his way at incredible speed back to the mainland of the British Isles, to meet his future head-on and begin the rest of his very long life.

Burger Anyone?

They wandered down the wide street. Cars blocked the center but the hint of once bright yellow lines and integrated cycle route along the edge meant they could make slow but relatively obstacle free progress. Plants had managed to grow even here. Tarmac was still visible in places, but litter that had rotten centuries ago had given hardy grasses and butterfly loving buddleia a foothold. From there it had built, as plants died so they provided a fertile spot for the next to take its place. The line between road and pavement was blurred, mounds of soil clumped into hillocks, moss covered and sprouting with ferns, the dampness and shade from the buildings providing perfect conditions.

They zig-zagged between it all as best they could, odd patches of tarmac feeling alien underfoot. Occasionally noises could be heard that might be human or animal, but nobody came out from hiding. Marcus could see the presence of a few people behind the walls, their energy shining out like tiny beacons of hope amid the ruins.

Weapons held in deeply veined hands, two young girls and a naked man trailing dreadlocks behind him were far from a welcoming sight, so those that remained in the city hid from what was sure to be an encounter that was bad for their health.

Inevitably there will always be one though, thought Marcus, as he saw the movement from a squat building up ahead to the left. The windows were gone and plant-life was heavy around the doors where the once familiar M had fallen and shattered. Plastic and polystyrene could still be seen sticking out of the grass and the weeds, the old promises of rapid decomposition revealed as a lie so many years later. Marcus saw the movement in The Noise, a dark sparkle of energy pushing forward from the back of the building, a few others holding back, letting the bravest come forward alone.

The man's character was obvious to one such as Marcus, Fasolt too. Both men looked at each other, nodding sadly at what they knew was coming.

"Stay here please," said Marcus, to Letje and Arcene. "We won't be long. Just don't move, and absolutely don't come forward until we tell you it's safe to do so. Okay?"

"Okay."

"You going to go get food?"

Once again Marcus sighed. Where did she put it all?

Marcus and Fasolt strode toward the man in silence. There was nothing to say, his intent obvious. The girls.

He was remarkably friendly looking. All smiles like he was meeting friends he hadn't seen for some time. He wasn't fooling anyone. "Hi, I'm Badger." He put out his hand, the left Marcus noted, smiling at such an obvious ruse. When there was no response the friendly appearance was gone in an instant. True objective replaced the facade of friendliness. He pulled the gun out from behind him, the right hand steady and confident. "Are they Whole?" He pointed at Arcene and Letje, bad thoughts about what he would do to them emanating in The Noise like a loudspeaker.

"What if they are? It's not your concern."

"Maybe I'm making it my concern. My wife is almost useless now, The Creeping has her, but she's still warm, so she does for certain things." He smirked, believing he had the upper hand. Marcus had only knives in his hands, Fasolt had nothing but his nakedness, his small satchel and plenty of hair.

Marcus had flashbacks to the first time he had used his knowledge of The Noise to protect a woman in his home-town, and the way he had made the two assailants fight each other until they were a bloody mess — dying as he walked away. It seemed like after all these years he was coming full circle. He didn't want that, but what choice was there?

"So you abuse your wife? You treat her like she is nothing?" Fasolt was truly sorry for this man, he was like he used to be, a creature that was no good, not deserving of life. But could he be saved, just as Fasolt had been?

"She's mine. I can do what I want. And you, why aren't you wearing any clothes?"

"My body is mine, I can do with it what I want." Fasolt smiled, wondering when the man would realize what had already happened.

Here it comes, thought Fasolt.

"You think you're funny eh?" The man pointed his gun at Fasolt, at least that was the intention. He frowned, his face turning red as he strained against forces he didn't understand. "What the hell...?"

"We don't like you. We think, we know, you are not a good man. You're an abuser, and we do not have time for the likes of you. We have other matters to attend to. Marcus?"

Marcus felt the man's fury, knew it would be bad for those huddled in the back of the building if he was allowed to return. "Yes, I'll do it."

"You'll do what? What's going on here. What have you done to me? I'll get—"

Marcus turned to Letje and Arcene, beckoned them forward as the man fell to the floor, all that made him an individual gone in a single command through The

Noise. It was as easy as flipping a switch. *Too easy*, thought Marcus. Feeling worse than he did all those years ago when he made the men pay for their deeds.

"I would have done it Marcus, I know what it does to you."

"Thank you Fasolt, but it was my duty. If taking a life didn't hurt what kind of a man would that make me?"

Arcene came running up, seemingly over her refusal to move deeper into the heart of the city. "Is he dead? Did you kill him Marcus?" Arcene poked him with her foot, the body moved, but the man made no sound.

"No, I didn't kill him Arcene. Not his body, just his mind. It's gone, like the last stages of The Lethargy. He will die soon though, so I suppose I did kill him. Yes, I did."

"Um, okay Marcus, you could have just said yes then, right?"

Marcus put an arm on her shoulder. "Very astute Arcene. You are wise beyond your years. Now, would you mind stopping kicking the man on the floor, it's really rather unladylike you know."

"Oh, sorry." Arcene stepped away, then bent and pulled something that caught her attention from a thick clump of moss. "Hey, what's this?" She opened and closed the carton, making roaring noises, like it was the gaping mouth of a fierce creature.

"It's what we used to have burgers put in when we bought them from places like this. It's supposed to have degraded by now."

"And they were horrible anyway," said Fasolt.

"Why?"

"Why what?"

"Why would they be put in this? And why would you buy them if they weren't nice to eat?"

"Convenience."

"Convenience." The men stared at each other and laughed.

"Snap," said Marcus.

"Haha. How odd it all seems now Marcus, the way things were."

"What, and things seem normal now do they?" asked a rather bemused Letje.

"Touché."

"Toosh what?" asked Letje.

"Never mind. Look, let's move on, there's nothing more we can do here. This was not a nice man, and his family is in the back, but they are beyond our help. We need to move, we have to go somewhere."

"Are we going to have a burger? I want to see what they were like. What was it exactly?"

"I'll tell you all about it on the way, can we please go."

~~~

"So they put perfectly good meat in a grinder and make it as flat as possible and really thin, and then put lettuce in with it, and tomatoes and all kinds of other weird things then put bread around it and then make it even flatter then give it to you once it isn't very warm any more. You think I'm going to believe that?"

"Well, now that you say it like that it does sound kind of odd," mused Marcus. "You didn't think about it like that then though. It was just really cheap food that you could get quickly. Lots of places you didn't even get out of your car. You gave your order to a box and then drove forward and picked it up out of a window." Arcene and Letje were staring at him funny, annoyed they were being the butt of a joke. "Look, it's true, I know it sounds odd but it's how it happened. Fasolt?"

"Marcus is telling the truth I'm afraid. It all seemed perfectly normal at the time I assure you."

As they walked Marcus tried to keep Arcene and Letje occupied by talking of how things used to be, how the city worked. It was obviously keeping them a lot more relaxed, and the distraction was helping him to feel less out of place as well.

The chatter continued as dusk settled on the already shadowed streets. Main crossroads were eerily quiet, the larger spaces seemingly off limits to plant and animal life alike. They kept going, Marcus guiding them silently. George was subdued by the menacing buildings that were obviously out to threaten him personally. He stayed close to Marcus, almost rubbing against his legs, even giving up his penetrating stares at the others, preferring to use his anger on the buildings themselves.

While the girls chatted about what life must have been like, Marcus and Fasolt held a silent conversation in The Noise, joined by Yabis. Although Yabis was nowhere near the level of the two ancient men he contributed to the plan for what he was told was coming. The Eventuals were getting close and Marcus assured him that by the next day things would be coming to a head, to a conclusion.

They were interrupted by Letje.

"Why are we here Marcus?"

"Well, that's a philosophical question better people than me have struggled with since the beginning of our history Letje."

"No, I mean why the city? Why not somewhere else?"

"Okay, but it gets confusing. I'll try my best though."

Marcus explained about the future, and that he had seen what it held. Although not a guaranteed outcome it was the most likely path if they followed the things he had seen. It was why they were in the city. Fasolt had questioned the wisdom in coming to such a place — surely the open country would be safer? Marcus tried to explain that the best way to protect the females was following the future that saw them coming to this place. It was an impossible conundrum, even to Marcus. The future he had seen was one where they were in the city, so that was the path he had to follow. But it was only his decision to come to the city in the first place that meant that timeline was a possibility. And that had been decided by him seeing it in the best future available. It was all based on events yet to happen so there was no way to logically explain it, it was simply the way it was, nothing more, nothing less.

"Well that makes no sense at all does it?"

"No, absolutely none," smiled Marcus. "Time makes no sense, but what I saw happens here."

"But you saw other futures too, didn't you?"

"Yes, lots of them. And trust me when I tell you that they were not ones that any of us want."

"And me Marcus, did you see me?"

"Well, that's the thing. No, I didn't see you in any of them Fasolt. Which means I'm unsure exactly how things will happen from this point on. It's all closed off now, we are too close to things for future events to show themselves."

"Or I have interrupted the flow? Changed what could come to pass? Maybe I can convince Varik to cease his vendetta. After all, I was a much worse human being than he, and I am to blame for the person he has become."

Marcus stayed silent, not wishing to influence what he thought of as an old man, who in reality was as close to Marcus' own age as to make the difference meaningless.

"Let's get shelter for the night shall we? I wonder if..."

"What? What?" Arcene was getting excited, the long days, the attacks in the woods, the eclipse, Bird, the danger of the city, it had led to her becoming more manic by the day. She would burn out soon, Marcus knew. Rest and comfort were what was needed.

"Well, I did kind of do a few experimental Rooms here a long time ago. I wonder if the buildings are still standing? Let's go find out shall we."

"Oh, yes please. I've never been in a Room before, what's it like?"

"Neither have I. Not a proper one," said a sullen Letje.

"Arcene, you will just have to wait and see. Letje, you remember those words a few years from now. You will be so sick of Rooms that you will wish for them to be somebody else's problem." Marcus winked at her, reminding himself to continue Letje's lessons later on in the evening. It might be the last chance he got.

You Crazy

"Well, it looks like the old place is still here, that's good news at least," said Marcus, staring appreciatively at the facade of the rather austere looking building.

"It looks like it's gutted to me," said Letje, staring at the broken windows, the graffiti on the battered old door.

"Looks can be deceiving Letje, it's all part of hiding in plain sight."

They stepped up cracked tiled steps to an entrance that was a mixture of boards, original door, and a lot of tarnished hardware. Marcus placed his hand just to the right of a door knocker with the head of a lion, and his left just below the sealed up letter box. A series of dull thuds could be heard from within before the door swung open on perfectly oiled heavy hinges. Stale air greeted them, pleased to escape after centuries of confinement.

"Why don't you go first eh George?" Marcus frowned at his long time companion, already in the foyer, pushing past the rest to ensure they knew he was still in charge. George just turned and stared blankly at Marcus.

"Please, do come in." Marcus waved the others into the expansive foyer, dark tiled floor and a sweeping baroque staircase leading upward.

"You were right Marcus," said Fasolt, giving a whistle of appreciation, "looks really can be deceiving."

"I'm just glad it's still standing. I did put in some quite good protection but nothing can stop decay if the surrounding buildings burn or fall down."

Letje and Arcene ran into the spacious rooms, exploring the fake walls and windows that gave the impression from the outside that there was nothing to see within apart from ransacked spaces of no use to either squatters or looters.

"How is it still light, with the fake exteriors?" asked a genuinely interested Fasolt.

"Mirrors, carefully placed mirrors." Marcus winked.

Fasolt knew not to ask for more details, he was getting used to Marcus and his secrets.

"Arcene? Letje? Do you want the grand tour?"

They came running, eager to see what was behind the numerous doors on the ground floor, wondering what Marcus could have done to what looked like a rather lavish townhouse from the inside, a derelict pile somehow still standing from the exterior. George, more tired than he had been in his life, stared incredulously at Marcus, turned in a circle three times, lay down and was snoring before anyone had the chance to take him on another adventure.

Marcus opened a small panel hidden behind a painting of a rather stern looking woman and flipped a number of shiny black switches. "Okay then, it's safe to proceed, we don't want anything exploding on us do we?"

"Exploding! Is the place booby-trapped?" Letje looked around, trying to spot trip-wires, or maybe motion detectors.

"You bet it is. I can see a lot behind these walls Marcus," said Fasolt, making Letje jealous for the benefits those truly adept in The Noise seemed to take for granted.

"There may be a few hidden safety features built into the house, yes. But don't worry, it's mostly safe now."

"Mostly? Um, okay." Letje grabbed Arcene's hand to get her under control, the young girl was becoming manic, hopping rapidly from foot to foot. She probably wanted feeding again. That or sleep. More likely both.

~~~

"What's that?" asked Arcene, running over to the strange contraption before fearlessly poking at it.

"Um, please don't pull that lever Arcene. Thank you. I think maybe we should try another Room, this one should be off-limits really."

"Why? What does it do?" Arcene reached out for the shiny gold topped lever that stood in the center of a contraption made up of gleaming chrome tubes, cogs, chains and the strangest looking chair anyone apart from Marcus had ever seen.

"Come on, I want to show you something." Marcus hastily grabbed Arcene and guided her away from the chair and quickly out of the Room. Marcus was pleased that the building was still standing, he didn't want to change that fact by letting young hands pull levers or press down on deadly plungers.

"I think you are going to like this next Room very much, I built it a long time ago. Actually I built it for my son, but he never got to see it. I got caught up in Commorancy business and never did return here, but not to worry, at least it will hopefully get some use now, before it's too late." It was hard not to feel a tinge of regret for the missed opportunities of fatherhood — what had seemed the right course of action long ago felt very different with centuries of hindsight.

Arcene was hopping from one foot to another again, arms waving like she was controlled by a demented puppetmaster, making Marcus seriously doubt how great an idea this was. Would she like it? Would it be too simplistic? Or would she love it and never go to sleep? Only one way to find out.

"Ta da," shouted Marcus dramatically. Arcene, Letje and even Fasolt craned their heads around the door to see what all the fuss was about.

"Oh, it's just a black Room." Arcene smiled weakly, patting Marcus on the arm reassuringly. She knew adults liked different things to girls her age.

"Hey, wait a minute, we have to go in and start it up." Marcus knew that girls of Arcene's age liked to patronize what they thought of as the oldies. He smiled as he walked into the Room, a beckoning finger inviting the others into the bare space.

Black, totally and utterly black.

Once over the threshold the door slammed shut and the Room was plunged into not just darkness but a complete absence of light. As dark as The Void itself and almost as empty.

"Over here," came Marcus' voice from somewhere inside. "Follow my voice and hold on to each other."

"Marcus, what's the name of this Room? It's not something like The Really Dark And Scary Room is it?"

"Haha, no, don't worry. Actually it's The Space Invaders Room. And get ready, the game is about to begin."

"What game? We don't know the rules of any ga—"

The Room exploded into noise and streaks of light as huge blocky pixelated creatures descended from a point overhead in the middle of the space, spreading out across the ceiling then descending the walls. Each alien vibrated as it scrolled from left to right, lowering its height each time it made a circuit of the Room.

Marcus crouched low, arms extended in front of him, hands held together holding an imaginary pistol. As he aimed at the descending hordes he made a *pew pew* sound. Letje and Arcene just stared at each other dumbfounded. What was he doing? What kind of a noise was that?

"Pause," whispered Marcus. "Sorry, got all carried away there. You wanna play?"

"Me, me. I do," shouted Arcene. "What's a pew pew?"

"Ah, yes, sorry. I guess you don't have much experience of virtual laser sounds from the twenty first century do you. Let me explain the rules. Although if you want you can go *ratatatat* or even *takka takk*. Up to you." Marcus just got blank stares for his trouble. "Okay, right, space invaders goes like this..." He explained the rules. The one thing you had to be sure of was that under no circumstances were the aliens allowed to touch the floor. Marcus made sure to highlight just how dangerous this would be, and that if they valued their lives then they better be sure to stop the attackers before then.

"Right, ready then?"

Fasolt was first to take his stance, the end of a dreadlock held out in place of a real weapon. Letje and Arcene stood back to back, legs bent, focus deadly. Marcus smiled. "Let the games begin again. Play." The aliens began their attack once more, a menacing **dum dum dum** screaming out their descent in amplified surround sound.

~~~

"I need a lie down," said Fasolt, his skin a sheen of sweat, breathing labored.

"I need one too," croaked Letje, voice raw from going *pew pew pew* too many times.

"If this is what it was like when you were growing up Marcus, then I think I'd have liked it. That was cool." Arcene's eyes gleamed manically, she was more hyped up than if she had eaten a whole hive of honey.

"It's not a normal way to play the game I'm afraid, I found this version at a warehouse where more interactive games were being developed right before... Anyway, it never did go out into mass production. Shall we go to the kitchen? Have a bit to eat then off to bed? Tomorrow won't be fun and games like that was, but it seemed like a fitting end to the day."

After a few quick bites and some rushed slurps, Marcus was left alone in the kitchen, everyone else was too exhausted after a day that seemed like a week's worth of experiences all bunched up into a knot of concentrated stimuli. He had to admit it, he was exhausted too. He would switch off soon, that was a promise. First he just had to have a little alone time, being around people constantly was exhausting.

Today had been the worst — way too much had happened. Not to mention the other him, the one that was no longer him in the strictest sense any longer. With experiences now diverging at what point would they truly become different people? Did a brief time apart, with life unshared, already mean they were no longer the same man? It's what shaped you after all: the life you led, the things you did. If another person's memories were different to your own then surely that made them that — a unique entity? But how long did it take? A second? A day or a month or a year? Finally he gave it up as an abstract contemplation that had no answer. He was him, the other Marcus was now unique. They had shared memories, but their futures would be very different.

He wondered which one of him had made the right choice? Or maybe that was the wrong way to look at it. Maybe it was like he was lucky enough to have two of him so that both right choices could be made. Or both choices were the wrong ones. He dared not think that though. Way too much was depending on the outcome of the lives they had both now chosen for themselves.

Marcus went to bed, leaving George snoring where he lay, curled up, still dreaming deeply.

Bird's Eye View

Bird cocked his head to the side, listening intently to the house as the sounds died down within.

Bird was nervous, on edge, feeling wrong. It wasn't just the death of a young one, nor even the strangeness of the city — a place he definitely felt was wrong on so many levels. No, it was more than that. It was the decision he had made to no longer call Varik Master, the betrayal that was actually his, Varik not knowing of the family Bird had, so unaware of the misery he had caused. It was also the emptiness.

Bird had masked his mind for the last few days, hiding his presence from The Noise, making him untraceable to Varik. It felt strange, like part of him was missing, even if it was a part he no longer cared for. But he was slowly getting used to it, knew that he would be the puppet of Varik for maybe only one more day, and then only to complete his revenge.

He shifted on his perch, a crumbling brick chimney topped with the remains of a small birds nest, long abandoned. Even if occupied their owners wouldn't dare to venture near to a creature as intimidating as Bird. He called out to the night — *screeee* — ruffling his feathers, huge wings dislodging the brittle twigs and dried up moss, sending them tumbling down the slate roof, then falling to the ground far below.

How he hated the cities, with their strange architecture and sense of sadness, as if embedded in the very bricks used to build the empty buildings. The depression of those left alive was palpable to Bird's sensitive mind, the cleansing caused by The Lethargy somehow stripping the larger, once proud places of man, leaving behind a sense of the wrongness of it all. It was as if the city itself had a form of Creeping Lethargy, slowly losing its character and its soul, becoming dead and oozing malevolence, crying tears of glass, brick and wood as it splintered and collapsed in on itself. It was no place for Bird, he knew that. Too alien, too thick with a fog of human despair and isolation.

Not long now though. Soon life would be very different for him, for the humans he knew, for the girl who had welcomed his painful perch on her shoulder, his test of her, his beginning of her rite of passage to be allowed into his life, be a part of it, and he a part of hers.

Her future was an interesting one. Bird saw much opportunity in having her be present in a life that extended far out in front of him, hopefully able to soar eventually above such cities as this and see nothing but trees, grass and wild meadows, no dark blots on the landscape oozing decay as they did now.

But that was long into the future, a future that had many outcomes, only one of which he had seen that was of interest to him.

He would make sure that he got to see his destiny, and Varik was definitely no longer a part of it.

Bird took to the wing, a silent silhouette against the sky, deadly and carrying infinite knowledge.

He returned to his family. The journey was long but worth it.

Tomorrow he would seek out Varik, open himself to him for the last time, lead him to those within the crumbling house below, so that all of their games would finally come to an end.

Alone Again

Marcus couldn't sleep — it was the city, he didn't like it.

He made his way through the house, the musty furnishings tickling his nostrils, making him focus on trying not to sneeze. Which of course meant that he found it impossible not to.

Achoo.

Marcus had managed to close the front door quietly behind him before he could control his sneeze no longer. He sniffed the clear night air, watched his breath dissipate, then stepped out into the night.

It was a strange feeling, being alone in a place that would once have been constantly buzzing with nightlife. London was once the capital of the world, now all it was doing was waiting to be eaten up by the Thames and the ever encroaching plant life. Familiar landmarks from long ago still dominated the skyline in parts, other large tourist attractions had found new homes as part of his own. A wry smile was impossible to suppress. Who would have thought it? A skinny kid able to orchestrate the removal and rebuilding of The London Eye for his own amusement, and that of the odd guest of course.

But what a price to pay for such extravagance. The death of nearly everything, everyone. If he could go back to living with his mother and sisters then he would give it all up in a heartbeat. Wouldn't he?

His sisters — he hadn't thought of them in a long time. He was still so very young when they were taken, the beginning of the injustice that was The Lethargy. The impetus for what he had become, what he had done. He didn't want the sorrow to spread, to continue forever. However hard he tried to battle this curse on humanity though, it still prevailed, turning the world as dark as the night he found himself in. Stood at the brink of humanity's fate, trying to cling to the frayed edges of mankind's history, its future.

What a life.

Such a way to spend so many normal lives. It seemed like an impossible dream.

Maybe it was.

Could it have all been a dream and right now he was just rousing from a restless night and would wake to hear his sisters arguing about who got to use the bathroom, and his mother in her dressing gown, shouting at them to hurry up or they would all be late for school?

He wished that it was true, but knew it wasn't.

No, his was a world where his son had left him, left to grow old and not even tell him. A world where he was the most powerful man in the country, where others would see him dead and dance on his bones, crushing them to dust while they welcomed the beginning of The End.

Marcus stopped, finding himself in an open space. He stared at the statues. *Still here.* He smiled, walked over and climbed upon the back of the lion still proudly standing guard, yet nothing left to guard against, or for — Nelson had been toppled from his column centuries ago. Marcus rubbed the back of the statue, the bronze still shiny from countless hands before nobody could care enough any more to climb onto the beast's back.

He stared around him, the menace of the city seemingly creeping out of the very fabric of the place as the night deepened and the air grew colder, threatening to leave a frost — something that would never happen when the traffic and the people warmed the streets by a few degrees.

A hush filled the air above, the huge Bird passing silently overhead. Marcus waved, he liked that creature, liked what he saw in the future. It was a sign things were coming to their conclusion, events were coalescing. He knew that the great Bird had his own priorities, didn't begrudge it reporting back. This was right, as things should be.

After it passed there was a flurry of movement, the ground of Trafalgar Square suddenly alive with pigeons. It seems that he wasn't the only one that had been aware of the huge eagle passing overhead. The pigeons had awoken, a message signaled between them of the danger, now it had passed they were in search of food.

Some things never change, thought Marcus. Even after all these years the pigeons were still active, acting like the tourists would still feed them overpriced seed from the hawkers that made their living from them. Wait, hadn't some Mayor or other banned even that? It didn't matter anymore, and the birds seemed fine either way.

Clip clop. Clip clop.

Marcus looked up, a pale apparition forming through the damp night.

Hello my friend, do you feel it? The wail of the city?

Haha, I don't think it's quite that bad, but yes, I feel it. Things are about to change, for better or worse, but they will change.

And this is your doing, yes?

Marcus shook his head sadly. *Not really, no. The Eventuals will know where we are this night, and tomorrow will see things come to a head. This is no place for you to be. And for that matter, what are you doing here anyway?*

Well, we were passing close by the city and I felt the difference, figured maybe you needed some help. I knew it would be something to do with you, I could feel the disturbance in The Noise.

Marcus frowned. *What kind of difference?*

Ahebban stamped a foot, snorted deeply, breath condensing on the base of the raised lion statue. *It's hard to explain, I suppose you could call it a ripple. No, that's not right really. Not sure, like manipulation was possible, like strong forces were coming together.*

Ah, right. That would be a combination of me, Fasolt, maybe even Letje, her father and even that Bird that now seems rather fond of young Letje too.

Okay, you lost me. I don't know anything about a bird, and who's Fasolt?

Long story but it's Varik's father.

Through dilated eyes Ahebban stared at Marcus with as serious a face as he could muster being a horse. *I hope you know what you are doing Marcus, this seems very dangerous. This isn't The Commorancy you know. Are you sure you are up for this? There aren't all the safeguards you're used to out here in the crumbling sadness.*

Thanks, I'll be fine.

Or at least one of me will be I hope, thought Marcus.

Suit yourself.

You should go, it was good seeing you again, but I don't want any more people, um, friends, caught up in things, you have done more than enough for me already. Go back to your team, that's where you belong now.

Can't say I'm not relieved. Towns and cities give me the creeps now, it all seems too alien for this body.

Tell me about it. I still have a human form and it feels wrong to me too. Too much time has passed, things are too different now. I like my buildings intact and with less reminder of what used to be.

The horse turned, tail swishing slowly. He looked back over a well muscled shoulder. *See you Marcus, you take care, you hear?*

I will. You too. Hopefully we will meet again my friend.

Marcus was alone once more, but his friend had cheered him somewhat. As the dawn hinted at the beautiful day to come, Marcus jumped down from his silent seat and made his way back to the others.

There were things to do before the day washed away the sadness of the night.

It Comes to This?

Bird kept fidgeting on Varik's shoulder.

He could feel the edginess even through his dead flesh. The shifting, the eyes darting from side to side. Bird was becoming lost to him, and he didn't know what to do about it. An emptiness was there where once there had been companionship — familiarity over the endless years. It made him sad to think that his closest companion was no longer connected to him, they were once like part of the same creature.

Varik's shoulder was testament to how much love and trust he had in his old friend, what had he done to lose that bond?

He shook away the emotion, recognizing it for what it was: another reason why life was such an abomination. If Bird no longer wished to be his closest companion then that was his prerogative. He was, after all, a blessed creature, not a cursed one. Bird had been closed to him for days — behavior totally out of character. He felt the whispers of longing through The

Noise, felt that Bird no longer wanted the intrusion on his mind, resented being kept away from... What was it that had driven a wedge between them? What had he done for Bird to be so closed off to him?

Pale blond hair lifted as Bird took flight, his work done. Varik now knew where Marcus was. It seemed he no longer had as much company as before. Bird reported there were but three companions in human form, a rather cryptic message with no more information forthcoming. Still, he knew the location and would be there soon enough.

Marcus' presence had gone dark some time ago now, obviously to do with the fact that he had powerful company, enough to hide them totally from The Noise. They kept moving away, hiding from the acolytes that were scouring the land in ever increasing numbers, but to no avail, nothing but hints and whispers were all Varik had to go on most of the time. It was getting more and more frustrating by the day, but finally there was to be a reckoning. Eventuals had dropped out of The Noise a few times now, and the search was becoming more focused on smaller and smaller areas. Now he had the information he wanted. Varik smiled at the thought of dealing with his nemesis personally, it would be him that put an end to the madness once and for all.

Still, he wished that Bird wasn't so distant.

Damn these emotions, I don't need him, I don't need anybody. Soon it will all be over and I can finally have peace myself.

Varik knew he was kidding himself. Even if he did destroy Marcus there was still much work to be done to ensure that the rest of humanity died out once and for all. But Marcus was the main threat to Varik's desire for humanity's end. So once he was dealt with he would spend some time formulating a plan that would see his work, The Commorancy, razed to the ground and done with at last.

Varik turned as he saw Bird take the meal left for him. The rabbit was on the ground, freshly killed and plump. But Bird, rather than eat it where he was, grabbed it with the talons of one foot and flew out through the open flaps of the large tent.

Something strange was going on, too many quirks were filtering into his friend's behavior. He put it out of his mind, he was too tired to think about it any longer, he had to get his priorities right. He settled back into a comfortable chair, deep cushions providing a comfort he seldom took advantage of.

The traveling had been exhausting, too much time focusing in The Noise, trying to stay abreast of the reports sent up from acolytes, many overly eager and giving information that was nothing but dead-ends, wasting Varik's valuable time.

Still, Bird had come through in the end. Now Varik just wanted to rest a while, enjoy the peace while he could. He needed to restore his depleted energy.

He leaned forward, plucking a leg from the roast chicken on the low wooden serving table he was using to rest his feet. He munched absentmindedly, occasionally stroking his shoulder — it felt bare without the tickle of feathers next to his cheek, the occasional pain as Bird nipped gently on his ear lobe. Time away from his home had worn him down, he was actually feeling his age for the first time. It was amazing just how tiring traveling through the country actually was. When he had last done such a thing he didn't recall the aches and pains, the monotony of it all, the disgust at himself for not actually enjoying it more. After all, it was what he wanted, the country turning green once more, less and less of man's footprint visible. But it felt different to when he last roamed for any length of time. It just felt, well, kind of pointless.

It took so much focus to deal with his Eventuals, co-ordinating things, talking to the idiots and directing operations. It wasn't that though which took such a toll on him, it was the discomfort of being away from familiar surroundings. As he forced himself to eat he came to a realization that Marcus had understood much sooner: he too was institutionalized. Hundreds of years of constant familiarity with his environment, one built and adapted by him to suit him perfectly, meant that anything else simply felt wrong.

Where was the control? The ability to order changes made, mistakes instantly rectified? Where was the food he wanted when he wanted it, the company he wished for appearing with appropriate deference to his station above them?

He missed his daily meditations, performed naked and at his leisure. He wanted to climb his tree and stare at his home, knowing he was in charge.

Out here, traveling, having to put up with the constant erection and dismantling of his tent and the lack of proper amenities simply drained him like a leak in a bottle. He needed to finish what he had come here to do and get back to his rightful place within The Sacellum.

Standing, Varik paused for a moment to let pins and needles pass.

His foot felt dead.

He stared at it, brow creasing at such a thing. He had complete control over his body, this kind of sensation had not happened for as far back as he could remember.

"I really am getting old. Time to be done with all of this."

He made his way over to the bed, a huge wooden thing piled high with pillows and blankets. He hated the indulgence, but appearances were important: he had to be seen to be above the rest. He had even contemplated getting The Ink, just so he didn't have to keep dying his skin every few days, but in the end he dismissed the idea. Soon enough he would be back home and reveling in the purity of his body, the untarnished beauty of it.

A strange sensation ran through him. Varik craned his neck to stare at his shoulder. He could feel it, feel the muscles under the knots of scar tissue, as if his body was already mourning the loss of his friend.

A tear trickled down a red-stained cheek before Varik stripped off his clothes and got under the covers.

~~~

Sleep would not come, it eluded him just as Marcus had. He chased after the nothingness, the blank space of slumber, but it was no use, he could feel the tremors of the events of the next day echoing back and forth in his mind, teasing him with victory, chasing him with doubts of defeat and twisting his mind with insecurities. It didn't help that his shoulder kept itching, an unconscious call for his friend to come and comfort him — a call left unanswered.

Varik mumbled to himself as he sat up in bed, deciding there was only one thing for it. Varik went deep. He went as deep into The Noise as was possible, to search out his friend. He knew Bird was blocking him, but it didn't matter. If he focused hard enough he could break the shielding.

Sweat beaded his brow as he concentrated, ignoring the dull thud that pounded at the inside of his skull, a warning that he was coming close to dehydration as such mental gymnastics took up fluids rapidly. Calories burned at an incredible rate as brain power honed in on a tiny pinprick in the vastness that was billions of creatures, minds large and small that could be accessed by those with the necessary power and knowledge.

Varik actually jumped from his bed as he suddenly gained access to Bird's mind and vision. He saw his own home from the rooftops, The Sacellum gleaming, taunting him with its distance from his current location. Then Bird glanced down at a beautiful female, almost as large as him, with a streak of white running from beak to brow. She was feeding a scruffy chick, all squawks and desperate need for food. Then Bird startled his family, wings flapping wildly, mind screaming at the intrusion as he took flight.

A message of intent came through The Noise directed strongly at Varik, along with an image of a dead chick lying far below, dashed to the ground, bloody and mangled. Then an image of Bird called far away at Varik's command, the fault his, the blame placed squarely on his scarred shoulder.

There was more. Not words, for Bird had no language as such that Varik could understand, but the message was clear.

You are my enemy now. You killed my chick, you are to blame. I have a new friend now, not a 'Master', a friend.

And a vision of Bird sat on the shoulder of the girl, that damn Letje.

Varik was on his knees, the connection, or rather, the intrusion, at an end. There would be no more contact between the two. Bird had let his intentions be clearly known, and Varik felt a part of him drift off into The Void, never to return.

What had he done?

He hadn't stopped to think of the increasing burden he was being to his friend. Hadn't taken time to even think about Bird wanting, needing to be somewhere else. But why had he hidden his family? If he had known then things would have been different.

Wouldn't they?

All Alone

It was a surprisingly warm breeze that greeted klt as he walked down the middle of a stone bridge, so high he dare not look down. His face was a mass of pustules, oozing into his mouth, the taste enough to make him want to rip his own tongue out right there and then. It was certainly dry enough to grip. He had been here for what felt like a lifetime.

He couldn't get in through any of the damn doors.

He supposed that he had been one of the lucky ones, although it certainly didn't feel that way at the moment, and hadn't for weeks now. He wondered how much longer he could carry on in this way. Nobody to talk to, nowhere to go, food becoming a real struggle to find, and the dogs, always the dogs, haunting his dreams and his waking hours with equal ferocity.

At least some of the pain had gone — finally.

For the first few weeks he couldn't even bear the feel of his clothes on his skin, and had to walk around naked, carefully dressing only when the temperature got so low it put his life in danger. His arms, face, legs and neck had been a mass of cuts, bites, stings, boils, and all manner of extreme allergic reactions that made it impossible to actually know what hurt the most. All klt knew was that it did hurt, and like nothing he had ever come close to experiencing before.

He had assumed that he was going to die, at the time it had certainly felt that way. Along with others he had found himself descending steps on the inside of the defensive walls only to be confronted with a beautiful field full of flowers. He could hear the bees, watched delicate butterflies fluttering in the breeze, and heard countless insects going about whatever business it was that insects involved themselves in.

Then it had all turned on him.

The butterflies ripped his skin, the bees stung him, bringing huge hives bubbling to the surface instantly. Gnats, midges, mosquitoes and who knew what else joined in the attack until he was swallowing the black dots of pain and trying to snort them out of his nostrils. Insects clogged his airways, got into his eyes, up his nose and in his ears.

It was unbearable — then it got really bad.

The plants themselves attacked him, adding wounds to his already damaged body. They stung, they released pollen that gave uncontrollable sneezing fits, and then his airways reacted. Anaphylaxis was the result.

But somehow, as he watched it happen to others, and he heard dogs howling hungrily in the distance, he managed to stumble on, amazed his body didn't shut down completely. He made it into the vast grounds of The Commorancy, and climbed carefully up walkways and crossed bizarre bridges until he found himself on the very top of a huge stone viaduct, seemingly serving absolutely no purpose that he could figure out. No matter, at least he was safe — for now.

He had awoken the next day in absolute agony. There was no doubt he was being tortured by a madman with access to very sophisticated equipment, something that could flay open every nerve in his body then tease them with something very sharp. So he was surprised to find himself alone when he managed to prize open a sticky eyelid and get onto all fours to look around.

The following weeks had been nothing but a continuation of the nightmare.

It became apparent that he was the only survivor of the attack. There were bodies strewn around the different levels, shot down from their paragliders. They soon disappeared, dragged off by the dogs he watched from a safe distance, ever aware that his fresh meat would only become more desirable once the remains of fellow Eventuals began to turn putrid. There was not a sound in The Noise of any survivors, and it seemed that the Bishops, Cardinals, and even Varik himself had simply given everyone up as dead and had left.

Left him.

Alone.

He caught sight of somebody once, a man walking off down a long cobbled walkway. He shouted after him, then ran as fast as he could, all pretense of staying hidden and fulfilling his mission forgotten long ago. It was no use, by the time he made it down the convoluted walkways and bridges that let him get to what seemed to be the actual ground level, the man was gone. There was a door, but as usual it was locked, impossible to gain access to. He had tried so many doors, so many strange entryways, only to be turned back over and over again. Not once had he managed to get inside any of the buildings, all he could do was walk, and walk and walk and walk.

It was dizzying, and damned annoying. The place was beautiful, but it also made absolutely no sense as far as he could tell. Why would so many buildings, so many bizarre buildings, be needed to house just seven people? Something wasn't right here, he was sure of it. He had to fight his teachings, his indoctrination, to even begin to try to figure it out. Since the earliest of days, back at the beginning of The Commorancy and the rise of The Eventuals, the one constant was that Marcus' home was for seven guests at one time, and that only when one left did a Room become available.

Now he suspected it was so far from the truth that he wondered what else he had been taught was actually a lie? Did Varik really believe that? Did his teachers?

Marcus had kept his secret well, and there was little doubt in his mind that if Varik really knew the extent of what was surely going on behind the all too secure doors then he would have moved heaven and earth to eliminate what was undoubtedly a much bigger threat to The End than he could have ever imagined.

It didn't matter now though, how could it? klt was alone and he was hungry and his clothes were hanging off his malnourished frame and there was no escape. If there was a way back out of the sprawling conglomeration of buildings and walkways that made up The Commorancy then he sure as hell couldn't find it. The only ways out were lethal. Much like the only way that people could get in, unless expressly invited by Marcus, and that wasn't about to happen, he was sure. No, he was going to die here unless he found a safe exit, and soon. At least if he was able to roam the rest of the island he had a better chance of finding a way off somehow, maybe a boat? Maybe not, but there would surely be food, meat to hunt, something, anything.

A scratch at his nose brought tears to his eyes, once again forgetting quite how delicate his skin was. Blood dripped off the end, the loose skin breaking under the most gentle of touches. He cursed Marcus, cursed Varik too, and not for the first time.

He began to walk, again.

Maybe this time he would find a way to escape. Maybe.

~~~

Approaching the box carefully klt looked around, turning slowly, trying to take everything in, to sense a trap if there was one. It gave little reassurance, but it was better than just walking up to it without at least checking as best he could.

Since he had been marooned he had come across some impressively bizarre objects and he had learned from experience that Marcus had a rather perverse sense of humor. Once he had spent a day staring at a tiny hole at the base of a wall where little mice dressed in formal-wear came out, then scurried off, only to return later with little lumps of cheese. It took him all day to realize they were some kind of projection, and if he hadn't been tattooed bright red already he was sure he would have looked as embarrassed as he felt.

There were numerous such strange encounters, from invisible walls to doors that receded as he approached, to bridges that simply stopped mid-air, leading nowhere and seemingly pointless.

So he was wary of the box.

It was large. A brown box, just a simple brown thing, about as high as his chest. There were no wires he could see, no disturbances emanating from it that he could sense in The Noise. To all intents and purposes it really was just a big box, made of some kind of hard paper by the looks of it. He could see it moving ever so slightly if the wind picked up.

"Do not open this box," read klt.

It was written on the top of the box, the black writing done hastily with a paintbrush or so it seemed. The lid was taped shut, the writing written once it had been sealed.

That was it.

Nothing more. No clues, no buzzing, whirring, ticking or any kind of hint at all as to what was inside it.

He walked away.

"Stupid. Stupid, stupid stupid. Who needs to look inside?" No good could come of opening it. Why else would it be there? It was a test.

~~~

On the other hand, maybe it was a test to see if he was courageous enough to risk opening it? Maybe it would be a way out somehow? Maybe there would be a key to a door inside? It could be, couldn't it?

Damn, this is the third day now I've been back here. Stupid box. Walking away yet again he turned to look back at the box, shook his head and turned back towards it.

Well, I've got nothing to lose now anyway. I'm gonna die soon if I don't get something to eat, so it's now or never. I may as well open it while I have the energy to do it, before I can't even move.

It had been getting hard to summon any energy at all, and klt knew he was beginning to lose his grip on reality. He kept finding himself coming to in places he couldn't remember walking to, and his limbs felt heavy whilst his head felt light at the same time. And the hunger, the ache in his belly, it just got worse and worse. Plus he kept fainting, just keeling over, ripping his skin. His head was covered in bumps from the falls.

He had to do something.

Right, let's see what's so special about you then shall we? He pulled out his knife and sliced the tape. He grabbed the flaps of the box and opened it.

"Definitely don't open this one," read klt. There was another box within the outer box. Same material, same tape, same writing, it was just smaller.

He sliced the tape and opened it.

"Or this one either," he read on the top of the third box, about half the size of the original. "Oh, c'mon, you have got to be joking."

He opened it.

"Last chance. Really, this is serious. Under no circumstances open this box. You have been warned," read klt in a croaky whisper, the words close to his last. His throat hurt so much when he spoke now. He stood up, cricked his back and thought for a moment. What was the worst that could happen? Toxic gas? A biological agent? A bomb? It all seemed ridiculous. Why in His name would anybody go to the trouble of making such a bizarre thing and then putting something inside that could damage the rest of The Commorancy as well? Then again, why would anybody build such a complex development in the first place — normal rules obviously didn't apply here.

Ah, who cares, let's see what you've got then you stupid bloody boxes. klt tried to lick his lips, but his tongue just rasped across cracked lips. He couldn't even summon up saliva any longer. He didn't have long to go, he knew it.

He bent over and grabbed the smaller box.

Nothing, it wouldn't budge. Just like the others it was weighed down somehow, impossibly heavy. So with an aching back and legs trembling he once again cut through brown tape and pulled the flaps of the box back, revealing its contents.

That Was Unexpected

He couldn't stop, the laughter bubbled to the surface, using up what little energy he had left. The man now known as klt, once called Enos, sank to his knees and let the madness consume him.

The laughing continued until his chest hurt too much and his throat rasped painfully, then it faded away, leaving madness in its wake.

Ah well, I guess I really should have stopped at box number five, he thought. *It's not like I wasn't warned about opening them.*

Bemused by his own actions Enos shook his head at his own folly, then died.

What Front Door?

With grumbles from Arcene about a lack of breakfast, although she soon fell into a funk of silence along with the others, Marcus directed them towards the still relatively open spaces of Hyde Park. He didn't want to be surrounded by the decay of the city for this day of reckoning. Although the park had spread to join with the other recreational areas, slowly taking over the streets and buildings, it was still nature overlaid on man's work. Marcus wanted pure soil and trees grown in it to be the sights and sensations on this morning.

Even better would be being back at The Commorancy sitting in a chair that matched his outfit, performing Orientation as he had done countless times over the years. Still, it was no good wishing for things that were in the past, changes were afoot and he had to keep his mind occupied, sharp and totally in the present.

The buildings that surrounded the park had been demolished soon after The Lethargy hit — people did a lot of crazy things when life began to change, and London had undergone some of the biggest transformations. With nature worship rising dramatically, people returning to pagan beliefs and rituals, streets and streets had been dug up, buildings detonated, and the park increased to become a circular green space that extended for miles. Before they too succumbed to The Lethargy those with the will thought that the sacrifice of part of London would appease what seemed to be a scourge on humanity for the desecration of the earth — it made no difference, they all died in the end.

The parkland lifted the spirits of Marcus, and he could see that it was doing the same for the others. Chatter slowly began to build, voices getting louder and louder as if to try to fill the openness after the cloying suffocation of the cramped streets at the center of a once thriving hub of business and money making.

Marcus took Letje to one side and pulled out a leather cord strung around his neck. On the end was a small plain key. Marcus played with it, turning it over and over in his hands, the light glinting off the dull metal.

Letje watched him in silence, he had yet to speak or do anything. Marcus was feeling pressure building, knew that things had to be done now, had to be taken care of.

Marcus pulled the cord over his head, then dangled the key in front of Letje, letting it spin in the gentle breeze.

"I want you to have this Letje, it's yours now."

"Okay, what's it for?"

"The front door, so don't lose it." Marcus smiled weakly, then grew serious. "I mean it, absolutely under no circumstances are you to lose this key." Marcus held his arm out, waiting for Letje to open her hand to receive her gift. He felt bad doing it, felt the weight of years of responsibility shifting onto her shoulders, knowing the battle she would face for her own sanity. But this was what her future held, what was right. Her destiny.

"Wait, what are we talking about here Marcus? Do you mean the front door to The Commorancy? I didn't think it had one. And why are you giving it to me? It's your key, your home. You're in charge there, not me. I haven't even been in a Room yet."

"Letje, of course there is a front door. There is *always* a front door. It's actually pretty impressive too. The carving above the door is magnificent, done by a very skilled man." Marcus had a flash of what had happened to that man, part of the memories that were now his, given by the other him before they parted ways. "Look after it, keep it somewhere safe, and please ensure that you never try to gain entry to The Commorancy any other way than through the front door using this key. Don't touch the door until you have unlocked it, that's very important."

"Marcus, Marcus. This is moving too fast, what's going on? Why are you giving me this now? You need to explain yourself. I'm not ready to be going there and doing, well, what exactly am I supposed to be doing anyway? What's happening? I'm confused."

Marcus felt her sadness, felt the understanding coming to her, even though she didn't want to admit it just yet. Was he doing the right thing? Was this fair to her? Too late now, she was The One, the rightful heir to humanity's hopefully continuing future.

"You are the new owner of The Commorancy Letje, it's yours now. I know you haven't had a Room, are not even fully Awoken yet, but that doesn't matter. Soon enough you will be. Very soon. It will grow inside of you, making you stronger every day, as it already has since your father let himself be known to you. That was your first Awakening, as far as most people ever get. You are different. You are like me, like some others that have gone beyond what we ever thought possible, to become truly Awoken. You will see the world differently, have knowledge unavailable to others, and you must learn how to channel it correctly, and stop yourself from going mad at the same time. I'm sorry." Marcus took hold of her arm, prised open her fingers and wrapped the cord around her hand. He put the key in her palm and then closed her fingers over it.

"Don't lose it."

Letje opened her hand and stared down at the simple key. She picked up the leather cord and held it up to her face. She looked at Marcus. It broke his heart, that look of innocence, the inquiring mind behind those big brown eyes. "You need a haircut, cut those bangs." Marcus smiled at her, his depth of sorrow knew no bounds.

Letje swiped a hand across her brow, shifting the hair away from her eyes, smiling at Marcus' chiding despite the seriousness of the situation, the responsibility just given to her. "How can I do this though? Am I supposed to run things? I wouldn't know where to begin. Marcus it's *your* home, not mine."

"Not any more. Yes Letje, you are to run The Commorancy, all of it. And don't worry, you will learn as you go. There is a book, a rather large book, so sorry about that, but it lays out what you are to do, how you are to run it, how to act, what Rooms to use for what purpose. Plus it gives you all you need to know about how it was built, kind of like a diary that part, and how it all works. It's rather complex, granted, but once you read The Book all will become clear. There are rituals to be followed, ways of doing things that must be continued, don't let the traditions I have started die, they need to stay in place. The myth and power of The Commorancy must continue. People need hope."

Marcus felt funny, like he was drowning, pressure building all around him. He was being squashed, cocooned in a watery grave. He knew he was a little stressed, but had definitely done what needed to be done to control his body, keep him calm and slow his heartbeat, limit adrenaline until it was needed. This was something else.

"Ugh, don't feel well at all." Marcus collapsed to the ground, gasping for breath, unable to get his body to function as he ordered. It seemed like it was a day for firsts — he always had control over his inner body. Always.

"Marcus, Marcus! What's happening? What can I do?"

Fasolt and Arcene came running over. They had kept their distance, Arcene being uncharacteristically observant, knowing Letje and Marcus were having a private conversation. "What's wrong with him? He looks like he's turning blue."

"I don't know, we were talking and he just collapsed. His eyes went all distant and glazed and then he just fell over."

"Let me take a look," said Fasolt, kneeling down and lifting a closed lid. Marcus was gasping for breath, unable to get air into his lungs. It was as if he no longer found the air of any use to him, like he wanted something different.

"He's in the ocean, air's no good to him. Leave him be, he will either resurface or he won't. There's nothing we can do, it's too deep for even me to bring him back from this. It must be his decision."

Marcus thrashed on the floor, hands tearing at his throat, chest heaving heavily, a deathly rattle bellowing deep in his constricted chest.

"What are you talking about? He's right here." Fasolt was making no sense at all to Letje.

Fasolt stood suddenly, turning at an interruption in The Noise he knew all too well.

"Well, this is a surprise. Hello Father, I didn't expect to see you again, especially as you were dead. And what's wrong with him? This looks like it's going to be a little bit too easy. How disappointing." Varik sighed, he was expecting an epic battle to the death, powers pitted against each other, forces unleashed. It was a bit of an anti-climax if he was honest, a bit of a let-down after all his expectations. Varik had dressed suitably. Marcus would have been proud if he could see how well turned out he was.

Varik swung his arm from behind his back, a sword gleaming in the bright crisp sunlight, sparkling with cold beauty as it arced high overhead, an appropriately antique way to send Marcus to The Void, Varik felt.

"Wait, wait just a minute," whispered Fasolt, all his focus on the sword arm, fighting for control of it, failing to totally halt it from the commands of its owner.

Varik frowned, lowered the sword voluntarily, inquisitiveness getting the better of him. "Okay Father, I was wondering what you were doing here anyway. What happened to allow you to beat your own death and why on earth are you walking around naked? Pray tell your son that much." Varik put the tip of his sword to Marcus' throat, he didn't want to be one of those people that failed to kill his foe at the right moment — nothing would see him miss this opportunity. He pushed down slowly, skin breaking.

This was more like it. He would cut through Marcus' body slowly, while his traitor of a father and the girls watched. Then they would be next. It was obvious that his father was now somehow connected to them all, remarkably clean too. Varik hated him more than he ever had in his life.

"This is wrong Son, I was wrong. There's no need to kill. You and him," Fasolt pointed down at Marcus, the blade edging in deeper, "are more alike than you would care to think. Not all people are evil, there is a place for us here, we belong here."

"You dare try to preach to me? The man that let his dying wife suffer? That abused his son? That turned me away whenever I needed him, when I needed a father? Nobody deserves to live, least of all you."

"I know what I did, and for that I will be eternally sorry. It doesn't even feel like me any longer. I can't even begin to pay for all the bad I did, your forgiveness would be a blessing, but I know that is too much to ask. But please, understand. People, most people, are good. I know that now. I know that what we have both done has been wrong. All the killing, you wanting to eliminate humanity, it's not right."

"Spare me, please. You think too much of yourself old man, that your opinion counts, that it was only you that influenced what I have become. You're wrong. I have seen it all, seen the misery mankind causes, seen the way they spoil everything, contaminate it. It must end." Varik put both hands on the hilt of the sword, about to plunge right through Marcus into the grassy ground.

Letje and Arcene both screamed, knowing that Varik would not be swayed, even by his father, that Marcus' death was all that interested Varik.

"Prepare for The Void Marc—"

Varik flew past Marcus' head, the sword clattering to the ground. George, until now silent and unobtrusive by simply staying still, crashed into Varik from behind, head down, horns slamming into him and sending him spread-eagled onto the ground before he could deliver the death blow.

Varik laughed. A goat, a stupid goat. Then darkness crossed his face, his powerful will clamping tightly around the strong but still animal mind of George. George was motionless, unable to follow up on his attack. Varik reached for, and got, the sword and in a movement too swift to follow he swung fast and hard, executing George in a split second. His head rolled along the ground, bumping into the still prone body of Marcus.

Marcus gave a bubble of a cough, choking on unseen substances, and Varik, sneering at his father, winking at Letje and Arcene, swung high once more and the sword fell in a lighting fast arc at the throat of Marcus. Another head was about to roll and Varik screamed his pleasure at the emptiness around him.

Finally the abomination would be dead.

Epic Battle

Things got confusing very quickly.

Letje found it impossible to fathom what on earth was happening, what happened when, to whom, and even where she was. One minute Marcus was coughing on the floor, with Varik's sword arcing toward his neck, the next he regained his color, a huge spout of water gushing from his mouth, a salty tang dissipating instantly in the breeze as Marcus rolled away. The sword sliced at the crushed grass where his body had been a split second before.

She heard Varik howl, saw Marcus roll and stagger to his feet, then a strange sensation came over her, a tingling that was there, then gone again. But it felt strange, like time was no longer important. She could have been stood there tingling for a split second or a thousand years.

The next thing she knew was that Marcus and Varik were in swapped positions. It was Marcus holding the sword, Varik was on all fours, bent over on the ground wheezing. She went to run to the fight, to be there if needed, but as she moved Varik turned and stared at her. A silver light danced in his eyes, the power of The Noise burning behind eyes sparkling with the delight of battle.

Then the tingling again, this time darker, more malevolent, and she found herself staring at empty space, the two men far away across the open parkland, running, dancing in circles, hands held high, shouts impossible to decipher, lost on the breeze.

Letje grabbed Arcene, seemingly too stunned to do anything but sit on the grass and shake her head. Fasolt came up fast, shouting at her through a fog of incomprehension, the air feeling heavy, buzzing as if with electricity.

"Come on, we must try to help, they can't go on like this, it's too much of a disruption." Fasolt was frowning deeply, his hair gone wild, caught in the eddies of power flowing in the charged air.

"What's going on?" shouted Letje, words seemingly unable to travel the distance, the air too heavy with the disruptions coming via The Noise from the two men fighting.

"It's time. They are both messing with time," Fasolt shouted back, his hair flying wildly at Letje and Arcene, forcing them to distance themselves from him. "They are trying to gain an advantage, each one fighting for dominance, suspending time apart from for themselves so they can move through the static and claim victory.

But they are doing too much damage, it's not natural. They are breaking the flow of history and futures. It's all wrong, things are getting out of control. We have to stop it."

Letje felt herself grabbed by Fasolt, so she pulled Arcene along and they ran right at the cause of the danger. Letje put her trust in Fasolt, begrudgingly but not knowing what else to do. She tugged back, grabbed the duffel and then was pulled once more.

Have faith Letje, this is the right thing. You must help, you must try to do something. It's your future that is at stake here, yours and everyone else's. Do what you can.

Letje didn't understand. *What can I do? I'm no match for these men.*

I'm sure you will come up with something my dear.

He sounded so confident, how could he be so sure? Blind faith of a father unwilling to let go of his little girl? Maybe that's all it was.

As they got closer Letje was released and Fasolt ran to join the fight but was rebuffed before he could get too close. Deep in The Noise and using up every ounce of energy they could summon, dragging up long neglected arts from deep in their past, the air was like a forcefield around the two men, impenetrable to anybody but them. Then something changed, the fight broke. The air cleared, the shimmer gone.

Marcus and Varik stood staring at each other panting deeply, energies waning. Then Varik smiled, turning to his father. "Remember the bats old man. The lesson you tried to teach me?" Before Fasolt could answer Varik turned to Marcus and held his arms up high.

"And I thought I was going to be disappointed in you Marcus. I thought for a minute there was no fight in you, what with you lying on the ground already half dead. This is more like it."

Letje watched as the sky turned black seconds later, a piercing screech and a thousand tin drums banging in the sky from all directions. Streaks of hatred ripped through the air, controlled by Varik. Once victim of a spiteful attack by his father, he was compounding the long ago action and unleashing bloody armageddon from all directions.

Marcus was covered from head to toe, disappearing under a chittering onslaught of countless bats. They swarmed and massed in ever greater numbers. Night had come to the open sky in a foul smelling cacophony of the creatures, unable to resist the pull from The Noise. Letje could see Fasolt through the furious beating of wings, his head hung in shame, shouting at Varik to stop. Didn't he know how wrong this was, how wrong it was all those years ago? Varik merely sneered, all hint of restraint gone. He was consumed with hatred for Marcus, for what he stood for. It was written large right across his face.

Fasolt and Varik were shouting at each other, Fasolt trying in vain to get Varik to stop, to understand that such invasive use of other creatures went against all he said he stood for, but Varik was beyond redemption. Letje had thought him a beautiful man, but no longer. His face was locked in a snarl of hatred that was directing his every action. He lifted his arms to the sky once more, shouting, but the noise was now drowned out by the bats that were descending in ever greater numbers to swallow up Marcus.

They whirled in great eddies. Spinning in unison all around him, a black fractal vortex of leathery wings and tiny pointed teeth tearing at his flesh. The noise was deafening, the whole onslaught terrifying. Arcene clung tighter and tighter to Letje until in the end she had to pick her up. Arcene buried her head against the older girl, her hair tangled, covering her eyes, wet from tears as she whimpered quietly, begging Letje to make it stop.

Then the world exploded into light, a blinding brightness that came with a searing heat that sent shockwaves through the ground and blew Letje, Fasolt and Arcene back before they were consumed by flame.

Letje felt the heat, shielded Arcene and the duffel bag as best she could, hoping they would survive. As they got to their feet the world was a changed place. Spreading out from the core of the event was a crater, ground scorched, earth hissing as it cooled rapidly. Marcus was at the center, black with soot, tiny trickles of blood and bites covering his body.

His face was a mess.

His clothes were in tatters, shirt ripped, outer coat gone. All around him were the bodies of the bats, history repeating itself, but on a grander scale.

He shone. His green eyes were luminescent, dancing with energy that threatened to consume Letje just by looking at them. And he was angry. It pulsed through The Noise, through the air, through everything, threatening to obliterate all in its path. Letje looked away. "Are you okay?" she asked Arcene, brushing her down and smoothing her hair away from her face.

"I think so. What happened? Is it finished?" Arcene looked around suspiciously, grabbing Letje once more as she realized it wasn't.

"I think this is far from over Arcene, they are too powerful to stop until one of them is dead."

Letje caught sight of Varik, stripped down to the waist, clothes ripped off before the burnt cloth attacked his body. His scar of a shoulder seemed to writhe with a life of its own, ripples of tissue threatening to jump from his skin. And like Marcus his eyes shone with an intensity that was too intimidating to do more than glance at for a second.

What are these men? They don't even seem human any longer.

They are old Letje. Old and very powerful. They are masters of The Noise and far from normal humans.

Father? Are you alright?

Yes, I'm fine Letje, but we still need to do something. You need to do something.

I never thought they were quite as powerful as this. Marcus seemed odd, but nice. Not like some...

Magician?

Yes, well, almost. I didn't know such power was possible.

Well, it is, and more. Time to do something Letje, before it gets worse, for all of us.

Varik screamed at Marcus, stared around him at the bodies of the bats, burned and dead. Marcus was distraught at the carnage, the regret and sadness emanated through The Noise, shockwaves of misery pulsing in the air.

"You have taken on the worst of what your father once was Varik. I thought you were better than this. Is this how you show your respect for the creatures you say should inherit the earth?" Marcus spoke calmly, as if death didn't surround him.

"My father used the bats to try to teach me a lesson Marcus, one I learned all too well." Varik glared at his father, then turned his attention back to Marcus. "It taught me to value life, but that sometimes the end justifies the means. A few lives to end yours is a price I am willing to pay, but if I can't do it with the animals, then it's time for the end for all of us."

"I don't think so Varik, you can't win. It's you and me, that's what you said. I am stronger."

"Well, maybe I changed my mind." Varik smiled, his eyes losing focus for a second as he sent a message though The Noise.

A silence descended, more threatening than the onslaught of bats. Letje turned in a circle as more and more of Varik's Eventuals came walking across the grass, emerging out of the trees, and making their way toward the one man they had been taught was what stood between them and His will.

Now was their time to eradicate the abomination. Their steady progress was terrifying as their eager faces smiled at the chance of being the one to finally send Marcus screaming into The Void.

"I think I need to do something," said Letje, frowning as the circle of Eventuals got ever closer.

To The Rescue

Bird felt it, felt the disruption, felt the call. He turned and went to offer his assistance. He wasn't alone.

Marcus calmed himself, tried to dismiss the hate, hard as it was. It was almost time. His path had been chosen some time ago now, he knew what had to be done for the future he had seen to become a reality. He looked around at the devastation at his feet, the death of the innocent creatures, the perversion of a man that had caused him to do such things.

All in the name of what we believe to be just, thought Marcus. And not for the first time he battled silently with who was right and who was wrong. Marcus for wanting to save humanity, Varik for wanting man gone. At least then such mindless acts of violence would be no more. But that was the point, wasn't it? It wasn't mindless, it was purposeful, done with full knowledge of the consequences.

Still, it was time, things were moving toward their natural conclusion.

It was deathly silent in the park. All that could be heard were the footsteps of Varik's Eventuals. At the fore of countless acolytes were pompous looking Bishops and Cardinals, all puffed up with pride at leading lost souls toward acts of violence.

Marcus smiled, he was ready.

He looked over at the charred corpse of his headless companion. They had some good times, even if George was one self-important goat. Marcus stopped his mind wandering back to The Commorancy, he'd had his time there, now it was ready for a new caretaker, new blood was needed. He was old, old and jaded. Probably completely mad — he finally accepted that as the truth.

"Do you still have it Letje?" shouted Marcus across the ravaged earth.

Letje paused for a moment until she understood the question. "I do, yes." Letje looked into his eyes, saw the resignation there, the purposefulness, a decision made. "No Marcus, no. You can't."

"It's what happens Letje, no point fighting the future. Take care of things for me. I know you will do a good job, and be careful. Oh, and try to get out now and then."

Letje shouted after him but he turned away, turned toward Varik who was staring at him in confusion.

Marcus walked forward, arms by his sides, head held high, confident what he was doing was right.

"Take up your sword Varik, I give you what you want. My head."

Varik didn't move. He looked around suspiciously. Seeing his flock approaching, Varik smiled, as if knowing Marcus was giving up because he couldn't win against the odds. He bent, picked up his sword and walked toward Marcus. The two men didn't say a word. As they closed on each other the air grew still and the crowd, now thousands strong, formed a circle around the two men. Letje, Arcene and Fasolt were in the circle but off to one side.

Marcus sat on the scorched earth, opened up his rucksack and rummaged around inside. Thousands of pairs of eyes watched mesmerized, wondering what would happen next. There was a flash of white and a hint of scarlet.

"Got to dress for the occasion, that's very important Letje," said Marcus, winking at her as he put his arms through the sleeves of the white ceremonial death robe then pulled the red sash tight at the waist. He knelt in front of Varik, back ramrod straight, stared him in the eye then nodded.

Varik swung his sword once again, and this time nothing stopped him. The blade descended and took Marcus' head off in one clean cut. The head rolled forward, and as it came to a halt Marcus winked knowingly at Letje before closing his eyes for the last time.

"Noooo." Letje screamed and ran forward, picking up the head and sending a message into The Noise.

As Varik's smile of triumph turned to one of confusion, and the jeers and cries of The Eventuals were silenced, the sky once again turned dark. A huge pair of wings blotted out the sun for a second, then descended, followed by a smaller but not insubstantial pair.

Bird's mate landed on Marcus' corpse and let out a *screeee*, the only sound that could be heard. But Bird didn't join her, nor did he go to perch on the dead shoulder of the man he had known as Master for hundreds of years.

Bird alighted on Letje's shoulder, talons once again digging deep, slicing the flesh. She didn't even feel it. Bird nibbled her ear gently in greeting, then turned his head to stare at Varik. Letje noted as if in a dream that Fasolt had hold of her father in one hand with Arcene held tightly by his other.

Letje had moved forward unawares, now standing next to the body of Marcus. She looked at the bird on his body, noting how beautiful it was, the white streak almost the same color as Arcene's hair. Letje communed with Bird silently, was told the story of how he met his mate, along with countless other tales, some happy, one especially sad, all told away from regular time, knowledge simply shared, there in an instant. Letje shared her short life back in return, the friendships, the losses — their bond was made, a connection that was deep and strong.

"Bird? My old friend?" Varik was obviously confused, his joy at the death of Marcus instantly replaced with a deep feeling of unease.

"Bird and his mate have chosen, and they choose me, Letje. They choose life over death Varik. Although yours is to be forfeit. They have chosen. I am the new ruler of The Commorancy. You think you have ended it? It's only just begun." Letje walked forward, the huge eagle on her shoulder, the head of Marcus held up high in the air by his long hair. She turned in a circle slowly, showing herself, her true self, to the amassed Eventuals and to Varik.

"Now, Bird, take your revenge," she whispered, her voice crawling across the crowd, her words clawing at The Noise, freezing the crowd to the spot.

Bird took to the wing, talons dripping beads of blood as he soared. His mate joined him. Varik reached out for Bird, to take control of him, to stop his old friend from doing anything rash — he hit a blank wall. A new power engulfed Bird and he was impenetrable.

"Bird is my friend now, and I protect my friends Varik." Letje gently placed Marcus' head beside his body as bird flapped his wings, breaking the air like a thunderclap.

Then he dove.

"I'm sorry my friend, forgive me. I didn't know about your children."

Bird heard, but Bird wouldn't forgive.

With his mate beside him they descended on Varik, who seemed resigned to his fate. He didn't fight, didn't call forth deep powers to battle with his old friend. He accepted, did nothing. Then he moved — his last act on earth was to rub his misshapen shoulder as the tears dropped from his cheeks before they streamed with blood.

Varik fell to the floor, descended on by Bird and the mother of future generations of Awoken eagles that would forever be tied to The Commorancy. They ripped and sliced with talons and beaks sharper than cold forged steel until all that was left of Varik's face was gore stained bone.

With their justice dealt Bird's mate took once more to the sky, screeching as she flew back to the distant nest. Bird would join her soon, but he had a little time. He knew that for the right timeline to continue he had one more act to perform.

He flew to Letje, tore at her jacket until it fell to the floor in tatters. With just her black vest left intact, her arms and shoulders exposed, Bird landed on her left shoulder, claiming his place, digging in talons so the blood ran freely. He stared out from vastly intelligent eyes at the silent crowd.

Letje never was sure if the crowd of Eventuals knelt because of Bird or because of her. But kneel they did, and as she took Arcene by the hand, took her father from Fasolt and picked up his duffel then walked back toward the city, the chanting of her name followed them until it was lost on the breeze that blew through the streets and the crumbling buildings, lost to her as she said goodbye to Bird, for now.

She knew she would see him soon enough, at The Commorancy.

A new home for her and her friends, and any Whole that could find their way to the last bastion of hope for humanity's future.

Tales From The Deep

Marcus felt his consciousness expand in a way that he had never known possible. What he had imagined and what it was actually like were so far removed from each other he was staggered by what was now open to him.

Marcus had never in his life tried to inhabit a creature so large — he had simply not had the time for such indulgences.

But he had made his decision back in The Room Of Permanent Decisions, and now time seemed of little import.

If only I had known, I would have taken the, haha, plunge years ago.

His brain was now more than double the size it had once been, allowing for his true potential to be accommodated.

What a revelation!

Within seconds of inhabiting his new body he felt his awareness change — as it would have to, but also his capacity for understanding and developing further thanks to The Noise. As he become accustomed to his new skin, and was welcomed by the aging current inhabitant, Marcus expanded and diverged, his life coming back to him in full, every second played out simultaneously until he was truly Whole for the first time since he had Awoken.

All of it, every last detail, was available for instant recall. But Marcus was not interested in dwelling in the past, he wanted to explore new possibilities, to go past what he had once been, to be something new. He communed with his host, knowing before he entered that the deal was welcomed, that he was readily invited to inhabit the creature and share the life it had left, to give solace and company to a loner that had lost touch with its herd and had been alone for years now. It welcomed him, and told of its gratitude for the shared experience of man — even though its ancestors had repeatedly hidden from them as their numbers dwindled from hundreds of thousands down to near extinction.

It opened itself to Marcus, as he did in return. The shared experience as delightful and amazing for one as it was for the other. They told their tales of good and bad, of fights and intrigue and of those that had Awoken, those that were Whole, and those that succumbed to The Lethargy. It wasn't just people that had bore the brunt of The Lethargy, it swept around the globe seemingly randomly, decimating populations that included man, insects, mammals, plants and countless sub-species without any apparent reason.

But Marcus was told this was far from fact. His host opened up the truth of the matter for him, showing him that there was a definite point to The Lethargy, and it was selective in the extreme.

For some species it was an ongoing fight for survival, for others there was an initial cleansing and then it faded back into The Void as quickly as it had appeared. It was only man that still had to fight for survival, the reset having never accomplished what it had set out to do.

The rest?

The survivors had all Awoken, each and every one of their number that remained alive was Whole and Awoken, completing in just one or two short generations what could have taken countless millennia. It was a shortcut to maturity for a species that had gone horribly wrong for one race only — man.

The Lethargy had failed humanity.

It had failed to produce a race that was truly Awoken to their future potential, merely leaving them on the verge of extinction and unwilling, or unable to take advantage of the culling and become what they should have been after such a catastrophic event.

His host did not think it would end well for Marcus, at least, Marcus that was, and his kind. It had every sympathy for the fact that what should have been a great Awakening and thriving for humanity had gone so thoroughly wrong. Human beings had strayed from a path they knew in their hearts they should have followed.

It must be the price they are paying for the things they have done, for the way they treated their home and those that shared it with them, came the ponderous voice of the aging creature. *They lost their way so long ago, they weren't ready to see what a gift they had been given. What they could have achieved if they had taken advantage of the new-found freedom left to those who remained Whole.*

Marcus didn't think it was that simple, there was something else at play. Not enough people had been given the opportunity to make a change to the course of human history — things fell too close to utter destruction. He didn't want to argue however, his host was gracious and he didn't have a better answer for the ponderous thinking animal that was the largest creature currently inhabiting the earth. He forgot that his very being was now open to the creature though, and soon enough was in a long discussion with his new friend that ended up taking years to complete.

There was no hurry.

The blue whale was not the fastest thinker, its body mass put it on a timescale alien to Marcus' human brain. Life was slow, thoughts took an age to formulate. Silent conversations were ponderous. It took hours even for a few short sentences, rather than seconds or minutes.

It took some getting used to, and to begin with communication was extremely difficult. They worked at different speeds and Marcus had to train himself to slow down his thoughts until he was eventually so much a part of the whale that there was no longer a choice in the matter.

The large brain, and the extreme mass of what he had become, meant that over the days that morphed into months he settled into his new way of being.

The slow way of life was not just second nature, it was *his* nature now.

The End

Author's Note

Sign up for The Newsletter for news of the latest releases as well as flash sales at Alkline.co.uk

Book 4 in the series is Resurrection – The Rise of Letje. Find a full list of titles at the author's Website.

52483176R00240

Made in the USA
Charleston, SC
20 February 2016